"Curbside Curses is a trillion times more fun than a yard sale and a lot more terrifying. Quaint, mysterious, and full of hidden treasures, this collection will make you think twice about rummaging through other people's cast-offs." – **Mark Towse**, author of such tales as ***Chasing the Dragon, & Nana***.

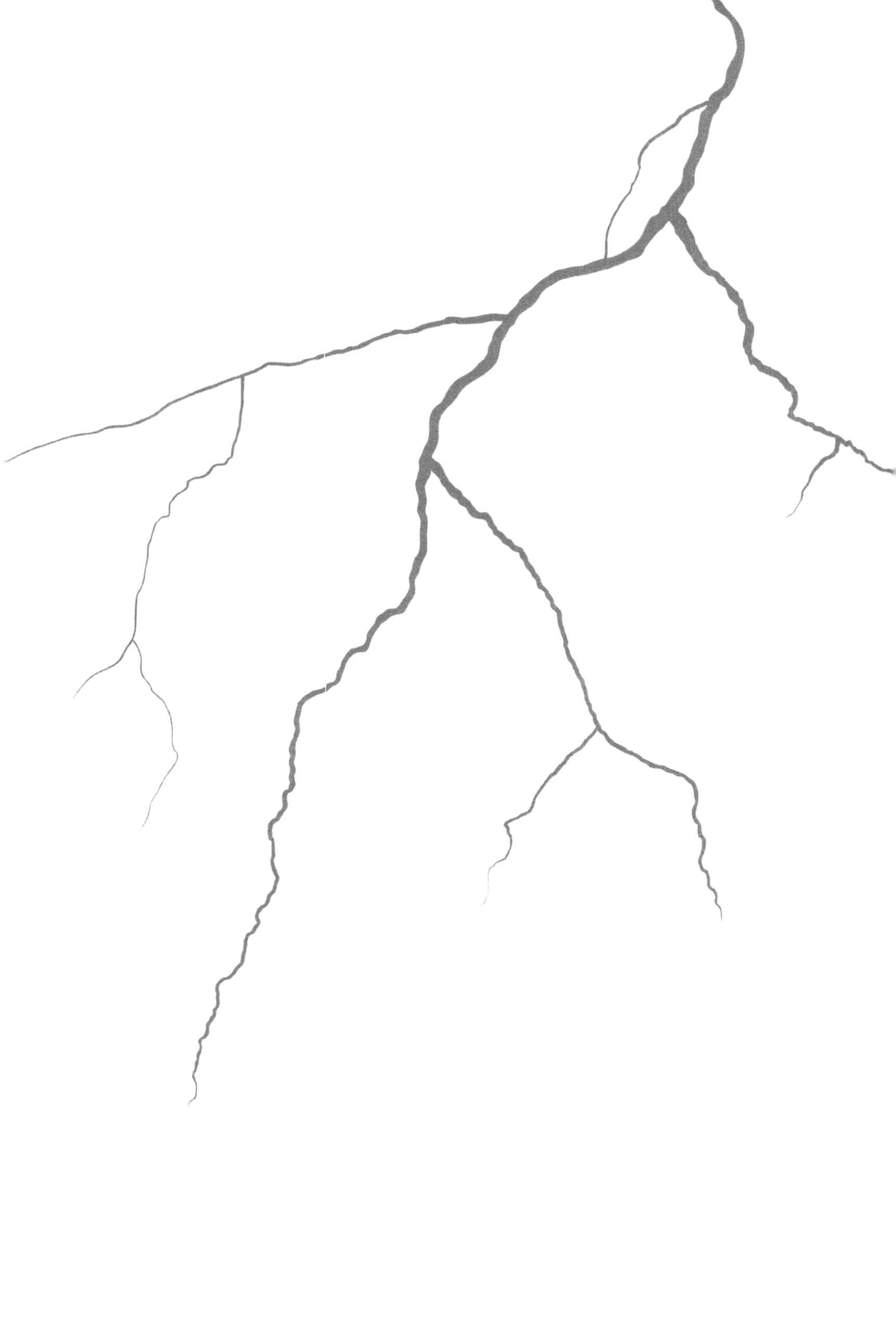

HOUSE OF THE MACABRE

For my mom and dad who have always encouraged us kids to follow our dreams and pursue the arts. And to my dad who I owe any talent I have at this writing thing to him. Thank you for always believing in me.

~N

Table of Contents

Table of Contents Continued...

TITLE	AUTHOR	PAGE #
Any Which Way You Slice It	S.C. Fisher	209
Room For Two	Bert S. Lechner	218
Fishcore	Connor Boyle	226
Epilogue	Nadine Stewart	234
About the Authors		239
Acknowledgements		249

Prologue

BY NADINE STEWART

She could almost still see him standing there. Moving through the house like nothing had happened. A mere shadow of a ghost but still there. It had only been a few hours since her husband had succumbed to the darkness, and she knew she wouldn't survive the night.

You couldn't see it, not really. Not to an untrained eye, and not to a trained eye either, apparently. But if you sat very still letting your eyes adjust to the dusky room as the last rays of light from the setting sun streamed through the blinds and hit the air at just the right angle then you could see it floating there, lingering and swirling around the room like stale cigarette smoke. A dark, smoky curtain, shrouding and enveloping everything it touched, creeping its way through the house like spirits, twirling in an otherworldly dance. How long it had been here she didn't know. Was it unleashed from a recent acquisition or had it been growing for years? Threads of forgotten secrets, intertwining and weaving an invisible web throughout their home.

The ledger sat next to her on the sun-faded floral couch. She had spent most of the afternoon going over every line of it, wondering what went wrong. What had they missed? What would happen now? They had contingencies in place. Protections. This wasn't supposed to happen like this.

"I still can't believe Mom and Dad are gone," Rae remarked to her brother Donavan as she emptied the contents of yet another box onto one of the folding tables in the driveway. It had only been a week since the funeral of their parents, but the siblings decided while they were all together in the same place at the same time that it would be best to work together to clean out their childhood home. It was fitting that the majority of their junk and collectibles were now on display to be rifled through by strangers when so many of the knick-knacks had been bought and collected from similar sales and flea markets over the years.

"Is it just me or do some of these things really weird you out?" Donavan asked as he unpacked an odd bear-like doll with a baby's head. "Like where did Dad say he got this thing again?"

"I can't remember, but Tabatha said she found a whole cabinet full of old things like that in Dad's study that gave her the creeps. You know how obsessed he was with all that paranormal stuff." They all liked to tease him for his weird hobby and fascination with Creepypasta or some supposed supernatural legend he'd watched on the internet. Mom was out unearthing ancient civilizations as an archeologist while Dad was playing Ghost Hunter in his spare time. "Do you remember this?" Rae held up a Mexican wrestling mask she took out of a box. "You were obsessed with Jack Black and *Nacho Libre* as a kid ... hey D, do you see that dark cloud moving in? I thought today was supposed to be sunny. It was beautiful, clear blue skies when I was out an hour ago putting up signs. Maybe we should postpone the yard sale."

"No way!" Tyler yelled from the garage as he placed a box of old VHS tapes on a table next to the old boxy tube TV and VHS player that they hauled up from the basement. Donavan stood next to him and looked out at the dark cloud, shrugging and returning to his work. "I can't take any more time off work and need to get home to my animals. It'll hold off or pass us by. Look ... it's still clear all around. It's probably just a rogue storm cloud that will be gone anytime."

"Ummm, I could use a little help here," Tabatha huffed as she struggled through the garage door with a clunky old vacuum cleaner dragging behind her and a box balancing on her hip that was labeled "Kid's video games". "I don't know why I got stuck hauling out all this heavy crap when D and Tyler are here. Why aren't you guys taking apart the old waterbed from the spare room? And don't say it's because you're waiting for it to drain. After all, you've both walked past the hose over there a dozen times and water hasn't been coming out of it for like an hour now."

Donavan and Tyler both rolled their eyes at their sister as they quickly unburdened her. "Ya, ya ... we'll get to it," they both snapped in unison. "Jinx! You owe me a pop," they blurted out at the same time.

Rae laughed as her brothers playfully socked each other in the arm as they went back in the house. It was a nice moment of levity that felt like old times for a brief second. The last couple of weeks had been an emotional roller coaster. The atmosphere had been tense the last few days as her siblings bickered like they were kids again while they dug through long-forgotten memories tucked away in every corner of the house. She wasn't sure if it was because their parents had died here or if it was just the stress of their grief putting them on edge, but the once lively, happy home had just felt unsettled since they'd all been back here together this time.

No one expected this. Her parents were active and healthy traveling the world as they always wanted to do together when Mom retired. So, it came as quite a shock when their neighbor, who had been stopping by to borrow Mom's cake stand for a lady's luncheon, found them. The toxicology report said it was from carbon monoxide poisoning, but it was a mystery as to the source because the gas fireplace had been broken and hadn't been used in years. But the fire marshal said that an improperly maintained or ventilated gas fireplace can create an unstable environment, producing carbon monoxide, and causing the toxic gas to linger. It was quite possibly a ticking time bomb. The only mystery was that all the carbon monoxide detectors were working perfectly fine when the investigators tested them. Their deaths were simply a random accident, or so it seemed.

Rae and Tabatha finished laying out the last of the boxes under the tables while eyeing the ominous dark cloud lingering overhead. The guys lugged out the last pieces of the waterbed frame and the old mirror from over the bar in the basement and placed them on the side of the house. Standing in the driveway with their arms around each other, the siblings watched as the first cars started to pull up on the street. Like vultures circling their prey the bargain hunters were descending, ready to pick through and scatter the remains of their childhood out into the world.

Lampshades

By Ivan K. Conway

"**M**y God," uttered Ruth with shock.

A rotted, maggoty corpse was hanging from their basement ceiling by a hemp noose.

Maud clenched Ruth's shoulders as she cowered behind her. "You see?! I told you!"

Ruth tugged their lamp's beaded string. Said light immediately winked out. She then turned on her flashlight and directed it to where the carcass had hung. Nothing was there.

"Sorry for doubting you," Ruth conceded before relighting their lamp. The appliance's scarlet glow filled the room and seemingly webbed it in dark red veins.

Maud's hands cupped her mouth and nose as she began coughing. "Good heavens! The smell!"

She wasn't wrong. The thick air was putrid. It also felt ten degrees colder. Yet, when Ruth turned off their lamp, these changes completely vanished. Just like that dead body.

Ruth's attention returned to the new appliance. "Where'd the hell you get this?"

Its base was teal and covered in pink flowers. A maroon lampshade crowned it. The lamp currently stood on a nearby dresser.

There came a pause as Maud bit her index nail. "Gretta Norton gave it to me. Mentioned buying it at an estate sale months ago. Couldn't remember where. Was in an awful big hurry to get rid of it, too."

The news made Ruth frown in pity. Gretta Norton had been a sharp bank clerk once. These days though, the senile woman had a habit of wandering away from home.

Another click sounded when Ruth pulled their lamp's switch. Sure enough, the corpse was back again.

Faintly, Maud could be heard chewing that fingernail. "Think we should call the police?"

"And tell them what? You found a cursed lamp that makes ghosts appear in our basement? We'd be committed to St. Lotus in a heartbeat."

"Sheriff Rodney—"

"Would drive us to the looney bin himself."

"Not if we had evidence," was Maud's hopeful rejoinder.

That was true. He and Ruth had formed a mutual respect during her years at the *Dry Rose Gazette*. They'd even become friends since she retired. Yet, she'd still need proof to sway him.

"Damn," Ruth grumbled as she studied the spot through her smartphone screen. "It doesn't show up on camera."

"Who do you think it is?" whispered Maud as she resumed cowering.

The question made Ruth sigh hesitantly. "If I were to guess, Ted Jordan. He hung himself here after murdering his wife and daughter."

A predictable gasp preceded Maud's eyes bulging. "You never told me that!"

"How do you think I got this place so cheaply?" asked Ruth with a shrug.

Before Maud could protest further, Ruth approached the carcass.

"What are you doing?! Don't touch it!" was Maud's alarmed murmur.

Already, Ruth had poked Ted's white undershirt. It felt completely solid but abnormally cold. Almost to the point of being painful. Her prod made his corpse sway gently.

She turned back to her friend. "Try this lamp anywhere else?"

Maud's head shook before pointing to the dresser her gift sat upon. "Haven't dared to. Hated how dark it gets down here, so I've been hunting for a nightlight to put on that bureau."

Promptly, Ruth unplugged the appliance and began carrying it up their basement's creaking wooden stairs.

"Please tell me you're going to throw that awful thing away!" begged Maud creeping after her.

"Not a chance," Ruth grinningly replied as she entered the kitchen.

Sunrise poured through a window over their sink. This coated the room's cabinets, oven, floor tiles, and four-seated table in gold. Also gave the women's trilling tea kettle a bright gleam.

Maud began hugging herself before taking the kettle off the burner. "Don't think I'll ever sleep again knowing that ... that thing ... is down there."

Ruth nonchalantly set the lamp on their table. "Ted's presumably been around for the last five years. He hasn't hurt anybody."

"Should've told me what happened here!" groused Maud while seeking teacups in one of the kitchen's white cupboards.

That earned Ruth's perceptive sigh. "Would you've agreed to move in if you'd known?"

"You know I wouldn't've," replied her pouting housemate.

Ruth's short gray curls bounced as she nodded. "Well, there you go."

They had a good deal. The two childhood friends were both retired widows whose kids were off raising kids of their own. Fact they got this house so cheap offset anything else in Ruth's mind.

After petulantly stomping to their table, Maud paused with tea kettle in hand. "No tea until I get the truth about this place! The full truth!"

"Alright. Alright," relented Ruth with a blithe wave. "You want this house's ugly history? Well, here it is. Ted was a high-strung businessman with a secret gambling habit. The debts got so bad that he was on the verge of losing this house. Rather than admit it to his family, he murdered them and committed suicide. Least that's what his journal suggested. Happy?"

"You're well informed," Maud grumbled before setting the kettle down.

Their teacups tinkled as Ruth helped arrange them. "It pays having lunch with Rodney once a week. I keep saying you oughta join us."

"Wouldn't want to spoil your little lunch dates," replied Maud rolling her eyes.

"You're the one he's interested in, sweetheart," Ruth relayed beamingly. "Think he only invites me in hopes that you'll tag along one of these days."

That made Maud redden before she hurriedly fussed with her silver blouse, blue jeans, and long white locks. "N ... n ... never mind that! What are we going to do now?!"

"About what?" quired Ruth as she poured the tea.

Maud motioned anxiously around them. "About this! Surely, we can't stay here!"

Shrugging rustled Ruth's azure pantsuit. "Why not?"

"Why not?! There's a ghost under our feet!" wailed Maud jabbing a frantic finger at their basement stairway.

Ruth's response was another shrug. "Like I said. A ghost who hasn't made a peep in the last five years."

Suddenly, Maud shriveled into her seat. "Wait. What about the others? Did the rest of the Jordan family die in this house?"

Instead of answering, Ruth chose to sit and sip some tea.

This clearly did nothing to ease her friend's nerves. Maud's voice rose to a shriek. "They *did* die in here, didn't they?!"

"Calm down," admonished Ruth giving her housemate a steaming cup. "Have a drink."

Maud's hands shook even as she lifted some tea to her lips. "Are they in this room?"

"Not sure," Ruth admitted while eyeing the lamp between them. "Going to have to test your little nightlight and find out."

"Please don't," pled Maud glancing all around the kitchen.

"I can wait until you go shopping," offered Ruth with a nod towards the door behind her.

The other woman bit her lip and looked down. "I don't want you dealing with this alone."

Hearing that made Ruth tear up a little. She quickly wiped her eyes before taking Maud's hands. "That's brave and sweet of you. But I doubt the Jordans are in any position to hurt me."

"You say that as if there are ghosts here who can," observed Maud with a furrowed brow.

Rumors about their property made Ruth wonder. Yet, all she could do was shrug again. "I honestly don't know. And I won't know until I take your lamp for another spin."

"I just have to pull the switch?" warily repeated Maud.

Ruth reassuringly nodded from across the table. "You got it. Ready?"

Maud grimaced. "We really shouldn't be doing this."

"Last chance to go shopping while I investigate," was Ruth's warning before she closed their kitchen's window curtain.

Her housemate gave the front door a longing glance. But she then groaned and shook her head. "Say when."

"Count of three. One. Two. Now."

There was a familiar click as Maud tugged their lamp's string. Then the room went red. Webs of pulsing veins seemed to cover everything. Meanwhile, a cold stench filled the air.

"Oh, good gracious. There's that stink again," observed Maud before doubling over and trying not to vomit her tea.

Ruth's attention shifted to the chair on her right. As she expected, Susie Jordan sat slumped next to a bowl of cereal. The corpse was just as rotted and maggoty as her father's.

"Ted traveled a lot for work. Susie was homeschooled. And Viki was a stay-at-home mom," she recalled grimly. "So, it took a while before anyone noticed the Jordans were missing. By the time the police arrived, this was the sorry state their bodies were in."

For the first time, Maud seemed to spot Susie's remains. Ruth barely had time to catch her friend's puke in a plastic pail.

She patted Maud's shoulder consolingly and gave her friend a rueful smile. "Dug out this bucket in case we get trick or treaters tomorrow. Figured you might need it more, though."

"You knew she'd be here," declared Maud accusingly between ragged gasps over the candy pail.

This won another of Ruth's shrugs. "It was a hunch. Ted seems fixed where he died. Susie was found dead where she is now."

"Poor thing. She couldn't've been any older than my students," observed Maud lifting her head towards said child.

Noddingly, Ruth agreed. "Turned seven just a month before she was killed."

Her friend's mouth hung open in horror. "How?"

"Bastard poisoned her breakfast. At the very least, I doubt she felt anything," said Ruth with a sad sigh. "Viki Jordan, though, got wise to his plan and fled the kitchen. Ted finished her off with a shotgun."

Maud's body tensed. "And where's she?"

Ruth bit her lip guiltily. "Now, Maud. Your bedroom's the best one in the house—"

Her friend flung her hands up in outrage. "Ruth! Are you kidding me?!"

Something in Ruth's periphery made her peer over Maud's shoulder. A large brown leathery thing filled the kitchen corner beside the door.

Unsettled, Ruth stood up and backed away from the table. "Maud, behind you."

"You think I was born yesterday?!" demanded Maud with hands on her hips. "Don't change the subject! Where in the world do you get—"

"Maud!" shouted Ruth as the leathery thing began to stretch its limbs.

Understanding filled Maud's eyes and she went pale. The retired schoolteacher then turned around. "Oh, good heavens!"

Ruth's backward skulk continued until she bumped into the sink. "What the hell is that?!"

It'd been a man once. The bearded mummy looked ridden with bullet holes. Burn scars marked his face. He stayed crouched in the ceiling corner like some oversized insect.

"R...Ruth?" moaned Maud uncertainly as she also started backing away.

"Maud! No!" Ruth quickly murmured. "Turn off the lamp!"

"Why me?!" her friend softly squealed.

"You're closer!" she whispered back.

"Ruth!"

Meanwhile, the mummy began crawling along the ceiling. It gave the women a pearly grin as it advanced. Ruth could now see its nose had rotted off, and it sported a black rune on its forehead.

"Turn it off! Turn it off! Turn it off!" Ruth's voice had risen to a scream as the mummy's creep sped to an excited skitter.

"Alright! Alright!" Maud panickily shrieked back as she yanked their lamp's beaded cord.

Instantly, the red light, Susie, and that awful mummy vanished. But not before the monster greeted them with a raspy hiss. "Ruth Weaver. Maud Hawthorn. Welcome. I've been waiting for you."

All attempts to smash their lamp failed. Ruth couldn't say why. It looked as fragile as any other. Yet, even the lampshade seemed indestructible. So, she and Maud stuffed it into a cardboard box.

Afterward, Ruth tried forgetting about the antique. She hadn't built a journalistic career by being uncurious, however. This nosiness eventually drove her to spend the rest of the day sleuthing.

First, she tried learning more about the lamp itself. An internet search revealed it was one of hundreds made by a factory in Cleveland. None were reported cursed, though.

Uncovering who sold the lamp to Gretta was equally futile. The senile woman had vanished again, and her panicked adult kids were as clueless about the purchase as Maud.

With these inquires going nowhere, Ruth settled on identifying that fourth ghost. Nothing in her house's history gave any clue. So, she tried researching the land it was built on.

That probe proved more edifying. Their property had originally been owned by a Professor Pete Mathias in the late nineteenth century. Local legend held that he'd been some sort of warlock.

"You still up?" Maud mumbled blearily beside her. "It's almost midnight. Go to bed."

Understandably, Ruth's housemate felt reluctant to sleep where Viki Jordan had been murdered. Ruth offered to switch rooms, but Maud didn't want to sleep alone either.

Ruth doubted her newest discovery would ease Maud's mind. But she had to share it with someone. "Take a gander! It's a daguerreotype of our land's first owner! Look familiar?"

Maud irritably muttered while grabbing Ruth's smartphone. Studying the black and white photo it depicted seemed to wake Maud right up, however. "Is that …"

"I think we've found our mystery mummy," agreed Ruth with a shudder.

Pictures of him were few (most pertaining to his lethal confrontation with the cops). Yet, there was no mistaking Professor Pete's wild beard and burn scars.

Maud's eyes narrowed before she gave a grumble. "Let me guess. He died horribly in this house, too?"

"No. Police shot him outside of St. Melanie Convent after he broke in and attacked some nuns there."

Her friend gaped in shock. "But ... there were so many bullet holes ..."

She couldn't help checking the ceiling for signs of the creature. "Supposedly, it took eight gunshots to kill him."

"But ... why is he here? The Jordans are stuck where they died, right? Why isn't he?" asked Maud as she returned the smartphone and withdrew under their covers.

Meanwhile, Ruth's gaze anxiously darted between the bedroom's many shadows. "I wish I knew. His body went missing from the town morgue. Authorities assumed it'd been stolen. Guess he'd been associated with the Milk and Honey Fellowship."

Few grew up in Dry Rose without hearing tales of the infamous disbanded cult. Ruth began wondering if its members' alleged supernatural powers weren't all malarky.

"Great," Maud moaned miserably. "Not only are we haunted by ghosts. But one of them is an evil devil worshipper to boot."

"He said he's been waiting for us. Why? What could he want? And why'd he refer to us by our maiden names?" mused Ruth aloud as she resumed staring at the ceiling.

That's when it hit her. Ruth and Maud's ancestors helped shut down the cult, alongside Detective Lenoard Cliff. This common bond had kept relations friendly between their families for decades.

She murmured aloud, "Could that be it? Does he want revenge?"

"We've got to get out of this house!" observed Maud squirming.

For the first time, Ruth agreed with her friend on that.

They finalized an escape plan that morning. Their retirement checks would arrive soon. This money, along with their current savings, might suffice for a down payment on someplace new.

In the meantime, Ruth tried focusing on buying sweets. Halloween was tonight, and she'd just cleaned Maud's puke from that plastic candy bowl.

Said friend was clinging to Ruth's arm as they patrolled the aisles of Bounty-Mart. "Swear we're being watched."

As much as she hated admitting it, Ruth felt the same way. There were times when Professor Pete Mathias's pearly grin seemed to glitter in her periphery. Yet, she'd turn to find nothing.

"Don't worry," Ruth tried to reassure herself as much as Maud. "Whatever Professor Pete's become, I don't think he can touch us so long as we don't turn on that damn lamp."

Maud pointed ahead of them. "What's going on over there?"

A crowd was gathering in the produce section. On the wall of white concrete above it, streaks of black sludge were forming shapes.

Ruth froze. "Are those … letters?"

Sure enough, an invisible hand drew Ruth's name in jet slime. Then Maud's. The first woman recognized Professor Pete's handwriting.

Spectators began speculating who those names belonged to. Ruth dreaded being linked to the macabre graffiti. She was notorious enough in this small town for some citizens to recognize her.

Meanwhile, Maud's grip on Ruth's arm turned tighter than handcuffs as she read the scrawled message aloud. "Ruth. Maud. You know what to do. Turn it on."

"What now?! What now?!" moaned Maud as she paced their kitchen floor.

Ruth put on a brave face while digging through cardboard boxes on the table. "Just stay calm. Panicking won't help anybody."

Maud motioned to the front door. "You saw it! You saw what he did! Other people saw it too!"

The local news was still discussing that incident on their living room TV. Professor Pete's message had apparently vanished fifteen minutes after Maud and Ruth fled the store.

"We've gotta call the police!" Maud continued while biting her nails, "Rodney's gotta believe us now!"

Ruth's head shook. "Authorities have already concluded that it was some kind of Halloween prank. People would think we're nuttier than fruit cakes."

In response, Maud began pulling her hair. "Don't you get it?! He can affect things here! And he doesn't need the lamp to do it! That's what he was showing us!"

"If he could do whatever he wanted to us, why hasn't he? Why wait till now to send us a message?" pondered Ruth pausing to press a knuckle to her lips.

Tears were filling Maud's eyes. "Then what …"

"The Celts invented Halloween, you know. Samhain is what they called it. Believed it was when spirits were free to roam the land of the living," recounted Ruth.

Her friend blinked in confusion. "What's that got to do with anything?"

She studied Suzie's chair while continuing to speculate. "Maybe that's how Professor Pete is able to affect things in our world. Maybe today some border between us and him is getting thin."

It'd been Ruth's hope that Suzie might confirm her suspicions. But the child's remains remained invisible. Ruth did swear she caught a whiff of rot, however.

"*Getting* thin? You mean, this will get worse?!" exclaimed a mortified Maud.

"Wouldn't surprise me," Ruth admitted as she resumed rummaging through boxes.

Maud's pacing also restarted. "Then we should just go. Maybe hide in a church or something."

There was another pause from Ruth before she nodded. "Might not be a bad idea. You go ahead and do that. I bet Pastor Dean would take you in if you said you were scared tonight."

This made Maud wince worriedly. "But … what are you going to do?"

Junk jingled in the last box as Ruth opened it. "There's no telling how long or how far Professor Pete might follow us. So, tonight, I'm taking the fight to him. Just need to find … ah … there they are."

Great Great Grandma Juliet was said to have passed down three heirlooms: a crystal decanter of holy water, a hammer, and a spray bottle. Said relics were in surprisingly good shape.

"You're going to fight an evil witch's ghost … with some antiques?" asked Maud as her brow furrowed incredulously.

All Ruth could do was shrug. "These are the closest thing we've got to weapons. And I think I know just who to test them on."

"This is an awful idea," Maud warned while cowering behind Ruth again.

Admittedly, Ruth was having doubts too. Especially here in their haunted basement. The room's cold stench was as strong now as it'd been with the lamp turned on.

"Feels like Ted's ghost is already here," unknowingly agreed Maud.

Ruth's head bobbed. "It's almost Halloween night. Bringing his world closer to ours than ever."

A winging moan escaped Maud's lips. "Can't we go back?"

"I'm not facing Professor Pete before testing these weapons. Is the lamp plugged in?" asked Ruth with a brief nod to the appliance on their dresser.

Her friend grunted affirmatively before pleading, "Please don't tell me you mean to turn it back on!"

"Not unless we have to. And, if so, only for a second."

Maud was searching the room anxiously. "But ... what if Professor Pete's already down here?"

She had no good answer for that. "It'd only be for a second."

Determined to act before she lost her moxie, Ruth walked up to where she recalled Ted Jordan hanging. She then fired holy water using her ancestor's spray bottle.

Maud's hands covered her mouth after she excitedly gasped. "Thank God! It's working! It's working!"

Clouds of fetid steam wafted were Ruth's holy water hit unholy flesh. Ted Jordan's remains were becoming translucent but visible. All without the use of that accursed lamp.

"Okay. Let's see what this does," Ruth decreed before spraying her hammer and then smacking Ted with it.

The tool left crumbling holes wherever it touched that ghost. So, Ruth began whacking him like a pinata.

"Yeah! Keep it up!" Maud cheered.

After seven blows, Ted's remains disintegrated to nothing. And Ruth didn't even have to use the crystal decanter in her pants pocket.

With a relieved sigh, Ruth wiped her brow and gave an improvised prayer. "May you go to your final rest, Ted Jordan. Wherever that is."

That's when Maud gave a little hop. "Fantastic! Think we could do the same for Sus—"

Suddenly, their lamp's red light clicked on. Holding its beaded string was none other than Professor Pete Mathias.

Ruth tried lifting her spray bottle, but the grinning mummy was quicker. He grabbed Maud and held a bone knife to her neck. "Now now, Ruth. Let's not do anything rash. My hand might slip. Wouldn't want our friend's throat cut, would we? So, why don't you put that wretched thing on the floor?"

Recognition raised Ruth's brows. "Those scars. I thought they were acid burns or something. But you've been sprayed by holy water before, haven't you? What you get for assaulting a bunch of nuns, I bet."

Remembering the incident seemed to make him wince. "My god was in the process of changing me into the blessed form you see now. Making me sensitive to that vile brew. But enough reminiscing. Unless you want Maud to become another resident ghost, you'll put the spray bottle down. Now."

All Ruth could utter in response was a frustrated growl. Reluctantly, she set her spray bottle on the concrete.

"Hammer, too," he smugly ordered.

She complied with a glare.

He nodded in approval. "That's a good woman. Now, Maud and I will meet you in Viki Jordan's room. Bring the lamp and nothing else. Otherwise, I can't guarantee our friend's safety."

"Ruth!" screamed Maud tearfully as the mummy rushed her up the stairs.

"Maud!" Ruth yelled back as she ran after them. Yet, the moment Professor Pete left their lamp's scarlet light, he and Maud disappeared.

Sunset gave a bloody glow that almost matched the lamp's. Ruth held said appliance in her shaking arms as she sprinted to Professor Pete's rendezvous.

Viki Jordan's tastefully decorated boudoir was already open. Ruth found it seemingly empty. However, a familiar cold stink mixed with gunpowder in the air.

"Well done," was Professor Pete's unseen coo. "Now, set the lamp on Viki's dresser and plug it in."

Ruth put on her fiercest face even as she fought not to cry. "Where's Maud?! If you hurt a hair on her head, I'm sending you back to Hell where you belong!"

He chuckled at this. "Not to worry. She's safe with me. Isn't that right, Maud?"

"Ruth! Don't do—" Maud's outcry suddenly got muffled.

"I think that'll suffice for now," he stated wryly.

More muffled screaming became audible. Yet, it didn't sound like Maud's.

Ruth's eyes narrowed suspiciously. "Who else is here?!"

His answer was nonchalant. "Turn on the lamp and see for yourself."

She felt her shoulders and throat tighten. But Ruth complied. What became visible in that veiny crimson light shocked her.

Their walls and the ceiling were covered in black runes and geometric shapes. Matching candles encircled the bed. Viki's ghostly corpse lay beside it. On the bed itself laid an unfamiliar woman.

It took Ruth a moment to finally recognize her old acquaintance. "Gretta Norton?!"

The prisoner looked unkempt and thin to an unhealthy degree. She was also bound and gagged by hemp ropes. But it was undeniably the same woman who'd given Maud that horrible lamp.

"Thought she could escape me by giving the lamp away," was Professor Pete's smug explanation. "But she was too late. The borders between this world and the land of the living have grown far too thin, and I was still able to snatch her."

Maud and that mummy emerged from the adjacent bathroom. Professor Pete then released Maud before closing their bedroom door. "Ah, together at last."

Ruth's teeth gritted. "What do you want?!"

"Simple. I want you and Maud to take the life of Gretta Cliff," he answered while motioning blithely to the woman on their bed. "Do that, and I promise to set you both free."

Fear and confusion wracked Maud's face. "Gretta Cliff? But ... that's Gretta Norton."

"By marriage, yes," agreed their cadaverous captor, "but it's her bloodline that concerns me. Just as yours and Ruth's does."

Ruth's eyes knowingly narrowed. "This has to do with the Milk and Honey Fellowship's disbandment, doesn't it?"

Great Great Grandma Juliet spoke little of her role in the affair. Yet, history credited her with helping uncover the cult's illicit activities and turning them over to police.

"Indeed," said Professor Pete with scorn. "Juliet Weaver, Detective Lenoard Cliff, and Stan Hawthorn all conspired against our world's eternal salvation. But their future relations will finally set things right."

"You want revenge?" was Maud's fearful squeak.

His head shook. "Not revenge, my dear. Redemption. Redemption and salvation for us all. My fellow believers and I still have work to do. Work that's hampered by being trapped on this side of the veil. But your sacrifice of Gretta Cliff will permanently tear the boundary between your world and this one, freeing us to finish our god's divine plans."

"You're nuts," Ruth observed gaping.

"Far from it," the undead madman retorted while brandishing a grimoire made from bone. "All has been prepared as instructed in *The Book of Everlasting Love*. So shall it be."

At last, Ruth remembered the decanter of holy water still in her pocket. She subtly grabbed it while approaching Professor Pete. "Alright. We'll help you. Just promise to let Maud and me go and leave us alone."

"Ruth!" was Maud's admonishing yell.

The mummy nodded in approval before offering his bone knife to her. "Very good. Now, you and Maud take this blessed blade and stab Gretta together. Then, the ritual will be complete."

Before reaching out for the knife, Ruth gave Maud a contrite smile. "You were right all along, Maud. Never should've played with that damn lamp. Sorry for dragging you into this."

Then, instead of taking Professor Pete's dagger, Ruth grabbed his wrist. She next used her free hand to smash the decanter on his head. This broke that flask and spilled holy water all over him.

The mummy shrieked and thrashed madly as his body sizzled. "Wicked harlot! What are you doing?!"

"Finishing what our ancestors started !" Ruth declared still holding his arm. "Time to die, bastard!"

As they struggled, Ruth kicked a glass shard Maud's way. "Take this and cut Gretta loose! Then, turn off the lamp! Hurry!"

Maud quickly snatched the shard before jumping onto her bed.

Meanwhile, Professor Pete used Ruth's distraction to free himself from her grip. He then turned to pounce on Maud.

"No you don't!" yelled Ruth tackling the mummy to the floor.

She next grabbed the nearest piece of broken glass and started stabbing him. The shard still had enough holy water on it to make his body boil with each puncture.

Professor Pete howled even as his body began disintegrating. "Heathens! This isn't over! My fellow believers will continue our sacred work! Just you—"

The undead warlock crumbled to dust before he could finish his threat.

At the tug of their lamp switch, those black sigils and candles disappeared. Gretta fell sobbingly to the floor as Maud did her best to console the traumatized captive. "There there, Gretta. Come on, let's get out of this awful room."

As they entered the kitchen, Ruth called Gretta's kids to explain where their mother was. She also planned on contacting the police but had no idea what to tell them.

Maud's lower lip trembled while she gave Ruth a haunted stare. "Is it over?"

"Good God, I hope so," answered Ruth before slumping against the sink.

Her friend shuddered. "I still think we should move out."

Ruth suddenly felt her neck hairs rise. On a hunch, she plugged in the lamp and turned it on. Sure enough, she could see three mummified cultists leering back at her through the kitchen window.

Hurriedly, Ruth unplugged the appliance. "You know something, Maud? I couldn't agree with you more."

Spinning Out of Control

BY A.W. MASON AND G.M. PUGLIESE

An Edison bulb hung like a precarious piece of mistletoe, casting a pale-yellow light over Beckett and Magnolia's repurposed barn door dining room table. In the center of it, a dark-stained walnut Lazy Susan sat empty, a glass plate top ready for overpriced artisanal cheeses and club crackers. It was a recent purchase from a yard sale and the couple's first time using it. Neither knew it would also be their last.

"So, we have Caiden and his boyfriend Jaxon bringing their small batch hummus and Kiki said she'd perform a few of her new poems if she felt 'inspired' enough," Mags said as she sliced small pieces of Manchego. "If she even shows."

"I'm more excited for the hummus," Beckett responded. He was bent in front of the fridge, door open, scanning the array of craft beers for their upcoming tasting. "Sometimes Kiki can be a bit of a cuckoo."

They both laughed. Beckett closed the fridge, stole a piece of cheese from the small pile Mags had made, and sat down at the table. He savored the buttery flavor of the Manchego while he absently spun the Lazy Susan, watching each slow rotation.

"It's a shame it's supposed to rain later. Having this outside under the pergola would have been nice," Mags said. "Do you think we could chance it?"

Outside, the sun was high in the air and not a cloud in the sky hung around to conceal it. If there was a storm coming, it was miles and hours off. Mags grabbed a block of sharp cheddar, aged in the former coal mines of Kentucky, and started the slicing process again.

"Beckett?"

The Lazy Susan continued spinning, Beckett zeroing in on the knotty wood. His vision tunneled and he began to feel lightheaded. A small bead of drool peeked out from the corner of his mouth.

"Beck, I asked you a question," Mags said, stopping the Lazy Susan so she could outfit it with the cheese.

"Hmm? Sorry. I think I just zoned out a little. Like I was off in another little world."

A heavy pounding on the door, produced by an antique cast iron door knocker in the shape of a ship's anchor, echoed through the tiny bungalow's front hallway. Beckett shook his head and rubbed his eyes, trying to shake the feeling of dread that had slowly enveloped him.

"Never mind the pergola now. Jaxon and Caiden are here. Please go let them in," Mags said, oblivious to the drool on Beckett's lip.

As Beckett moved out of the room and down the hall to the foyer, Mags glanced around for last-minute needs. Not seeing anything out of place she returned to the Lazy Susan, giving it a nice steady flick to deposit a few squares of cheese in an open slot. As it spun, she found herself hooked to the colorful patterns of the artisanal meats and cheeses. Then from nowhere, a voice echoing the rhythm of the Lazy Susan softly came into focus.

> "Around and around, adorned and ordained,
> through the will of Theid, Grace of pain,
> unbound and unwound, embossed and enameled,
> Time to gift, to bleed, your blame, Vain"

Mags, completely enveloped in a trance, raised the imported Japanese blade from the countertop and mindlessly posted behind the door. Waiting. From the hallway, the cordial sounds of Beckett greeting their guests drifted into the kitchen.

"Oh no, the traffic was dreadful. Jaxon just had to take the expressway though ... " One voice started, before being cut off.

"Yes, yes, again with the expressway hate," from the other new guest.

"Oh fine, I'll drop it then. Beckett, could you be a dear and point me to the powder room? The drive has left my hair in a dreadful state," from the first voice, accepting there may be nothing he could do about it.

"Oh sure, it's just down the hall, through the dining area, first door on your right," Beckett said smiling.

From her hiding spot, Mags stood fixed in her trance, knife raised and ready to plunge at the unlucky guest. As the footsteps in the dining area grew more raucous, a sudden series of noises, each one louder by volumes, began. First a soft thud from a leather boot hitting the hardwood. Then, a half curse cut off by the next sound: the shattering of porcelain. It rained down so loudly that Mags was shaken from her trance. Loosening her grasp on the knife, she blinked, trying to make sense of why she was hiding behind the door.

"Oh my god. I'm so sorry!" Caiden shouted from down the hall. On the ground lay a Hummel figurine, Boy with Toothache, shattered into little pieces. The porcelain shrapnel spread down the hallway from the bathroom.

"I hope it wasn't a family heirloom or something," Jaxon said.

Beckett grabbed a dustpan from the hallway closet.

"We got it from a garage sale last week over in Vernon. No biggie," Beckett said, sweeping up the mess.

From the kitchen, Mags laid down the blade, confused from the macabre sensation that flowed through her seconds earlier. *What was that voice? That sing-songy voice chanting something about grace and pain. And why was I holding the knife like …*

Jaxon, Caiden, and Beckett walked into the kitchen. Mags tried to clear her head and welcomed her guests. After the cans and bombers were put away, the four sat at the table digging into the cheese and crackers, the weird sensation a distant memory in Mags' brain.

The friends talked about the new coffee shop uptown, debating whether their java was fair trade or some bulk blend from a commercial bean farm. Soon the cheeses would need to be refilled—each of them had eaten a healthy share—but Mags was happy enough chatting with her group for now.

Around and around, adorned and ordained …

Mags looked up to see the Lazy Susan slowly spinning. Jaxon absently thumbed at its base as he argued water rights with Beckett.

Through the will of Theid, grace of pain …

Her hand scanned the top of the table, feeling for the cheese knife. Her jaw hung slack as the conversation around her dulled.

Unbound and unwound …

The voice, it was so sweet and inviting. Mags drank it up like a mix of milk and honey.

Embossed and enameled …

Mags felt something touch her hand. Caiden's fingers wandered the tabletop like a lost dog, his eyes distracted by the Lazy Susan.

Time to gift …

Caiden clutched Mags' ring finger.

To bleed …

He caressed her fingertip with his thumb.

Your blame …

He squeezed.

Vain …

And snapped the finger back with a quick jerk. The phalange bone tore loose from its connective tissues as it bent back to Mags' wrist. Tears welled up in her eyes, but her gaze remained upon the Lazy Susan, watching its slow rotations.

Jaxon and Beckett continued their debate, moving onto gerrymandering, oblivious to the trance that held the rest of the party. Mags felt for the cheese knife again, nowhere to be found. Instead, her hand wandered into her purse slung over the chair she occupied and fumbled for something sharp. Something to stab with. Finally, her fingers wrapped around a fountain pen.

"I'm telling you local government is letting this get all out of hand. It's like we're—" Jaxon felt a hot sharp pain in his thigh and looked down to see the fountain pen sticking out of his leg meat.

The Veil of Theid, long ago trapped inside the useful, yet unnecessary kitchen utensil, felt itself come more alive. Blood had been spilled and that was a good thing, a needful thing. With each spin of the Lazy Susan, the old deity felt stronger, more confident, ready for release from the banal prison it had been locked up in for so many years. Now all it required was murder. Spilled blood from the innocent, to be set free.

"Yeoww! What the hell Mags? You fucking stabbed me!"

Jaxon ripped the pen from his thigh, little spurts of blood jetting out from the hole. The Lazy Susan stopped as Jaxon pressed down on his wound with both hands. Little red rivulets squirted between his clasped fingers.

At the same time, Mags looked down at her cockeyed finger eyeing the broken digit before screaming. There was pain, yes, but the shock from seeing the impossible angle of her finger sent her into fits of shrieks.

Caiden sat up from his chair, almost knocking it over. His face flushed but the rest of him broke out in a chilly layer of gooseflesh. The realization of what he had done sank in, and he didn't know why he did it. His stomach churned and his bowels became watery.

Beckett froze, unable to process the scene unfolding in front of him. He looked over at Caiden, face screwed up in a confused grimace, and retched.

"What's happening?!" Caiden yelled. He opened his mouth to scream but a chunky avalanche of Manchego and brie spilled from his lips. His hands went to his throat as the stream continued to splatter the old table.

Beckett, feeling his own guts start to gurgle, spewed a magnificent fountain of Havarti. The firehose-like blast dribbled down the front of his shirt. Caiden hunched over, the yacking continuing. Next to him, Jaxon started swaying in his seat. Sweat ran down his waxy face. He began to heave, letting the cheesy vomit run down his chin while still trying to maintain pressure on his leg.

That's when the world began to fade away for Mags. Her head felt woozy, and the bile creeping up her esophagus burned like molten lava. She watched her hand reach into her purse again, barely aware she was doing it. She rummaged around until she felt the old familiar rectangular shape of her phone. She unlocked the screen, dialed 911, and retched.

Patrolman Hart heard the dispatch call for a possible domestic disturbance, reported by a neighbor, then heard the address and just knew he was going to owe his wife that ten dollars. They both understood the couple that lived there were odd, but she was convinced something was amiss in their household.

Hart called in to dispatch to let them know he could take the call. He was already around the corner from the neighborhood. Turning into the large gravel driveway of the ultra-modern monstrosity that now dominated the once quaint neighborhood, he chuckled to himself at the mismatching of outdoor decor and wondered if they'd ever visited a store and not bought the gaudiest item they saw. Parking behind the pale pink G-Wagon, Hart radioed that he'd arrived and was heading to the door to make contact. He noticed they had removed the doorbell, relying on the large knocker, and laughed again. He reached to his belt for his Maglite to give the door a good knock. But Hart realized immediately that there wasn't any kind of activity coming through it and his gut told him something was wrong. Backing away from the doorway, Hart reached for his shoulder radio mic.

"Dispatch, 2942, no response at the door. Be advised, there is zero movement in the house. Any details on this 5188? Over," Hart spoke, the uneasiness not yet creeping into his voice.

After a few more seconds of silence, the radio crackled back, "2942, Dispatch Actual. No further info from the call. We got a 911 hangup to a cell phone that pinged at the same address about thirty seconds before this call. Dispatcher advised female caller, sounded like crying then the call terminated. Two more units en route already. Advise perimeter check. Over."

Hart grumbled to himself that of course he'd be doing a solo perimeter walk, but nonetheless called in an acknowledgment and started walking away from the driveway. At the third window his gut feeling proved gruesomely correct: the lifeless legs of a man clumped together in a large pool of blood. Things happened in a weird mixture of slow motion and fast forward for the next minute as Hart would later recall in his statement. He rushed away from the window, one hand going for his radio, the other to unholster his sidearm.

"DISPATCH, DISPATCH, 2942, visual one on male, unconscious inside, looked like a lot of blood. Request EMS. Attempting ingress on front door."

"So, what's the preliminary?" Detective Gannon asked his partner. He held a handkerchief to his nose to mask the stench of regurgitated cheese.

Detective Robichard looked at his little spiral notebook as he chewed on the end of his pencil.

"EMS says some kind of poisoning, maybe from what they were eating, but they seem to think it could be from the Lazy Susan."

Gannon raised his eyebrows as Robichard continued.

"It's an old one, 1960s or 70s judging by the design. See that glass on the serving platter? The era in which that monstrosity was produced used leaded glass. The cheeses being served had contact with the toxic surface and then were consumed by the victims. Best they could tell."

"And him?" Gannon said, nodding towards the man with the bloody pants. The fabric was saturated, sticking to the bare wood floors.

"I guess that's for us to figure out," Robichard said.

The crime scene folks had already packed up and left; EMS gone as well. Now all that was left was a visit from the coroner. Gannon stifled a retch and moved towards the front door.

"No use waiting in here for the meat wagon to show up. I'm going to go outside and get some fresh air," Gannon said.

"Right behind you, partner."

Robichard waited for Gannon to leave before moving back into the kitchen. He was careful to step over the bodies strewn about the floor, making his way to the table. He stared at the Lazy Susan. *Too bad about the lead poisoning*, he thought. *The wife would love this thing.* Robichard reached down and thumbed the glass. It moved. He applied more force and tilted the Lazy Susan, realizing the glass was removable.

"Well, I'll be ... "

The detective set the Lazy Susan back down on the table, spinning it to clear the remaining cheese. Once it was empty, he removed the glass, setting it carefully on the table, and stared at the rotating wood. It held him like a trance, he couldn't look away. Robichard started to hear something in his head, faint at first. A voice. A dark, gravelly voice.

"Hey, the body baggers are here," Gannon said, poking his head in through the front door.

Robichard blinked and shook his head, the fog lifting.

"Yeah, okay. Let 'em in."

The detective heard the door open all the way and his partner calling the coroners in. He looked back at the Lazy Susan, contemplating taking it now but made a mental note to check the evidence room later in the day. It would be tricky getting it out of the station, but he could do it, and his wife would be thrilled with the new centerpiece.

Watered Down

BY AudraKate Gonzalez

S he looked into my eyes like she could see into my very soul. As if everything I was feeling was bubbling up through my irises and spilling out of my sockets. Her own eyes searched behind her rose gold glasses. Her lips used fancy words to pry into my secrets.

After all, that's what I was paying her for. One hundred dollars for these suffocating thirty minutes. Suffocating minutes that, deep down, I knew I needed.

"So, you've moved past the affair then?"

I watched as she jotted notes down on her notepad, already on her third page this session. My brain was distracted by what she could possibly be saying about me.

"Elaine?"

"Huh?" I blinked. "Oh, right. The affair. Yeah, totally over it." My fingers located my cuticles to strip them away. Dr. Porter lasered in on them.

"Mhmm. And how is the communication going? Have you guys worked on the exercises I spoke with you about?" The pen moved furiously in her hand.

We have. Every day. He still gets mad at me every time I remind him of it. He gets frustrated every time he has to reassure me. And I still don't trust him. Her perfume hangs on him like a spirit not ready to leave. No matter how many times I wash his clothes. The thought of his hands on her every time he tries to touch me. Any time he tries to kiss me. I want to vomit.

But I love him. I hate him. I …

"Yes. The exercises have been a wonderful help." The hand on the clock next to Dr. Porter said I only had five minutes left. I could do five more minutes.

"Have you talked to him about maybe coming to one of these sessions? I feel it would help both of you tremendously if you're actively seeking guidance together."

Fat chance.

My cuticle bled. There was no sting. Not anymore. Just numbness. "Yeah. He actually wanted to come today." Lie. "But he's picking out—" A boulder lodged in my throat.

The pen stopped. "He's picking out what, Elaine?"

I coughed past the boulder. "A new bed." After he ruined the last one. With *her*.

Dr. Porter put the notepad down. Her manicured hand reached across the space to grasp my fidgeting one. "That's good, Elaine. Getting rid of reminders is a good step. Those things only hurt your relationship in the long run. And that's what you said you wanted to do. Fix your relationship, right?" She squeezed my hand as if she could sense the thoughts I'd been fighting with all day. All month.

I wiggled my hand free, pretending to use it to brush a strand of brown hair away from my face. "I want nothing more."

The clock struck. Time was up.

The trailer on Ryan's truck was empty when I pulled in the driveway. He either didn't find a new bed or he and Lyle, his brother, already carried it in the house. I was hoping for the latter.

Dr. Porter said part of healing our relationship would be to sleep together again. There was no way I was going to sleep where she had. As it was, I had slept there for two weeks, not knowing, before I caught Ryan.

He was annoyed that I wanted to get rid of our bed. He was lucky I didn't want to just sell the whole house.

My hand shook as I went to turn the doorknob. I knew it was stupid. Lyle was with him. But I couldn't help the invading thoughts of walking through the front door and catching him with another woman.

"Ryan, I'm home!" I called out, giving him ample opportunity to redress.

Stop it. He's with Lyle.

"In the bedroom!" Ryan shouted back.

I threw my keys on the stand by the door and jogged up the stairs.

I hadn't been in our bedroom in a month. The night everything happened, the night I came home early from visiting my parents out of town, I gathered up all my things and immediately moved out, and then eventually back in, choosing to stay in the spare bedroom.

Our old bed, deconstructed frame and all, was leaned against the wall outside of the room. I averted my gaze, edging around it. I never wanted to see it again.

I was honestly surprised walking into the bedroom. Ryan and Lyle had worked hard to make sure it resembled nothing from before. There was new paint on the walls, forest green instead of bright yellow, and dark brown carpeting instead of beige.

And in the center of the room— "What is that?" I asked, staring at the wood framed monstrosity that Ryan had brought home.

Ryan placed his hands on his hips. "It's our new bed. Do you like it?"

I slowly sat down on the edge. The bed ebbed and flowed. "It's a waterbed," I said through a fake smile. When I had told him I wanted something vintage, something rustic, this was not what I had in mind. Maybe I should have given clearer instructions.

"We picked it up at an estate sale in the burbs. It's vintage." Ryan seemed so proud. And it was definitely vintage, I couldn't fault him there.

He was trying. I had to try, too.

"It's great." I gave him a quick peck on the cheek. A reward. A sign that I was moving forward, giving him a chance. "It's exactly what I wanted." Wasn't it?

Small steps. That was what Dr. Porter had emphasized during our sessions. What she recommended when I told her I wanted to try and work things out. First step was speaking to him again. Second step was moving back into the house.

Third step ... I slowly leaned back onto the bed, my head gently resting on my pillow as the waves rolled around me, adjusting to my weight. The smell of vinyl invaded my nostrils, at first unwelcomed, but then I breathed it in, enjoying the fact that it didn't smell like another woman's perfume.

I stared at the wall until my eyes grew too heavy, ready to drift to sleep. The bed rocked as Ryan's body relaxed next to me. I could sense him scoot closer. I winced, hoping he couldn't tell I did in the dark, and inched closer to the wall.

I felt his hot breath on my neck as he breathed in. His arm was still damp from his shower as he wrapped it around me.

The bedroom door creaked open and light blazed through my eyelids. I shot up in the bed, fully alert, believing an intruder had just entered our room. Ryan stood next to the light switch by the door.

"Sorry, didn't know you were already in bed." Ryan looked at me, a towel wrapped around his waist. He had still been in the shower this whole time.

I glanced down at the empty space on the bed.

Then who had I felt next to me?

Work was grueling. The holidays were quickly approaching, and everyone wanted to make their last-minute hair appointments before seeing their families. This meant that my usual eight-hour day was going to turn into a twelve-hour one.

I ran to the break room while my eight-thirty client was still processing. Picking my cell phone out of my purse, I pulled Ryan's name up on my contacts.

My gut always told me not to call him. If I called him and gave him a heads up as to when I'd be home, he could easily hide anything from me. But Dr. Porter discouraged that type of behavior. She said that it wouldn't help us continue to move forward if I was constantly trying to catch Ryan in the act. And I wanted us to move forward, right?

The phone rang and rang. Finally, there was a click and Ryan's tired voice came through. "Hello?" he asked. I must have woken him.

"Hey, I just wanted to let you know I'm going to be a little bit later than normal." I cupped my hand around the speaker so he could hear me more clearly over the hair dryers in the background.

"Oh, that's okay. I was just watching a movie in the bedroom. Must have fallen asleep. This waterbed is almost too comfy."

I scoffed. Not in my opinion. I was about to tell Ryan that, but a laugh in the background made my eyebrows raise. Not a laugh coming from the salon. A laugh coming from the other end of the phone. A high-pitched female's laugh.

"Who is there with you?" I demanded.

"What are you talking about?" Was that shock in Ryan's voice? Shock at being caught again?

"I just heard a woman laugh. Quit playing with me. Who is there with you?" Irritation laced my voice.

"Are you seriously going to do this, Elaine? No one is here. You must have heard the TV." Was he gaslighting me?

I immediately hit the *Video Call* button. I needed to see things for myself. I heard Ryan give a deep groan of annoyance from the other end of the phone. His face appeared on the screen as he connected the video call. He was lying on the stupid waterbed, shirt off and hair mussed.

He spun the phone around the room, a dizzying effect as my head and thoughts spiraled out of control. "See, no one here." The phone landed back on his exasperated face.

Ryan was right. There was no one there. It was all in my mind.

"I'm sorry. It's been a long da—"

"Are we going to spend our entire lives going through this? I've apologized, Elaine. *Thousands* of times. I can't keep apologizing for something that you've said you've moved past. It's not fair."

No, it wasn't fair. It wasn't fair that I had been faithful our entire marriage. Stood by his side through *everything* only for him to throw it all away for some blonde hotshot.

But you wanted to stay.

You want this to work.

You love him.

You hate him.

"I know. I'm—I'm working on things with Dr. Porter. Just … bear with me, please?" I couldn't believe I was practically begging him. He *never* begged me, not even when I had moved out of the house. He never begged me to come back.

Ryan rolled his eyes. "I need to go shower. I'll see you when you get home."

"I love—" *Click.* He hung up.

My heart sank and my feet felt heavy as I walked back to my client. I slowly pulled the foils out of her hair, my mind completely numb.

I carried the used foils over to the trash can and a damp sensation seeped into my shoes. I looked down to see a puddle of water sloshing over my shoes.

What the—

Turning around, a woman stood behind me completely nude, water bubbling out of her mouth, moisture dripping from her dark hair. Body bloated and decaying.

I dropped the foils on the floor as fear swept over me.

A cough escaped her. "*You must have heard the TV,*" she said in a gravelly voice. A voice made raw from screaming underwater.

I fell to the ground, and just as quickly as she appeared, she was gone.

My client rushed over to my side. There was no water on the ground. "Are you okay?" she asked.

I slowly nodded. I had just seen … a ghost? An omen? What was that?

But then what she said sank in, and the idea of her being a ghost was no longer important to me.

You must have heard the TV.

That's what Ryan had told me. Images of the video call came blurring around me, and in every single one, the TV was off.

Days passed since the salon incident. I didn't bring anything up to Ryan about it. As it was, he had already spoken to my family about how paranoid I was being. How I was imagining him cheating any time I wasn't near him. And of course, because my family didn't believe in failing marriages–in my mother's words a failed marriage was a *"family scandal"*—it was all my fault that Ryan and I were in the situation we were in to begin with. They were all concerned with my mental health. A thought that Ryan had put into their heads.

The way they were all reacting had already made me second guess myself that night after I left the salon. Had I really seen a ghost? Had she really spoken to me? Was I one hundred percent sure the TV was off? Was I paranoid? Maybe I should be concerned about my mental health, too. I'd ask Dr. Porter about prescribing something at our next session.

After all, Ryan was being super attentive after the whole ordeal. He'd bought me a beautiful black lace dress and roses. I had found them spread out on the waterbed next to me when I woke up, feeling a little seasick. There was a little note on top of the dress that read, "For a romantic evening tonight. I have a big surprise planned."

I was elated.

Maybe I shouldn't have been. It could be more proof that there was a woman here that night.

Stop it. Those thoughts aren't helping.

Or it could be because he felt badly about the way he'd been treating me. The latter, I hoped.

I didn't have to go into the salon, so I spent the time tidying up the house, trying to make it look nice for when Ryan got home. I had even put silk sheets on the bed. I wasn't sure how I felt about moving on to the next step with Ryan in our relationship again, but I was hopeful that maybe this night would turn things around for me.

"Babe, I'm home," Ryan called from downstairs.

I rushed down to greet him in my brand new dress, paired with some flashy, but classy, red heels. I had put my hair up into an elegant ponytail, the way Ryan liked it, and light makeup because Ryan preferred to see my freckles.

Ryan looked speechless. "Wow. You look amazing. I mean, I knew that dress would look great on you, but ... I did not expect this."

I felt my cheeks redden at his compliments. "You definitely picked out a good one," I said as I did a little twirl. Ryan moved behind me and wrapped his arms around my waist. My breath caught, and I couldn't tell if it was because I enjoyed his arms around me or not.

He draped his jacket over my shoulders. "Let me go get changed, and then we can head to dinner." He kissed my neck, sending a shiver down my spine.

Was it a good shiver or a bad shiver?

I watched him go upstairs, and I turned to hang up his jacket. A red smudge on the collar made me freeze. Why would there be a red smudge there? What would cause a red smudge other than ...

My stomach churned. Lipstick. A woman's red lipstick.

Ryan jogged back down, changed into a button-up and navy blue pants. His chestnut hair swept back off his face. "Ready?"

I didn't say anything. I was afraid if I opened my mouth I'd just throw up. Instead, I held the jacket out, collar facing toward him.

His jaw clenched, and he ran a hand down his face in frustration. "Don't tell me you think that's lipstick." His face turned red. "Don't tell me you think that I'm still cheating."

That was exactly what I thought. All of the above.

He tore the jacket from my grip. "It's red ink from a pen that leaked."

"On your collar?" I said in disbelief.

"The pen leaked on my hand at work, and I had already grabbed my jacket before I noticed it was even there. I washed my hands right after." He brushed past me. "I'm going to go start the truck." The door slammed behind him, and tears streamed down my cheeks.

Was I losing my mind? Here Ryan had planned this wonderful evening, and all I could do was accuse him at every single turn.

I let out a shaky breath and strode into the bathroom to get rid of my tears and salvage what little makeup I had on. My eyes were rimmed red, mascara puddled around them. I took a tissue and dabbed to get rid of the inky blackness.

The bathroom door slammed shut, startling me. I tugged on the door, but it refused to open. "Ryan, is that you?" My voice sounded so small.

Water flooded from underneath the door, pooling at my feet. I jolted backwards, hitting the back of my knees against the side of the bathtub, sending me sprawling into it.

From the water, the woman arose, this time with red lipstick smeared across her face as water dripped all around her. The red made her gray skin seem even bleaker. She rubbed her bony fingers over her lips, smudging the lipstick even more. "*It's red ink from a pen that leaked.*" She spat out water as she spoke.

Was she mocking me for believing Ryan?

I stood up in the bathtub on unsteady legs. "Who are you?" I wanted it to be a demand, but my voice trembled.

The woman cocked her head. "*I was you.*" She pointed a bony finger at me. In the blink of an eye, she moved across the bathroom, wrapping her hand around my throat. I gasped, but she didn't squeeze, didn't try to choke me. She caressed my neck. "*He is stealing your air. They always steal your air until you can no longer breathe.*"

The bathroom door barged open with Ryan standing on the other side, huffing as if he was out of breath. "I've been banging on this door. Did you not hear me?"

I was in a daze. Did he not see the woman? I mean, she was gone now, but had he not seen her before she disappeared?

My eyes flicked to the floor, looking for a puddle left behind, but there was nothing.

"We're going to be late for our reservation. Let's go."

Dinner was had in silence. I had thought the restaurant was nice until I remembered where I'd seen the name of it before. *Iago's.* It was the name printed above a receipt I had found in Ryan's pocket a couple of days after I'd caught him with *her*. He took her here. And now he was bringing me here. Was this some kind of sick joke?

He acted like everything was fine. Like what happened at the house and the lipstick accusation didn't happen. And then when I made a tongue-in-cheek comment about the restaurant, he didn't even acknowledge it. He had to have remembered that this was where he brought her.

I couldn't even touch my shawarma. It came home with us in a to-go box.

I tossed the stupid box and marched up the stairs, Ryan following close behind.

"Hey, hey." Ryan gently grabbed my arm, spinning me toward him. "Look, I know you're still feeling some kind of way about what happened earlier."

I clenched my teeth together.

"But, I still have that surprise for you." Ryan quickly spun me around to face away from him, and then blackness surrounded me as he tied a blindfold around my head. He guided me, and I couldn't tell where we were going until he sat me down on the edge of the waterbed, the water jiggling all around me.

I hoped he wasn't trying to do some blindfold thing as a way to introduce a weird kink. I was not ready for any of that again under normal circumstances, let alone blindfolded.

I felt Ryan move up behind me on the bed. "Ready for your surprise?"

I nodded, and then my heart hammered in my chest as something tight wrapped around my throat, stealing the breath from my lungs. I fell back onto Ryan as he gripped my neck from behind with a rope. He pulled and pulled. So tight. My throat burned. My lungs burned. I clawed at the rope, trying to release some of the pressure around my throat.

He is stealing your air.

Ryan was trying to kill me.

I ripped the blindfold away from my face and kicked and slapped, but Ryan still held firm. My vision was beginning to get hazy.

Then the bed began to violently slosh. The waves beneath us crashing like the ocean in the middle of a storm.

My mouth opened in a scream. I tried to suck one last breath in. And then the bedroom faded away as we dipped into the water.

Water rushed over us, and now Ryan, no longer focused on strangling me, was fighting for air too. I couldn't see anything in the dark depths of the vast water. It was too murky to make anything out.

I glanced up and could see the surface above us. The bedroom was up in the distance. I kicked myself away from Ryan and began to swim up. Ryan looked at where I was going, and he reached up, grabbing my leg, and pulled me back down.

I needed air. My lungs were screaming at me by this point.

He swam up my body, taking a fist full of my hair and dragging me beneath him. I kicked harder and tried to get past him, but then he wrapped his arms around me, holding me in place so I would drown.

I thrashed against him, and just when I was about to give up, when I thought there was no way I could be free of him, the woman from the water swam out of the darkness. She dug her bony fingers deep into Ryan's arms. He let out a scream, bubbles escaping from his lips.

The woman, with her fingers still embedded in his arms, held him in place while I pushed myself up through the murky water to the surface.

I glanced behind me one more time to see their shadows disappearing in the distance. Ryan's arms reached out toward me as though I would save him from his watery grave.

Fat chance.

Breaking the surface, I swam to the edge of the bed and crawled out of the water, landing hard on the floor, gasping for air. I turned around. The bed was completely back to normal. No sign of the body of water that led into a different world. No sign of the woman. No sign of Ryan.

And I could breathe.

"It's interesting how much better you're doing without him in your life. Based on our previous sessions, I wouldn't have expected this reaction from you." Dr. Porter looked pleasantly surprised.

I was, too. I thought losing Ryan would ruin me. I thought having a failed marriage would be the end all. And it was all because that was what the people closest to me always made me believe, but it wasn't truly my own opinion. I spent months battling against myself. I love him. I hate him. When in reality, my love for him was truly the bare minimum. I just hung onto that minimum like it was my life support. It wasn't.

And it was even easier for me to get over him when I found that forged suicide note he'd typed up on his laptop. He was going to kill me, take the insurance money, and go live a happy life with his side piece, all while making it look like I had done it. It's why he spent so much time making my family believe I was unstable. Making *myself* believe that I was unstable.

It took that woman from the water–waterbed–to show me what I already knew deep down inside. He was a horrible human being. And I was so incredibly grateful for her.

"Yeah, I feel like I have a lot less baggage in my life without him now." A genuine smile spread across my face.

"And you haven't heard from him at all?"

"I can honestly say that I have no idea where he's at." And I didn't. Not really. Somewhere in the depths of my waterbed, I guessed. But how ridiculous would I sound telling my therapist that?

A long day at work called for a hot and steamy shower. A shower that would make Satan say "ouch." With my hair and body washed, my comfy pajamas on, I slipped underneath the silky blankets on the waterbed. I curled up, relaxing against the current that flowed beneath me. There was sweet comfort in this bed. A comfort that wasn't there before, and I relished in it as the waves gently rocked me to sleep.

Mr. Ferry

BY KIRSTEN NOELLE CRAIG

Viola has worked up a sweat by the time she arrives at the last yard sale stop of the afternoon. It is a sunny, mild spring day and the perfect weather for oddity hunting. One might think a normal-looking suburb like this one would not be a great spot for finding weird items. Those people would be wrong. So far today Viola has found some unique treasures including a lucky rabbit's foot, a set of old dentures, and a lava lamp. The lava lamp is not technically an oddity, but she couldn't pass it up.

Stepping off the sidewalk and onto the driveway of the last house, Viola notes that the heat from the sun seems to have backed off a bit. She lifts her gaze to the sky briefly. The horizon now resembles a smudged line of grey. The sun is hidden behind several heavy-looking, grey clouds now. The wind picks up slightly and the sweat that has accumulated across Viola's back becomes chilly. *"Gotta get in and get out. Didn't bring an umbrella"* she thinks to herself.

Her strategy for yard sales is simple: go straight to the homeowner or family member sitting outside with the cash box and get the scoop. This plan has worked out very well for her thus far and she doesn't deviate from it today. Turns out this sale is being run by a couple of siblings who recently lost both their parents tragically. Viola gives the appropriate words of condolence. The oldest sibling, a woman who looks to be in her mid-fifties, gives Viola a warm but tired smile as she explains that her parents were pack rats. She further explains that her parents were "into strange stuff." In her head, Viola thinks *"Score!"* and gets to work on the boxes.

Right before Viola is ready to give up for today, she spots a box with the label "Mr. Ferry" scrawled across it in a black Sharpie. She leans down and pulls up the box flaps to reveal a scruffy, bedraggled taxidermy ferret. The ferret is almost completely dark brown with a band of white circling his eyes and mouth. The usual cute, button eyes of these animals are missing from Mr. Ferry and are instead replaced with milky white orbs that seem to gaze directly at her. Without hesitation, Viola tucks the box containing Mr. Ferry under her arm and heads over to pay the lady. She notices briefly that the woman does not even look at the item she has selected from the piles. She does not meet Viola's eyes at all during the interaction. "Grief is complicated," Viola explains to herself as she hefts her finds into her take-along wagon and heads for home.

That evening Viola sips on some sleepy-time tea while she listens to Lofi tunes and unpacks her spoils. Many of her finds for today will go onto her Etsy shop for other collectors to purchase. Mr. Ferry though will go onto her shelves with the several other taxidermy animals she owns. She is quite proud of the selections of stuffed critters she has curated. Among the more common ones like a cat, a crow, and a fox are the harder to find animals like a rattlesnake coiled to strike and a raccoon with its fangs bared. She thinks at her last count she owns close to thirty taxidermy specimens. Viola adds Mr. Ferry to the group of glassy-eyed animals and continues unpacking her haul.

After securing the yard sale treasures in their new homes, she shifts her focus to the items she wants to list online. She has an idea for how she can showcase the dentures, so she grabs her sketchpad to draw up a plan. The soft swish swish of her pencil lead across the slightly textured paper is soothing and Viola lets herself relax into the process. She is deep into her planning when a movement in her periphery pulls her attention taut. A flash of fur was what she thought she saw but that had to be her imagination running wild. She glances warily at the taxidermy shelves just to be sure. She can't stop the little hairs on her neck from rising when her eyes fall on Mr. Ferry. She tries to ignore the thought that pops into her head next: Mr. Ferry isn't in the spot on the shelves she put him in.

That night Viola sleeps and dreams of the swishing sound her pencil made during her sketches. When she tries to focus on her hand to see what she is dream drawing she realizes the pencil isn't a pencil but a ferret's tail. It swishes back and forth in front of her face like a metronome. Viola wants to scream but everyone knows you can't scream in a dream. Without interruption, the nightmare in front of her continues. On her sketchpad, she watches as the ferret's tail keeps up its ghostly writing. The only thing legible on the paper is the word "No" written repeatedly in blood. She jerks from sleep when her actual mouth releases a ragged scream. She can't go back to sleep for a long time.

"I swear something is off about that thing, Vi," her friend and fellow oddity aficionado Shelby exclaims.

Shelby had come over the next evening to check out all the fun stuff Viola had grabbed during the yard sale. She is pacing back and forth in front of the taxidermy shelves with a troubled look on her face. She stops to study the stuffed animals displayed on the walls. Viola watches as her eyes rove past the others and land firmly on Mr. Ferry. She briefly contemplates telling her friend about her dream last night but decides against it. She was being a weirdo and voicing the nightmare aloud may only give it more space in her brain.

A few moments of silence pass before Shelby turns away and shakes her head while muttering, "Seriously. Feels super messed up."

Viola shifts uncomfortably from foot to foot. "I know. I agree." Her reply to Shelby comes out so low it is almost a whisper.

She hopes the unease she feels didn't translate into her words. Shelby locks eyes with Vi. Vi feels her trying to assess if something more is going on with this situation. All her friend says as she heads out of Vi's apartment is, "Okay well, call me later and check in. Please?" Vi nods weakly as she shuts the door behind her.

Thin rays of moonlight are slipping through gaps in her curtains and spilling onto her bed when Viola wakes suddenly. Something roused her from sleep, but she cannot place what. She remains still in bed with her ears working overtime to discern any noises in the room around her. For the briefest of moments, Viola thinks she hears a clicking or tapping sound to her right. It doesn't come to her again after several seconds of listening, so her brain relaxes minutely.

"Well, I'm already up. Might as well go pee" she thinks to herself as she climbs from the bed and slides her house shoes on.

Passing through the room to the bathroom she notices a small lump on the carpet. She bends to pick it up. It is one of her stuffed frogs she keeps nestled at the top of her shelves.

"What are you doing here, little one?" she asks of its bulging, glassy eyes. It offers no explanation. Viola sets it gingerly back in its place and continues her late-night pilgrimage to the toilet.

Business finished; she pads softly back to her warm bed. Halfway there, something compels her to glance over at her taxidermy shelves. "Huh, I could have sworn I put Mr. Ferry on the top shelf … " She feels pretty shaken at the sight of the ferret being on the lowest shelf now, but she chalks it up to the excitement of the day and continues to her bed. She can't suppress the hairs that begin to rise on her arms as she goes.

Viola has just drifted back off to sleep when a thump jolts her into consciousness. Instinctively she sits up and peers into the inky darkness of her room. There is no longer moonlight illuminating her direct proximity, so she sees a whole lot of nothing. A tickling sense of unease is working its way up her stomach and lodging itself in her throat. Before she can again chalk it up to her long day, she hears a second thud. This is followed in quick succession by many more jarring thumps and bangs.

"The animals are falling off the shelves," she thinks with frightening clarity.

Viola stays as still as possible. The silence that hangs in the room after all that racket is absolute.

From somewhere on the floor, she hears a chorus of swishing noises. The heavy carpet of her room muffles the sounds, but the progression of the movements is clearly getting closer to her bed. She tenses every muscle in her body as her fight or flight response awakens.

"They are coming this way. The taxidermy animals are headed right towards me" Viola thinks with panic, and she must choke back a sobbing laugh with her hand. Soon she feels a tugging from the bottom of her quilt.

"Oh, hell no!" she screams aloud, and she kicks the covers frantically off her legs while sliding her body backward to meet the headboard. The movement at the foot of her bed ceases all at once and silence again takes hold of the room.

Violas knows she shouldn't want to see, but the urge to do so overwhelms her. She just has to know. She stretches her arm out slowly and fumbles for the small lamp on her bedside table. Her hand knocks into a glass of water sitting on the bedside table and it tumbles off onto the ground. Viola winces but continues searching for the lamp. Her hand finds it and pulls the chain. She keeps her eyes clamped tightly shut as she does so. She feels like a little kid in bed at night who is convinced the boogeyman is under their bed.

"If you don't look, you are never going to be able to go back to sleep, Vi," she mumbles to herself in a weak voice. She counts down in her head from three. On one she opens her eyes.

The last thing Viola thinks before the preserved animal corpses pounce on her is *"No wonder the yard sale lady didn't charge me for that last box."* Then the stillness in the room erupts into a chaos of claws and fur.

Las Pulgas Vestidas

By Alana K. Drex

Adults liked to tell Kelly Singleton how times were so much better for the previous generations, but judging from the familiar grey-streaked woman huffing a greeting with her hoarse smoker's voice from the top of the hill, she wasn't so sure.

"Look who it is!" Mrs. Singleton squealed, running up the hill and away from the bright day. Kelly watched her mom scurry underneath the strange cluster of fat, black clouds that seemed to only be hanging over the yard sale. "How's the sale been?" her mom asked, having reached the top and standing in a shade a few degrees away from night.

The woman, one of her mom's childhood friends, still lived on the same street decades later. Of course, Kelly remembered her because every time the two saw each other—at the odd funeral or wedding—it was required they outdo the other in acting like cocaine-addicted squirrels, a social display of how young and chipper they still were.

"Are you serious? Look around! Nobody wants to even sift through the items of old dead people these days. Too busy getting crunked or something—oh and these clouds have been here the whole time. Weird, huh?" her mom's long-time friend replied and watched the grown children of the dear old dead people—the children no spring chicks themselves—amble over. "I was just saying how now you two can have that truck come by tomorrow so you can get back to the party life! The Singletons are in the house!"

Kelly and James, her younger brother by a couple of years, passed an amused glance regarding all the cringey phrases the woman had managed to get into one breath.

"Kids! Come say hi to everyone!" Mrs. Singleton turned now to flap her hands at her children.

"It will all be over soon," Mr. Singleton reassured his teens as he stepped out and slammed the driver door.

And because this dreaded chore really did seem to be nearing its end, Kelly was able to feign a bit of excitement as she lugged her legs up the hill, James trailing a few steps behind.

"I just don't know why we had to come!" Kelly complained. She'd done so on the long drive out, but now that she knew they'd come only for her parents to pick up a pair of stupid vases and a gross little box of parasites she was even more rankled.

"I grew up on the same block as their kids, Kelly ... was practically like their younger cousin."

When do we even have flowers in the house? Kelly thought, checking her phone for service for the billionth time. The desert landscape streaked by her window, and she knew it would be some time before she could sufficiently distract herself, and by then home wouldn't be far.

"—so it was just the right thing to do," her mom finished.

"You've said that already. There are other things I could be doing," an explosive sigh escaped Kelly's lips.

"Like Matt? At least when the fleas do it, they're married!" James chortled, alluding to the parasites in the small cube he held up and wiggled in his sister's direction.

"Hand them to me, James. Heirlooms are not toys," came their mom's over-this-shit voice scolding from the front. That's when Kelly watched in revulsion as the box dropped from James' hands onto her lap.

She was getting ready to tear into James when the bubbles of irritation dissolved as quickly as they had formed. Thoughts of Matt played in Kelly's head.

"They better still be in there," Mrs. Singleton said. They, being the bride and groom—the dressed fleas of course.

There should have been strong feelings of aversion stirring inside Kelly at the thought of those nasty carcasses making contact with her, yet warm feelings rushed through Mrs. Singleton's daughter's body, unknown to the matriarch herself, who was currently jonesing to jump into the history behind this rare artifact.

"Can we drive past Matt's? See if he's home?" Kelly asked slowly and dreamily. A second later, she felt the light weight lifting from her lap, and James handed the flea box back to Mom. Her disgust returned. The blip of seemingly out-of-place emotion was not unlike when she would make a reel for Instagram, her facial expressions not quite aligning with the audio; lagging behind.

"Anyway, everything there was just tacky pieces of sh—junk," Kelly snapped with more vehemence than the situation called for. Dad cleared his throat in warning. She knew her tone had been overkill, incongruous with the situation, but something felt off, and it unnerved her.

"Sweetie, you're being a bit harsh. You guys didn't know them when you were little kids like I did," her mom answered.

"Haha! She was always drunk!" Mr. Singleton guffawed. Kelly and James exchanged an amused look while Mrs. Singleton glared daggers into the side of her husband's oblivious head.

"*Anyway,* we do these things for the ones left behind. And don't you want to at least know why dressing fleas ever became a thing?" Mrs. Singleton attempted to hijack the conversation, hopefully procuring a bit of calm for the rest of the car ride home.

"Sure," Kelly mumbled at the same time James quipped, "Hey! We brought home *fleas* from a *flea* market!"

"Yard sale, you idiot," Kelly said under her breath.

"So in Mexico, back in the 1800s, a group of resourceful nuns had this creative idea to make *las Pulgas Vestidas* to sell ..."

As the story unraveled, falling to a low drone, the marmalade-orange sunset started to dim. Purple smeared its edges as the car's tires crossed the Singleton family's city line. Visions of home—and Matt, thankfully less than an hour away—danced in Kelly's head as she drifted to sleep hearing no more of the silly 'history.'

The vision of a gargantuan face hovered. Nostrils led like tunnels to catacombs. Lips parted, and words tumbled down, drowning them. A language indistinguishable in its low, vibrating tones.

Yet, they could understand when the other *female voice spoke, her words crystal clear, her English not an obstacle. And there was an energy in the air. Had that awoken them?*

Where were they? When last they'd gone to sleep in each others' arms it was on a worn twin mattress in a stone room with a tiny perimeter and massively high walls. Bells would toll to wake them every morning. But bells had not tolled that day …

The history lesson progressed, and words became clearer. Soon it all came rushing back— albeit with many more details than this historian could provide.

For while the giant lady, lips caked in frosty pink, had covered las pulgas vestidas, she had not *covered their history as the disfrazado de pulgas—or the 'ones dressed as fleas.' No, Father Iglesias and Sister Maria—for their names had finally come back to them—had certainly not always been embodied in fleas.*

It was a witch or bruja *that had caused their entrapment, transferring their souls into the bodies of fleas, one clothed as a bride, one as a groom.*

The conversation in the car turned to the teenage girl and her apparent angst over someone named 'Matt.' Had this, the energy of possible true love awoken them? Because it had to be something about the girl 'Kelly,' since hers was the voice understandable from the start.

And it seemed the only problem wasn't the glue sticking them down (where they wore the garments that had mocked them for over a century) or even their still-frail bodies—they had to get the adults out of the picture.

Kelly awoke to the sound of the car door slamming. Excited to be back home, she opened her eyes, and—

They still weren't home. But to her delight, Matt now sat next to her in the middle seat.

So her dad *had* listened, always having been one to keep his "little girl" happy. Now Matt leaned over, kissing her gently on the lips. To that James made a pukey sound and Mrs. Singleton said, "Don't be rude."

Kelly twisted in her seat to capture Matt's cheek with a hand, then pressed her lips into his to draw the kiss out, ultimately provoking more pukey sounds from the other side of the car.

When the kiss ended Matt turned to take in James' reaction. "Did you know your sister is hot?"

"That's weird, Matt," Kelly laughed, even as she felt the rush of pleasant tingles from his words.

Inside their box held in Mrs. Singleton's hands, Father Iglesias and Sister Maria could feel the power of these two young people's forces. There was a visual orbit of their auras streaming like the aurora borealis over their box. Various colors swirled. Straw-like proboscises arose from the white surface each had been stuck to since before sliced bread had been a thing. No time was wasted sucking up the pinkish-reddish glows—even a color they had never seen before. Bodies that had been fragile and brittle seconds earlier were fortified; tough, and shiny, but still immovable under still-faded fabric.

And soon they discovered they could communicate telepathically, and so they conversed about how there seemed to be yet another power taking root—unfurling itself and growing inside them. It was not a puzzle they were frantic to solve because, intuitively, they knew it would be revealed at the right time.

In the meantime they conversed:

Is there an endless amount of these colors?

Only one way to find out.

We'll have to get to the source.

Sister Maria and Father Iglesias plotted, agreeing that the adults definitely had to go. Nothing could be allowed to get in their way.

Regardless of the nap Kelly had taken earlier, the teen found herself feeling tired again, listening to Matt's slow, heavy breathing next to her that could only mean he was on his way to sleep, too. This lack of energy troubled her. It wasn't like they lived far enough away from each other to squeeze in a sufficient nap during the short trip.

But there was something else bothering her too.

"Hey! Why aren't we moving?" Kelly wondered aloud. They were only a couple blocks past Matt's house, sitting at a stop sign with no cross traffic in sight.

Her dad was stiff in the driver's seat. His gaze was glued to the rearview mirror and frozen in shock; pupils tiny pinpricks surrounded by gleaming whites.

Mr. Singleton rubbed his neck slowly as if trying to snap out of something.

"Honey?" Mrs. Singleton nudged her husband's arm to coax a response. His arm fell away from his neck heavily at the touch. "Hon—" she tried again, voice dropping out after the first syllable.

Kelly turned her vision back to see what had shut her mom up. Her eyes didn't have a chance to fully take in the terror responsible for the sudden silence before a scream ripped through Mrs. Singleton's throat, turning her daughter's sight back to view her mother's too-wide jaws.

And when she turned back, there it was—the horrid sight. Mr. Singleton's head crooked back, eyes rolling around wildly. But perhaps worst of all, his tongue was now like a purple lolling grub leaking drool down the side of his chin.

The ambulance had come and gone with Mr. and Mrs. Singleton in the back. Since the incident had happened four blocks from home, the three teenagers didn't have long to walk, each in their dumbfounded silences. Kelly would have driven but at eighteen still didn't have her license. Before Mrs. Singleton had left, she'd hastily backed the car up onto the roadside. It now sat half in someone's yard and half on the edge of the road at a diagonal.

At least the EMTs had done their jobs efficiently enough, immediately shooting her dad up with epinephrine. That was what was most important. His breathing had regained a more steady wheeze before Mrs. Singleton handed Kelly the house key, reassuring them all that she'd call from the hospital just as soon as possible.

Kelly trudged with tired legs beside her boyfriend and brother, carrying one of the two vases from the yard sale that she was sure was responsible in some way for what had happened to her dad. *Some kind of delayed allergic reaction to that stupid sale,* she thought. *Maybe some old plant dust in the bottom of these ugly things ...*

"What is this, anyway?" Matt was first to break the silence as he held out the tiny container.

"How did you get that?!" Kelly snapped, quickly adding, "Sorry, I thought that was still in the car. It freaks me out."

"Whoa! Your mom handed it to me after she gave you the keys," Matt said, then his eyes softened as he reached around with his free hand to place a squeeze on her hip, simultaneously nibbling her ear. The walk became more of a challenge as both teenagers' legs became shaky and slow from their rushing hormones and tiredness.

"Sick!" James yelled and snatched the keys from Kelly, running ahead.

"Can I stay tonight?" Matt asked, voice low with a bit of huskiness to it that managed to touch Kelly's most intimate places.

She couldn't have dreamed of giving any other answer than the one that burst from her lips.

"Yes." The girl they'd come to know as Kelly replied, just as Sister Maria had conceded breathily that first time Father Iglesias had pressed her against the stone of the hallway outside her room with a warm hand inside the tunic of her habit, roving.

And soon Sister Maria was gushing to her close friend Sister Theresa about the paradise the young, handsome priest would take her to once a week. Then it became twice a week and then a few times until finally nearly every night.

Neither could refuse the temptation of the flesh.

It wasn't long before she confided, "I want to run away with him and get married somewhere far away."

"But I don't want you to leave me," Sister Theresa had said, looking wounded. "If you want to run away, I'll go with you. We can find a better heaven than the one you speak of—together."

It was true, they'd become fast friends even though the girl had only been at the convent for half a year, her parents having abandoned her due to the unexplainable things their daughter could do. Sister Maria had especially enjoyed the story about her friend's father losing his voice in the middle of a tirade, beginning to oink as a pig. The visual of a man turning red and running out of the house, oinking as he went, was enough to make her double over, belly hurting from uncontrollable laughter.

Yet for all their closeness and shared secrets, Sister Maria fell into an awkward silence at Sister Theresa's revelation, not knowing what to say. She didn't yearn for her friend's touch the way she did the young priest's. That was different, and Sister Theresa didn't seem to understand ...or maybe she did.

It was an overcast day in the church's garden when Father Iglesias proposed the very thing Sister Maria wanted, creating all the warmth missing from the absence of the sun. But Sister Theresa couldn't know of it. It would be horrid to hurt the girl who had been her best friend over something she obviously would never approve.

It would be better to just take off.

Except that it wouldn't be that easy for the sinning lovers.

"Flea bites! Or some kind of small bug bites, isn't that a weird coincidence?" Mrs. Single-ton relayed to Kelly about an hour later on the phone. "His blood pressure keeps dropping but they're working to stabilize it. I just don't understand ..."

After ending the call, Kelly quickly located the flea box from the entry hall table and stuck it in the back of the junk drawer in the kitchen. This drawer never got cleaned out, and the chance of the ugly thing being found in the next decade was slim.

The action may have been unfounded and silly, but those things were gross and she didn't want to see them. *Maybe it will find itself mysteriously in the dumpster*, Kelly thought as she recalled the bit her mom had relayed about how the nuns stopped dressing and selling fleas in the 1930s, when people started thinking more about diseases.

Matt came up from behind, enveloping her in his strong arms and interrupting her thoughts.

"What are we gonna do now?" he whispered. Stubble brushed her earlobe, and she shuddered.

"Whatever we want to," her response was automatic. She took one of his hands and twirled herself under his arm, then around to face him before passing him to lead him down the hall.

Once at the threshold of her bedroom—still decorated in the various shades of pink Kelly had insisted on at age nine—Matt lifted his girlfriend, marched her across, and threw her playfully down on her bed before diving on top.

Although Kelly had her own tricks up her sleeve, and she began tickling his muscled abs with fervor. Her boyfriend was the most ticklish person ever, and she found it endearing how he pretended she could actually hold him down. But eventually, like Matt always did after tolerating this a while, he lifted her off, springing up and running laps around the room. He faked fear until finally Kelly managed to convince him he was safe, and he joined her on the bed. They leaned against her Barbie pink chesterfield headboard, assuming their favorite position; Kelly with her back against his chest, his legs surrounding hers, and his arms wrapping her in a warm hug.

"So what were you thinking about back there?" he asked.

"What do you mean? When?" Kelly leaned her head back against the crook of his neck and shoulder.

"In the kitchen. You worried about your dad?" Matt rubbed then squeezed her thigh.

"Oh no, he's where he needs to be. I'm sure he'll be fine. I was hiding the fleas ..."

"You and those fleas," Matt chortled. But Kelly, not wanting to consider just what it was that made her so uneasy about those things, ignored his response, shoving his hand from her thigh and turning around to straddle him, pressing her lips into his.

It wasn't long before the couple writhed on Kelly's bed together, completely unaware of what was about to happen next.

Sister Scorned (for the name of who she once had been was long gone) floated in the tree outside the white clapboard and black-shuttered ranch-style home, vowing to make them pay. Their names were also gone to her, only the basest feelings associated with them remained. Only unadulterated hate fueled her now, literally blazing a searing pain deep in her soul.

She had chosen this fate when she sought out the ancient bruja. But it was worth it even if she couldn't quite recall all the details.

If she could remember who she once was, she'd remember how in the past no one had ever understood the girl named 'Theresa.' And before long she had been labeled a bruja because she spoke to nature more than people—eventually forming the ability to make the confounding happen on occasion. They swore it was because they loved her that they sent her away for her unwillingness to conform—rather than 'outing her.' Yet it didn't take long at the convent before she assumed she'd finally found love and acceptance in another.

But that very person was the same person she had ended up hating most. More even than her first abandoners. The young nun her heart melted for was worse than them since she had accepted who Theresa was before ultimately ditching her.

So the help from a more seasoned bruja was needed, and after stealing church monies such assistance was acquired from such a woman:

The sprinkling of special powder onto a pair of dressed fleas (that would be sold to some naive tourists later) and then onto her betrayers as they slept limbs intertwined, sweat still cooling.

The saying of the incantation that transferred the nun's and priest's souls and locked them away where they would lie unable to communicate a mere inch apart forevermore.

But it wasn't forevermore.

The bruja had told her this part was included for balance. The part was this: if a couple truly in love crossed paths with the doomed priest and nun, the ability to feed and jump into those bodies would present itself to them.

Sister Theresa hadn't believed it would ever happen because she would ensure the box would never have a chance to go anywhere. She couldn't have accounted for the most overzealous of the sisters, Sister Lupe, to spot the box, taking it upon herself to put it with the other ones where dumb fat tourists could purchase them to take home and show off to friends, another artifact to rub in how their money could afford them to go anywhere and find the rarest of curios. This meant the rest of Sister Theresa's short life had been lived wondering if and when the second part of the spell would take place.

After so much time, the second part of the bruja's spell was taking place—forevermore had ended tonight, *and Sister Theresa's damaged spirit (again, now simply Sister Scorned) had been taken to them as the three were linked for all eternity.*

The only way Sister Scorned could sleep peacefully again would be if the cursed lovers were recaptured. If she couldn't accomplish that, she would be cursed to roam the earth with that burning pain lodged in her phantom breast—an unrelinquishing hate filling her soul without a release valve.

"You must understand that you can't truly stop or destroy love—even with magic. You can only separate its players," the bewhiskered old bruja had explained. "And if the players find each other again through incidentally crossing true love's path, all that will be required for you to stop your torturous burning will be to kill the host bodies they seek to take."

And so hours ago, Scorned's spirit had awakened—traveling from where Theresa's corpse had joined nature—now floating closer and closer to a pinkish-red aura (and another nameless colored one) from the other side of the window glass. The colors throbbed in time with her dreadful burning pain.

After over a hundred years and thousands of miles, she would separate again what had once crushed her human heart.

James walked barefoot, his steps silent on the cold, white kitchen tiles before stopping in front of the drawer he'd spied Kelly stuffing the box into. *How could she hide away something so awesome?* Of course, he couldn't let anyone know his interest in ... well, anything. That's why he played off pretty much everything with jokes that even he found to be dumb if he were being honest. Opening the drawer, he removed and placed forgotten objects onto the counter as quietly as he could—not that they'd hear him over what they were doing.

He scooped up binkies (of which his mom claimed to still cherish—ugh!), an old cordless phone, an empty container of mints, a set of keys, some scissors, and sticks of glue ...

"There you are," James whispered to the pair of fleas. "I'm going to keep you safe in my room." But not long after the words were said, twinges of pain froze him in his tracks. Shortly after, his vision tunneled, narrowing into pinpoints, skin hot and swollen. The grab for the countertop proved futile and he collapsed bringing most of the junk he'd cleared to scatter around him on the floor—and the box escaped his hands.

Out came Father Iglesias and Sister Maria who now found they could move—thanks to feeding from the boy's essence as they had done his father's. They tore themselves away from their display, the backs of their garments ripping before traveling their insectile vehicles down the hall.

Now they were jumping as carefree as, well—the fleas that dressed them.

Not a single care was to be had, even as behind them James wheezed out a last squeaky breath.

From the room down the hall, Sister Scorned saw them approaching. She'd floated through the bedroom window only minutes ago, watching the young couple wrapped together on a bed, hungrily kissing and the devil knew what else under that comforter.

She'd wanted to throttle them, but sadly found she lacked the ability. Like a sort of instinct it soon came to her what was needed, but first she had to hide from those fools. Swiftly gliding, Sister Scorned took the opportunity to hide behind the bedroom door. *No wits about them ... but they wouldn't know about the* full *curse.*

Any body would do. Perhaps there was a pet around somewhere? She could use the family dog to rip their throats out.

Her targets now hopped through the door, and she slipped out into the hallway. Let them get comfortable; it would be better they get a taste of what they could have had again before she tore it away. The burning in her breast seemed to lessen a bit at the thought. Sister Scorned turned where she stood in the hallway to watch the scene in the room now behind her. The reanimated parasites bounced up onto the bed, seeming to hesitate. Perhaps they were communicating what to do next. But it didn't take long before they found a way into the bodies: Iglesias through the male's right ear, Maria through the female's left.

Suddenly Kelly jolted. One minute she was making out with her boyfriend, exhilarated, thinking this would be *the night*—the next she felt a tickle in her ear and was a mere passenger in her body. The world shook back and forth, and ... *Can you have fully formed thoughts during a seizure?* she wondered.

Then the shaking jittered to an abrupt stop. Kelly tried to use her voice but found she could not. Her hands began moving over Matt's body all on their own volition.

"Ha pasado mucho tiempo," Matt whispered what she knew was Spanish in her ear. He nuzzled her neck and she couldn't feel it.

What the hell? Kelly thought, while, *"Mmm,"* her throat purred silkily.

The scene brought a smile to Sister Scorned for the first time since returning to the mortal world. She floated on down the hall, wasting no time when she spotted what laid in a staring lump. Her soul with its own instincts, threaded itself easily into the vessel, like a needle poking through the tight crevice that was the boy's swollen tongue and palate. It didn't matter he was dead, this still qualified as the requirement of 'any body', and as an added benefit no stiffness had set into the cartilage and musculature.

She tottered the body, clumsily swiping the cleaver from the butcher's block as she passed it. The heated old lovers didn't even hear the threat coming.

But Kelly and Matt did.

And when the form loomed over where Kelly could see the face of her living dead brother she shuddered. *His eyes were different. They were his—and somehow* not *his.* The soft light of the moon filtered in, insisting on presenting the harsh truth: that James wore the unfocused gaze of the undead she'd seen in numerous zombie movies.

As James' hand gripping the cleaver rose up and arced down, his head shot back on his neck.

THWACK into her numb shoulder it stuck.

Hefting it out of the fresh divot, his head came forward—until the cleaver again arced down and his head shot back to stare at the ceiling. *TWHACK* (this time into the left side of Matt's skull). Matt's eyes showed fear, but like Kelly there was no scream.

Her little brother seemed like a marionette, strings pulled, head bobbing up and down almost comically as he alternated chops between Kelly and Matt's bodies. Blood sprayed black across the wall and bedsheets, and the last thing Kelly noticed, before everything went black, was how James' tongue was now also fat and protruding as her dad's had been.

And then—not that she knew it—even after death the cleaver continued jamming into her, then Matt.

Her, then him.

Her, then him.

And was it a relief for Sister Maria and Father Iglesias that they hadn't felt the pain? Or was it a new kind of nightmare, that they had known what was happening, known of their doom, but had not been able to escape?

Twenty-one thwacks to each, and the teenagers had been greeted by total blackness (long before that number), a blackness forever invading their vision and consciousness.

As for Sister Scorned, her soul was ejected after those burning pains were extinguished, snapping her back to from whence she'd come. Next, James' emptied corpse paused a few beats after her departure, before flopping to the floor limply.

Then Sister Maria and Father Iglesias used their fading energies to make their way despondently out of the dead hosts and back to their tomb.

The next morning found them still barely hanging on, when on their last dregs there was the light sound of a key turning in the front door. Forlorn steps shuffled past, and a woman sighed. The mom; back by herself. And with her came currents of black and grey—no energy to help their state.

The end was imminent now.

In these final moments they murmured "love yous" telepathically; each utterance quieter than the last, spiraling down into the sleep of the comatose. The last thing Sister Maria and Father Iglesias heard was the scream of grief. It lullabied them the rest of the way into a familiar abyss.

That primal wail had come from down the hall where Mrs. Singleton realized she'd lost everything that meant anything to her in the mere last twelve hours.

Even so, people were strange, and the woman would come to grow a strong attachment to *las pulgas vestidas*, believing they were in her life for a reason since she'd discovered the tiny things in their box, lying untouched in the melee of scattered refuse. They could have easily been stomped on or lost, but the fact they were unscathed must have meant they had been saved for a reason. For this she gave them a prime spot, hanging them above her bed only a couple of days after the funerals.

And that's where Sister Maria and Father Iglesias would lie unaware in slumber—waiting to be awoken, when and if true love's energy should ever spark the air once again.

Time To Go

By Carolyn O'Brien

Lucy rummaged through her bag in search of her cell phone. She fumbled with the bifocals that dangled on the beaded lanyard around her neck before glancing at the illuminated screen. That silly picture of her dog, Popcorn, always made her chuckle. She focused on the clock widget overlaying the wallpaper; it was time to go. Levi and his wife weren't due to be at her house for a few more days, but she still had to pick up a handful of supplies at the market before it closed. The couple was going to be staying with her while their house was being fumigated and she was going to make their stay delicious.

She paid for her find and was on her way. *Exactly what I needed,* she thought, *must be fate.*

At home, she plunked the sack of baking ingredients on the kitchen table and marched upstairs to her bedroom. She sat on the edge of the bed and unwrapped the digital alarm clock she had just purchased at the yard sale. Using her phone's alarm was adequate for a while, but over time she found it a burden to make sure the device had been fully charged before bedtime. A separate alarm clock was better suited for her needs.

The clock operated on batteries, the same size as the ones she used in her television's remote control. She opened the drawer in the nightstand and grabbed the spare pack of double A's. She inserted them into the back of the clock and turned it over. The numbers glowed.

"Seven, five, five, zero," she whispered quietly to herself, then shrugged.

She inspected the mechanism for a button, a dial, a switch, anything to adjust the time but nothing blemished the smooth plastic. She wondered how she could be so stupid as to overlook the verification of such important features before she bought it. She put the clock down on her nightstand. Maybe Levi could help her figure it out. Right now, she had some cookie dough to prepare.

When Lucy opened her eyes the next morning, the first thing she saw was the alarm clock. The numbers were now seven, five, four, nine. She was sure they were seven, five, five, zero yesterday. She played those numbers in the lottery. If fate had brought her to the clock, maybe it was showing her the lucky lottery numbers. She played, but not one number was a match.

She didn't give the mysterious digits another thought that day. She threw on an old flimsy house dress and headed downstairs to make her cookies.

On the third day, the numbers were seven, five, four, eight. Whatever those numbers were, they were counting down the days. *The days to what,* Lucy wondered. *To Christmas?* She bounded down the stairs and rounded the corner to the kitchen. Time to roll out the pie dough she made yesterday. Pretty soon the house was flooded with the smells of caramel and cinnamon.

That same night, as Lucy lay in bed, she stared up at a crack in the ceiling and pondered the significance of the four digits. Her mind swam with possibilities. She thought the numbers could have been a date, perhaps the last four digits of a phone number. She added the numbers together.

She heard the clock downstairs chime twelve times a while ago, and she instinctively rolled over to look at the digital clock next to her bed. The numbers were fuzzy without her glasses, but they were definitely seven—five—four—seven. She thumped onto her back. *Well*, she thought, *it's another day gone.* She snatched her phone from the night-stand, turned on a podcast, and fell asleep.

In the morning, Lucy stretched and yawned. The clock still read, seven, five, four, seven. As she finished getting ready for the day, she again started to wonder about the connection to the countdown. *Seven thousand five hundred and forty-seven divided by three hundred sixty-five days equals twenty years and approximately seven months*—a knock on the door startled her out of her trance.

"Aunt Lucy," her nephew called out from downstairs.

"I'm upstairs," she shouted. "Come here — I want to show you something."

Levi darted up the staircase, skipping every other step with each stride. He sauntered down the hallway and hopped across the threshold into his aunt's bedroom.

"What do you think those numbers mean?" Lucy asked.

"What numbers?"

"The four numbers on the clock—or whatever it is, I can't seem to find any means of setting the time."

"I suppose the numbers could *be* the time," Levi quipped.

Lucy wasn't in the mood for jokes. "Try again, smartass."

Levi looked at the clock. "Seven, five, four, seven. — Well, it's not military time."

"The number is subtracted by one every day," Lucy informed him.

Levi lifted the clock in both hands. He turned it this way and that, before viewing the screen again. There were five numbers now.

"Two, zero, eight, zero, five—what the ..." Levi blurted.

Lucy sidled up behind her nephew and peered over his shoulder. She grabbed the clock out of his clutch. The glowing numbers changed back to seven, five, four, seven. "I'm just gonna get rid of the thing."

"Wait, let me see it again."

Lucy handed the clock back to Levi. Sure enough, the numbers changed back to two, zero, eight, zero, five. "Do you mind if I take it?" he asked.

"Go right ahead, I don't want it."

"I'm here!" Levi and his aunt Lucy were startled. It was Eve, Levi's young wife.

"Up here," Levi yelled.

Eve climbed the staircase and joined her husband and Aunt Lucy in the bedroom.

"I guess you two can get settled in the bedroom down the hall," Lucy offered.

Levi picked up the duffel bag in one hand and carried the clock in the other before he led Eve to the room to unpack.

That night, Levi lay on his side and stared at the bright green numbers on the clock. He counted the gongs as the grandfather clock downstairs alerted the household that it was midnight. As the final gong rang out, Levi witnessed the five become a four. Making the numbers, two, zero, eight, zero, four.

"Twenty thousand eight hundred and four divided by three hundred sixty-five days equals approximately fifty-seven years—what if that thing is showing its owner the number of days they have to live?"

When Levi arrived at Aunt Lucy's house after work the following day, he went upstairs to change into a more comfortable set of clothing. He noticed that the clock now showed the number three. He felt something clamp onto his shoulder, and he flinched. He turned, "Oh, hey, what's up?"

Eve gave his shoulder a squeeze and then dropped her hand by her side. "I was doing some dusting today and when I moved your clock, I must have done something to change the number. I don't know how to change it back."

Levi couldn't move. He just glared at his wife, alarm and fretfulness overshadowed his features. "No worries," he said in a hushed tone.

"What? Is there something on my face," she asked, and combed her hair back with her fingers.

Levi couldn't tell his wife that the number three was quite possibly the number of days she had to live. He prayed that his theory about the digits was wrong.

Over the next couple of days, Levi did his best to hide his concern about his wife's foretold fate, but when that third day arrived, he took the day off of work to stay home with Eve. That morning, while he was talking to his mother-in-law on the phone in the bedroom, Eve waited for him to join her for a bath. She liked to lay under the water and stare up at the growing beads of liquid along the faucet. Her eyes closed, and when she started to fall asleep, she sat up quickly, banging her forehead hard on the solid chrome pipe. She blacked out before she plunged backward under the warm bathwater.

Levi heard the splash and tossed the phone onto the bed before sprinting into the bathroom. He bent on one knee and slipped his hand under Eve's neck, lifting her lolling head out of the water, a dark red 'L' indented the center of her forehead. He lifted her from the tub and carried her unconscious body to the bed. After covering her nakedness with a blanket, he picked up the mobile phone. His mother-in-law was still on the line, so when he heard Eve begin to gag, he tapped the speaker feature and dropped the phone again to roll Eve onto her side. She coughed and spat out water and complained about having a headache but seemed to have beaten fate.

Later that day, Levi and Eve made some pickled eggs, and Eve lit some scented candles. She stretched on the chaise lounge with a bag of ice for her head, and Levi popped some homemade bread into the oven. He wanted to make his lasagna for supper, so after reminding Eve not to fall asleep with the candles lit, he left for the market.

As Lucy trekked home from the neighborhood salon and neared the house, she could see smoke billowing out the window. She burst through the front door, and a mist of smoke wafted onto the patio. Through the haze, Lucy could see Eve passed out on the chaise. As she rushed towards her, piercing, beeps from the smoke alarms assaulted her ears. Her eyes watered and a fiery smell burned her nose. She hesitated briefly when she saw the ugly purple 'L' on Eve's head. She tried to wake her by shaking her and when Eve didn't stir, she tugged her arm. The young woman's upper body folded into her lap, but she didn't wake.

Some charred bread was the cause of the smoky ruckus. The clock was correct when it revealed that Eve had three days to live; ultimately, Eve died from a concussion. When your number's up, your number's up.

The Billiken

BY DAN RAFTER

I f you're driving to Iowa (not recommended) or just passing through (a better choice), there's a giant truck stop on Interstate-80. It's so big, it's billed as the World's Largest Truckstop.

What can you get there? You can slowly kill yourself with Wendy's, Taco Bell, or Dairy Queen. If you're one of those very rare travelers in the mood for it, you can even get an Orange Julius.

But that's just the beginning: You can get a haircut or have a tooth pulled at the Iowa 80 Truckstop, too. There's a place to give your dog a bath. You can visit a museum dedicated to trucks and throw your money away at the on-site chiropractor's office.

You can even pass the time at the truck stop's movie theater and library.

Now, if you're driving to Southern Illinois, where the state meets the edge of Missouri—also something that is not recommended—you can visit the second-largest truck stop in the world. Here you can stuff your face with Bluebeard's Burgers, U-Boat Submarines, and Taco House #56. And, yes, there's an Orange Julius here, too, but it's usually closed weekdays and holidays.

There's no chiropractor, but there is a small church run by a preacher who simply goes by the name Joe. There's no museum, but there's a Susie Scents Candle Factory outlet store. There's also a place that sells candy from plastic cubes so empty you need to stick your hand down to the elbow to scrape out the malted milk balls stuck to their bottoms.

Maybe it's because it's only the *second-largest* truck stop, but you'll never see a car with a bumper sticker boasting "I cracked my back at the Cairo Mega Truckstop and Mini-Mall" or "I downed a U-Boat at the Cairo Mega Truckstop and Mini-Mall."

There is one similarity between the largest and the second-largest truck stops in the world, though: They both have dentists.

The ash from Myrtle's cigarette dropped onto Mr. Sims' forehead.

"Myrtle!" Dr. Stan said. "What'd we say about smoking during procedures?"

Myrtle shrugged and tapped Mr. Sims' nose with her index finger. "I don't remember saying anything about it. Besides, he's out."

Dr. Stan shock his head. "Can you at least brush the ash off so when he does wake up it's gone?"

Myrtle obliged him, sweeping the black specks from Mr. Sims' forehead. But she didn't put out her cigarette. There was too much left to smoke.

Stan poked around Mr. Sims' mouth with his forceps, looking for a tooth that didn't have a filling. There weren't many options. Looked like a kid went crazy with a magic marker in there.

Molars were the best. Lucky enough, Mr. Sims had one perfectly unblemished molar stuck way back in his mouth.

"Which one you gonna' take?" Myrtle asked.

"Lower right quadrant. Number 31."

Myrtle blew smoke past Stan's face. "Don't crack it. That's a good one."

"Thanks, Myrt. Think we've been doing this long enough ..." Stan gave one big tug. The perfectly healthy molar popped out. He held the forceps in front of his face and grinned. "T.F. will like this."

Myrtle held out the red change purse so that Stan could drop the molar inside. She bent over the purse, shook the teeth already inside, and did the quick math. "That's 22. A good haul."

"Cheapest prices in the state," Stan said, dropping the forceps on a tray. "Thank God dental insurance is so shitty."

Stan waited in the Bluebeard's Burgers section of the food court. Marquis had already given him a large blue raspberry slushie for "free." Of course, Stan would have to give Marquis two $20 bills from T.F.'s envelope.

Stan poked his finger at the teeth in the change purse. Almost all of them were molars. That was a pretty good three weeks. It was amazing how many truckers were willing to trust their grins to a dentist who worked out of a truck stop.

"Hey, Doc! Thanks! Feel better already." It was Mr. Sims, holding a submarine sandwich in one hand and rubbing his chin with his free one. "Still a bit sore from the tug, though."

Stan nodded, zipping the coin purse shut.

Sims was a long-haul trucker, heading to California. "Appreciate the speed, too."

Stan took a sip of his slushie. "We think of ourselves as the Jiffy-Lube of dentistry."

Stan could tell that Sims was running his tongue along the hole where his molar had been. He'd be back next week for a false tooth that'd fill it.

"Y'know, I didn't even realize I had a cavity there," Sims said. "But once Myrtle mentioned that you had to yank one, I did remember that some of my back teeth seemed a little twingey when I drink a soda. That was probably a sign."

"Probably," Stan said. Most of his patients believed whatever he and Myrtle told them. Made life easier.

Sims nodded at Stan and turned away, off to his truck and his sandwich. And not a moment too soon: Striding past him and toward Bluebeard's was T.F.

T.F. doesn't look especially intimidating. What he does look like is a walking, talking noodle.

The guy is skinny. Stan never saw him without a shirt, but he could imagine the tips of T.F.'s ribs nearly poking through his skin. And the way T.F.'s elbows jutted out like bony apples always made Stan queasy.

Then there was the apparel. Stan never saw T.F. without a SpongeBob SquarePants shirt. Today's shirt had an image of SpongeBob smoking a joint, his bug eyes all glassy and bloodshot. And instead of carrying a briefcase, T.F. always had a bowling ball bag with two straps thrown over his left shoulder. Most days, the bag was bulging. Today it was, too. Stan had no idea what was in there.

"What's the word, Mouth Man?" T.F. asked as he approached the table.

T.F. always called Stan "Mouth Man." Stan hated it.

Stan slid the coin purse across the table, making T.F.'s eyebrows raise. "Hmmm ..." he said. "Looks like a nice set today."

T.F. dropped the bowling bag onto the table. "Tell me they're molars, Mouth. Tell me."

Stan nodded. "They are. Most of them."

T.F. held the coin purse up to his face, unzipped it and peered inside. A smile spread across his face, showing teeth that Stan swore T.F. must've filed into points each night. "Jee-bus," T.F. said. "Molar city."

T.F. never said "Jesus," either. That bugged Stan, too.

Stan wrapped a hand around his slushie. "I still can't believe people buy used teeth. I know how gross teeth are. I don't get it."

T.F. dropped the coin purse in his now open bowling bag. "People are stupid. And superstitious. My buyers think that they gain the strength and extra brain power of the teeth's former owners."

"Insane," Stan said. "What if the people who had the teeth were stupid and weak?"

"Don't matter. Any bit of extra brains and strength helps," T.F. said. "Even from a dumbass weakling. They consider it all a bonus."

"And let me guess. They shove them into their own mouths somehow, right?"

T.F. snorted. "Don't be gross, Mouth Man. They usually wear them on a chain around their necks." T.F. tossed an envelope on the table. Stan noticed that it looked full. T.F. carried several envelopes, choosing the right one after he saw how many teeth, and what kind, Stan provided. He reserved the especially stuffed envelopes for molars.

"And, because you've been such a good supplier as of late, I got something else for you, too," T.F. said. "A bonus gift."

He reached in his bowling bag and brought out what might have been the ugliest baby Stan had ever seen.

Well, that isn't quite right. It was a doll, the ugliest baby doll Stan had ever seen. The thing stood about 15 inches tall and had the body of a brown, fuzzy teddy bear. But its head was plastic, and looked, sort of, like a human kid's. The biggest problem? The doll's eyes were slanted, and its hair was jet black. The head's wide smile exposed a pair of oversized buck teeth.

"That looks a bit racist," Stan said.

T.F. scoffed. "Only if you're looking for that. It's a Billiken doll."

"Weird-looking thing. Where'd you get it?"

T.F shrugged. "A garage sale. When you travel as much as I do, you find these things. It brings good luck."

Stan tapped at the doll's nose. "Uh, if you say so. You can keep it, though. The envelope's more than enough ..."

"Nope," T.F. said. "Figure you could use a little luck. I mean, Jeebus, you're working in a fuckin' truck stop."

Stan picked the doll up and squinted at its slanty eyes. "I'd really like to paint over these eyes."

"Don't be so sensitive. These are collectors' items. Some school in St. Louis even uses it as their mascot."

T.F. was already up and walking away, the bowling bag slung over his shoulder.

"Wait!" Stan called out. "What about you? Don't you need good luck?"

T.F. didn't turn around. Just said, "Mouth Man, I got a purse full of chompers. What do I need luck for?"

Marquis didn't take long to hustle over. He had his cell phone in one hand and was pointing it at the ugly doll. In his other hand, he held a bag that Stan knew came from Susie Scents. It had the store's ridiculous logo on it, a lit cartoon candle pursing its lips and blowing out a match.

"That a Billy Ken doll?" Marquis asked.

"Think it's pronounced 'Billiken?'" Stan said. He reached into T.F.'s envelope and handed a pair of $20 bills to Marquis. Marquis might've been a scammer, but at least he charged reasonable rates for his silence.

Marquis set his bag on the table and snapped several photos of the Billiken with his cellphone. "These are collectors' items. You might get good money for it."

Stan thought about that. But then he also thought about T.F.'s next visit. T.F. wasn't the kind of guy whose gifts you sold.

Stan grabbed the ugly doll, and looked at the maniacal grin and slanted eyes. "No … I'll keep it. Supposed to bring good luck."

Marquis grinned. "Yeah, right. To me, good luck is selling something for big bucks." Marquis opened his shopping bag and held it in front of Stan's face. "What do you see in here?" he asked.

Stan saw candles in there, five of them. "Uh … candles? What am I supposed to see?"

With a sly look, Marquis looked up and over Stan's shoulder. The Susie Scents shop was located at the far wall behind the food court. It was closed now. Susie shut down when she went out for lunch, and she never ate lunch at the truck stop. Grinning, Marquis took a single candle out of the bag, a pink-colored troll doll wearing a bikini.

"This isn't a candle," Marquis said. "It's money."

Stan didn't bother to ask Marquis what he meant. He figured Marquis would explain. Stan was right.

"Trolls are big deals for collectors. And this is a troll that you can only get at the Cairo Mega Truckstop and Mini-Mall."

Stan waited and Marquis told him how much collectors would pay for this particular candle troll: at least $30. Then Marquis leaned forward and whispered, "And it's all profit. I stole that one."

"What?"

"Yep. Bought the other four. Susie didn't suspect that I had Ms. Troll here in my apron pocket. One of the bennies of working at Bluebeard's, an apron with big pockets."

"You stole from Susie?" Susie was a 60-year-old lady with a white bun of hair and Mrs. Claus glasses.

Marquis clucked his tongue, stuffing the bikini troll back in his bag. "You're one to talk."

Stan couldn't argue with that.

Marquis pointed at the Billiken doll. "You better hope you don't get any Orientals into your chair, man. You won't get much good luck if they see that thing. If you need me to sell it, let me know. We could split the profits."

Stan didn't bother telling Marquis that he should've said "Asian." And he had to admit: Marquis wasn't wrong. He'd have to keep the Billiken out of sight.

The first piece of good luck came later that day. A family had stopped in the bulk candy shop. Their daughter—maybe 6 years old—bit down hard into a chalky piece of candy shaped like a Lego brick. The dad heard the "crack" immediately.

Polly, the candy shop's owner, didn't panic. Rather than debate with the girl's dad about just how stale and hard that piece of candy was, Polly did the smart thing: She directed the girl and her family to Dr. Stan's and agreed to cover the bill.

This was a rare opportunity for Stan. Not only would he get a hefty fee for repairing the girl's cracked tooth—with a slightly inflated price for speed so that the tourists wouldn't miss their Disney World vacation—he could also pull an extra tooth from the young patient's mouth.

Baby teeth? They were rare. And T.F. paid a hefty price for them. Said his clients believed they sanded years off their actual ages.

The rest of the family members weren't overprotective types. Mom went shopping at the candle shop while dad and the other kids went to get tacos. It was a Tuesday: Five tacos for five bucks.

That left Myrtle, Stan, and the daughter all alone in what Stan had come to think of as the extraction room. The girl was already asleep; Stan had convinced mom and dad that because he'd have to both repair a cracked tooth and pull another one with a large "cavity," it'd be better to put her under.

Myrtle was typing on her phone with one hand and holding the Billiken with her other. "Says there are three kinds of luck with these guys," she said.

"Yeah?" Stan moved his mirror along the inside of the girl's mouth, looking for the healthiest molar. He was lucky. The girl still had three molars among her remaining baby teeth. But Stan had learned not to get too greedy. Even neglectful parents would think twice if he delivered a kid with three holes in her mouth.

"Good luck if you buy one. Better luck if someone gives you a Billiken. And the best luck of all if someone steals one from you."

"I'm at luck level two now?" Stan laughed. "It's all stupid."

Myrtle pointed the Billiken at the unconscious 6-year-old in Stan's chair. "What do you call this? That kid just happened to bite into the right piece of candy? I'd call that pretty good luck for a crooked dentist, wouldn't you?"

Stan frowned. "Don't call me 'crooked.'"

Stan saw that Myrtle was looking away from him and the girl, staring out the window toward the food court, where Marquis was sitting at an empty table, staring at his phone.

"Watch that one," Myrtle said.

"Mmmm ..." Stan said, staring into his young patient's mouth.

"He's probably looking up how much you could get by selling that doll right now," Myrtle said. "I'd keep it out of his sight. Guy has sticky fingers."

Molar number two seemed like the best bet. It was barely stained and had no cracks. No signs of decay, either. Stan edged the mirror along the side of the tooth and gave it a small push. He could feel some budge there.

Stan could already picture that fat envelope from T.F. next week.

"I'm going after number 2," Stan said, glancing up at Myrtle. "It's pretty pristine."

Myrtle said something in response, but Stan didn't hear her. Instead, his brain could only focus on one thing: the pain shooting through his thumb and index finger.

"Shit!" Myrtle shouted. Stan did hear that. He also noticed that Myrtle's eyes were bugging out and that she was staring at his patient.

Stan looked down and saw the blood dripping down his wrist. Saw, too, that the girl's mouth was clamped completely shut, teeth smashed together so hard that a crack snaked through the middle of her front incisor.

And, of course, he saw that the top halves of his index finger and thumb, the dental mirror still pinched between them, were hidden behind the girl's front teeth.

"Jesus!!!!!" Stan screamed. He yanked his hand backward but couldn't budge it. The pain was blurring his vision. He fell forward, his chin banging against the girl's bony knee.

Myrtle's hands dug into his shoulders. Stan felt her pulling him back. He saw his right arm stretching backward, his thumb and index finger still stuck behind the girl's clamped teeth, blood pouring faster down his wrist.

Myrtle gave him one more hard pull.

The tearing sound made him pass out.

When Stan woke up, the Billiken was looking down at him from a metal tray littered with mirrors, drills, and gauze. Stan could've sworn that the doll's ugly smile was stretched wider than it was when T.F. had set it on the table outside Bluebeard's.

Joe, the truck stop preacher, was kneeling next to him, wrapping gauze around Stan's thumb and index finger. "I'd keep these wrapped, and I wouldn't look under it too closely," Joe said.

"No?" Stan croaked.

"There's not much skin left." Joe cleared his throat. "I think I saw bone. But that could've been tendons or something. Not sure."

Myrtle cleared her throat. "Yeah. The kid, when she came to, had to spit out some of your ... uh ... finger skin? It was all balled up."

"Like a shed snakeskin," Joe added.

The preacher helped Stan to his feet and into the dental chair. Myrtle watched from behind Joe's shoulder. Her face had a greenish tint. Stan turned his head to the side and looked directly into the Billiken doll's eyes.

"Oh. And there's this," Joe said. He handed Stan a wad of crumpled bills—mostly fives and 10s—and five tickets to Disney World.

Stan took the money and tickets in his good hand. Stan swore he saw Myrtle licking her lips.

"What's this?" Stan asked, looking at the money. He'd become fairly good at judging wads of cash. He figured he held about $60 in his hand.

"They didn't have that much cash. Thought the Disney tickets would help make up for it," Myrtle said.

Stan still didn't understand. Joe filled him in: The girl's family didn't want to get sued for the damage done to Stan's fingers. So they shoved a wad of cash in Joe's hand and their Disney tickets.

"I figured it'd be OK," Joe said. "Um ... Considering your arrangement with that other guy."

Stan rubbed his forehead with his injured hand and immediately howled out in pain. It felt like someone had coated his injured thumb and index finger with thumbtacks.

Myrtle tapped the Billiken doll's stomach. "You could almost consider this a bit of good luck. Free Disney tickets don't just drop out of the sky," she said.

Stan groaned. "I hate Disney. And I don't have any kids."

Myrtle shrugged. "I have a granddaughter."

"And I have a grandson," Joe added.

And that's how Myrtle and Joe nabbed five free Disney World tickets between them. And Stan ended up with what turned out to be an extra $72 in cash.

Stan didn't want to unwrap the bandages, even with Marquis encouraging him.

"Aren't you curious at all?" Marquis asked, standing with Stan at the front of the dentist office. "Myrtle said it was really gnarly."

Stan had been practicing moving his thumb and index finger side to side and up and down. If he moved them slowly enough, the pain brought tears to his eyes. But it didn't cause him to scream, which is what he wanted to do whenever he accidentally bumped his hand against the side of his leg.

"I think I'm getting used to it ... a bit," Stan said.

Marquis clapped Stan on his back. "That's right. You gotta' be tough when you're working at a truck stop, right?"

Stan wasn't sure why that'd be the case, but he nodded anyway.

His hands on his hips, Marquis stretched backward. Stan winced at the pops and cracks that came from Marquis' hips. Marquis attributed that to too much standing, waiting for customers to request a Bluebeard's Bonanza Burger. That one came with three patties, a special sauce (that was just mayonnaise mixed with Thousand Island dressing), three purple onions, and four different kinds of cheese (or two, if Marquis was feeling lazy). It was a surprisingly popular choice among truck stop visitors.

"Well," Marquis said. "Gotta' get a get on, Dr. S. Shift is over."

He clapped Stan on the back once again, this time hard enough to jostle Stan's injured hand, sending a surge of lightning up the dentist's arm. Marquis didn't seem to notice as he sauntered though the food court.

But Stan, even through his pain, noticed something bulging in the left back pocket of Marquis' baggy jeans. Something doll-shaped.

And sure enough, when Stan hustled into his office and opened the bottom tray of the metal supply cabinet closest to the door, he saw that the ugly Billiken doll that he'd stashed there was gone.

Stan shivered. The best luck of all comes when someone steals your Billiken doll.

"Oh, shit," Stan said to himself, wondering what extra good luck might mean.

Marquis didn't come to work the next day. That counted as odd. Stan never remembered Marquis missing a day of work. Far as he knew, he came to work on Christmas and Thanksgiving, when Stan's dental office was closed.

But Marquis wasn't here today. Not that it mattered much. The few drivers wandered off to Taco House #56 to get breakfast burritos instead of Bluebeard's Pirate Booty Potato Wedges.

Others wandered into the candy store. Polly sold gummy candy fried eggs and chocolate-covered bacon. Stan heard the families joking that these counted as breakfast.

"Marquis isn't here today," Stan told Myrtle, as he placed a half-eaten breakfast burrito of his own on his desk. "That's odd, isn't it?"

Myrtle took a deep drag off her cigarette. "Don't know about odd. It's nice, though. Don't have to listen to him tell me how much he got for selling a vintage Donald Duck piggybank."

Stan looked across the way at Bluebeard's, a frown on his face. "Did you know that my Billiken is missing?"

"No shit?" Myrtle said. "Better get ready for a big day. You know the legend: The best luck comes when someone steals that thing from you."

Joe walked by the dentist office, heading toward his small chapel in the corner. He held a box of Milk Duds in one hand, purchased fresh from Polly's.

"Done with that?" Myrtle asked, pointing her cigarette at Stan's burrito. Stan noticed a small shower of ash drop onto his breakfast.

"Guess so."

Myrtle snuffed her cigarette into the burrito and then wrapped the whole mess into its greasy wrapper. "Good. Hate the smell of those things. You need to get the real stuff, down at the Junction."

Stan didn't answer. Myrtle grabbed the mess of burrito and cigarette and walked toward the food court. "Oh," she said. "Your first customer is here. Some guy with a toothache. Checked his files and he's only had five fillings his entire life. Lot to choose from there."

"Mmmm ..." Stan said, pressing his gauze-covered thumb and index finger gently on the surface of his desk. They still hurt.

"That's good luck already," Myrtle said, yelling across the food court as she dropped the remains of Stan's breakfast into a trash can that was already overflowing.

Stan hesitated. He gripped his forceps tightly, holding the metal inches from the sleeping man's open mouth. Myrtle was waiting.

But Stan couldn't help but look toward that now-empty file cabinet drawer.

Stan had to hold the forceps in his left hand. His right hand, which he'd normally use, ached too much. But all that this procedure required was a yank, one hard enough to rip that clean molar out with one tug. He'd just tell the patient that he couldn't fill in the real cavity. Make something up about nerve endings or the man's blood-sugar levels. Tell the guy he'd need to see his regular dentist when he got home.

And when the patient woke up? Stan would tell him that this molar needed to go. It was damaged, spreading poison through the man's gums. If Stan didn't yank it right away, it could lead to ear damage. He'd recommend that the guy get a crown to replace it, again from his home-base dentist.

Patients believed anything he told them. And if they were stopping here for dental work? They probably didn't have a regular dentist to blab to later anyway.

But Stan couldn't do it. He couldn't force his left hand—his pain-free, undamaged hand – into the patient's mouth. Not even with the thought of all that molar money from T.F.

Stan could still feel the force that little girl used to snap through the skin of his index finger. He could still smell the blood that poured down her chin and dribbled along his wrist as he tried to yank his hand free.

Myrtle was frowning at him, her thumb and index finger pinching the shrinking remains of a lit cigarette. "Stan? My smoke's almost done here. We doing this sometime today?"

Stan gulped and forced his left hand forward, so that the tip of the forceps moved just past the unconscious man's front teeth. He couldn't reach the molar from here. He'd have to move the forceps deeper into the mouth, pushing the tips of his fingers into the toothy cave. His hand started to shake at the thought.

"Maybe I'll just pull one of the front ones," Stan said. "Right in front."

Myrtle scoffed. "That molar is plump and clean, Stan. That's the money-maker. C'mon. You got good luck on your side, remember?"

Stan nodded and pushed the forceps deeper into the man's mouth. Now the tips of his fingers were inside, past the man's teeth. Sweat rolled down his forehead and burned into his eyes. His mouth was dry.

And then? Stan saw the man's mouth twitch. Just the slightest bit. But that jaw did flinch.

Stan let out a scream, jerked his hand back and fell backward, landing on his tailbone with a thud, the forceps still clenched in his left hand.

Myrtle dropped her cigarette, letting it flame out as it landed on the floor. Her eyes bugged wide as she looked at Stan. "The hell?" she asked. "What happened?"

Stan didn't answer. Instead, he jumped to his feet, still clutching his forceps, and ran out the extraction room, through the front door, and toward the empty, unlit slice of the food court watched over by Bluebeard's Burgers.

Stan had to sit on the floor. The gum that had been stomped into the grey tiles, the ancient cigarette butts scattered around the floor and withered pickles laying nearby weren't inviting, but if he stayed low, his back pressed against the freezer, the travelers couldn't see him. They wouldn't bother him for a Deep Sea Value Meal or Bottom of the Sea breakfast platter.

Sitting down there also kept him out of Myrtle's view. He pushed himself up an inch or two and peeked over the edge of the counter. He could see her talking with Susie in the candle shop. Susie was holding an orange-colored candle, but Myrtle was shaking her head at it. Smart move.

Stan took another sip of the blue raspberry slushie. Marquis had taught him how to use the slushie machine last year, a perk for the $20 bills that Stan funneled to him. The cold air floating off the paper cup eased the throbbing from his index finger and thumb.

In his other hand, his undamaged one, Stan still clutched the forceps. He wasn't sure why he hadn't dropped it yet. He took a sip big enough to give him a freeze headache, a feeling he sometimes liked after a long day of yanking teeth. But the slushie didn't do that today.

Instead, it shot a sharp, hot jolt through his back molar. Stan almost dropped the slushie, the pain was so bad.

It was strange. Stan had never had a cavity. His own dentist, Dr. Maxine, had told him when he was 11 that he had the strongest enamel that she'd ever seen.

The pain in his molar, then, was different, something new.

Gingerly, Stan took another sip of his slushie.

"AAAAHHH!!!" he screamed as the pain from his molar forced him to spit blue ice down the front of his shirt.

He ran his tongue along the tops of his back teeth. Didn't feel anything strange. No holes in any of them.

And that's when it hit him. That final, third stage of good luck, the best luck that a Billiken doll could give. This was a warning sign: His enamel was finally wearing out. His teeth weren't rotting yet, but they would be soon. If Stan waited long enough, cavities would sprout.

But if Stan could get at his teeth now? He'd have an entire mouthful of pristine, never-blemished teeth. That'd be 32 prime, blindingly white chunks of cash to hand over to T.F. Who knows how big T.F.'s envelope would be for such a haul?

Stan opened his mouth wide and shoved the warm metal of the forceps deep inside.

"Stan?"

He looked up. Myrtle was standing there, looking down at him. "What are you doing?"

Stan didn't answer. Instead, he pulled as hard as he could, ripping a chunky molar from his gums with one tug.

"Jesus!" Myrtle shouted.

Stan held the bloody forceps in front of his face and smiled widely. "Just 31 more," he said. "The best luck."

Estelle

BY BRAD WILKINS

Grant watched the houses as he drove from work. People were taking advantage of the warm spring day to clean up their yards. The light overcast kept the temperature comfortable. He had his driver's window down to enjoy the fresh air.

Ahead he saw a group of cars parked at the curb around a driveway. Some still had their engines running. As he got nearer, he noticed a sign on the lawn announcing a yard sale. He could see lights on through the open garage doors next to the house.

On impulse, Grant pulled to the curb between a minivan and a compact pickup. Checking for traffic, he opened his door and stepped out into the warmth of the afternoon. He made his way, carefully, to the sidewalk and approached the garage. Inside, under the lights he could see folding tables with a sparse display of household goods. The sale was, obviously, winding down.

He walked about the tables looking at the kitchen gadgets and old clothing. Nothing caught his eye until, near the door, in a corner, he spotted a rickety table made from two sawhorses and a piece of plywood. On top was a boxy-looking device with a lot of switches and a small, ancient portable television.

He walked over for a closer look. The device was a very old video recorder player. Chunky and square, it had a long row of peg-like switches across the front that ended in a row of oblong buttons. A big, rectangular door with a plastic window gave access to the tape on top. "JVC" and "Triple System" adorned the front panel. An ancient red LED display showed the time on the bottom of the panel, and a mechanical counter occupied the top between the switches and buttons. A series of wires ran from the back of the VCR to the back of the portable TV. Both were plugged into a long extension cord that snaked away into the shadows.

Under the makeshift table sat a dog-eared cardboard box full of old VHS tapes. Grant crouched and pulled the box into the light. He reached in and pulled out a tape. The label was handwritten. "May Day Picnic 1989." The next was in a cardboard sleeve with commercial labeling. "Desperately Seeking Susan" in yellow block letters hung above two young women on a white background. The next was another handwritten label ... "ESTELLE" and "Dr. Bancroft".

"Those were really well-made units." A tall, well-dressed man stood next to him. "I looked this one up. This model was the first commercially produced home video player recorder. JVC introduced it in 1976."

Grant rose and turned to face him. "Does it work?" He turned back to look at the display again. A small sticky label on the VCR said "$50." Another on the TV, "$25." There was one on the box saying "$2 each." Grant considered the possibility of watching some old movies over a plate of takeout. He looked around to see that he was the only customer remaining in the garage. He could just see the back of another walking away in the gloom of the driveway. "It wasn't yours?"

"All of this belonged to my Aunt Estelle. Lived her whole life near here, except for a short stay in a hospital. She died this fall, and we are just getting around to dealing with the remains of the estate."

The man reached over and turned on the TV and then pressed play on the VCR. "It comes with a wired remote." He picked up a small box from the table. It was connected to the front of the VCR by a long, thin black wire. The picture flickered and then steadied to show a group of men on horses firing six shooters. The sounds of hooves and gunfire filled the garage.

"Would you take twenty dollars for the VCR and TV?" Grant knew it was a low ball but hoped the lateness of the hour would motivate the sale.

"I could do fifty for the two." The man looked thoughtful.

"What about thirty for the pair?" Grant felt optimistic.

"Could you do forty?"

"Tell you what," Grant offered, "I could do thirty-five if you throw in the box of old tapes."

The old guy considered a moment, glancing down the drive. He was quite obviously considering his chances of selling anything else today.

"Done. It's yours."

Grant pulled out his wallet and extracted a twenty, a ten, and a five. He noted he had thirty dollars remaining to pick up dinner on the way home. He handed the bills to the old man who produced a large cardboard box that accommodated the small tube TV and the VCR on its side. Grant carried that and the old guy carried the box of tapes which they deposited in his trunk at the curb.

As Grant walked around to the driver's door, he watched the old guy pull the sign from the yard and close the garage door. He got in behind the wheel and drove to his favorite Indian food place. Later he dropped a bag of curry and rice on the passenger seat and headed for home.

At home he carried everything inside and set the VCR and TV on the coffee table in the living room in front of his favorite chair. He set the takeout with a fork on the side table and pulled the box of tapes over to his feet. He pulled out two from the top: the "Desperately Seeking Susan" movie and the tape labeled "ESTELLE, Dr. Bancroft."

Hadn't the seller said that his aunt's name was Estelle and that she had spent time in a hospital? He considered the two tapes for a moment until curiosity overcame him and he inserted the "ESTELLE" tape into the VCR. Turning on the TV, he hit play and picked up his curry.

As the screen flickered and steadied, he settled back in his comfortable chair and opened the takeout container. A deep male voice began a narration as Grant picked up his fork and began to eat in the glow from the screen. The rest of the room faded to shadows.

"December fifteen, nineteen seventy-seven, Beaumont Sanitorium, Doctor Eugene Bancroft. The subject is Estelle Campbell, age twenty-seven, admitted with hallucinations and non-suicidal self-injury." The picture showed a young woman with short, red hair, dressed in hospital pajamas sitting at an institutional metal table. Her complexion was greyish, and her eyes sunken in dark rings. She hugged her knees to her chest and stared nervously at something at the end of the table. "Estelle experiences hallucinations of a small child which apparently attacks her physically. Estelle, can you tell us what you see?"

"Don't you see her?" asked the woman incredulously. "She's right there." One hand released its grip on her leg long enough to point at the end of the table where she had been staring.

"No, Estelle," said the male voice patiently. "We don't see her. Can you describe what you are seeing?"

"But she's right there!" her voice rose with frustration. "A little girl. About ten years old. Skinny, dirty. Long dark hair covering her face. Except her eyes ..." her voice faded fearfully.

"What about her eyes, Estelle?" the doctor asked.

Estelle had averted her face, cowering behind her knees. "They are all black," she said in a small, quiet voice. "Shining with no whites."

"And what does she do?" prompted the doctor.

"She bites me, "said Estelle in a tiny voice, barely audible.

"Pardon me, Estelle? Can you speak up for the camera?"

Estelle uncoiled like a snake, lunging half across the table, both hands planted firmly at its edge. "I said SHE BITES ME!" she roared directly into the camera. Grant flinched and dropped his fork.

Estelle immediately subsided, resuming her previous posture. She avoided looking at the end of the table.

"Can you show us?" asked the doctor.

Estelle hesitantly extended her right arm. The camera angle changed slightly to get a clear view of the upper surface of her arm. There were numerous bite marks visible on the arm. Many of them had drawn blood and were scabbed over. Most were on the forearm with a few on the lower part of her upper arm.

"We believe the bites to be self-inflicted, although no one has witnessed the subject injuring herself," narrated the doctor.

"No, no, no," said Estelle quietly. "She does it." The arm she had been displaying for the camera swung left to point down the table.

Grant grabbed for the remote. It took him a moment to find the rewind button. He rewound the tape to the point where the arm was extended for the camera and paused it. The bites along the upper surface of her forearm extended from her wrist to her elbow with only one or two on her upper arm. He leaned forward and looked at the bites closely. It was hard to tell, the picture quality was not exactly high definition, but the bites appeared to be lower jaw toward the outer surface of her forearm. He looked again. Yes, the larger, upper teeth marks appeared to be toward the fleshier inner surface of the arm.

Grant hit play and watched as the arm swung toward the end of the table, exposing the outside of her forearm. He paused the tape again. There were clear bite marks all along the outer surface of the forearm.

Grant sat back and picked up his fork. He pressed play on the corded remote. He held his own arm up in front of his face. He twisted it, trying to expose the outer surface of his forearm to his mouth. He couldn't see how those marks could be self-inflicted.

On the screen the camera panned to follow her pointing gesture. The end of the table came into view. Nothing was beyond the table except an institutional greenish wall with a row of high set windows of reinforced glass. The camera swung back to Estelle as the doctor replied.

"There's no one there, Estelle."

"What the fuck?" exclaimed Grant as he punched rewind and then play. As the camera started back toward Estelle, he hit pause. He felt goosebumps rise all over his body.

At the end of the table, as if standing there was a dim, transparent image of a little girl. It was like a faint reflection on a sunny pool. A little girl. Head and shoulders above the level of the table. Long stringy, dark hair obscured her face. Dark shiny eyes glaring out between the strands. Her shoulders were clad in a grimy looking white shirt with ruffled sleeves. The straps of an apron or jumper were just visible.

Grant pressed play and the image disappeared as the camera swung back to Estelle. He rewound to the image of the end of the table and let it play again. Just as it began to swing back there was a brief flash of an image. If you weren't looking straight at it at that very instant you would miss it completely.

"Shit ..." Grant breathed.

Something moved in the corner of his eye. His blood froze in his veins. His heart pounded as he turned his head toward his side table. There was someone standing in the shadows on the other side of the end table. The shadows were deep enough that he could just make out the figure of a small child. His mind reeled. This could not be happening.

Grant reached slowly for the pull cord on the lamp on the end table. He could just discern a faint motion of hanging cloth. An apron or a jumper, draped fabric.

As his hand neared the lamp something slender and greyish separated itself from the fabric and moved hesitantly toward him.

He felt his fingers touch the chain.

They closed around it.

He pulled.

The lamp threw a pool of light around the table ...

Illuminating him ...

Illuminating her!

Black shining orbs glared at him through a curtain of lank black hair. She leaned forward, further into the light. The filthy greyish white blouse with ruffles at the shoulder left her pale grey arms exposed. They bent at the elbow, slowly thrusting her clawed hands with cracked, filthy nails toward him. As her face came fully into the light, her lipless mouth opened exposing a double row of cracked stained brown teeth before a wet black emptiness that writhed with obscene motion. She hissed. A stench like a charnel house filled the room.

Grant recoiled as she launched around the light, her teeth snapping shut where his arm had been a split second before. He vaulted the arm of his chair, falling to the floor on his back. The lamp toppled and went out.

Laying on his back staring up at the arm of his chair, Grant could hear the doctor on the tape droning on in his clinical analysis. In the dim light from the TV screen, the top of a head appeared over the edge of the chair. The hanging curtain of hair flowed across the arm and hung straight down toward him. Her face, exposed, held malicious evil, animal rage. As her hands crept over the arm of the chair and crept toward him, he remembered the remote he still held. His thumb sought and then pushed the pause button.

The thing, the creature in the guise of a girl child, froze. She hung, poised across the arm of the chair, reaching for him. Grant scrambled out from under her and rose to his feet. The thing in front of him flickered. It skittered like a video image paused at the wrong moment, caught between frames. Its head moved jerkily to turn its face toward him.

Suddenly the VCR began to play again. In a flash, she was on him, knocking onto his back again. The remote flew from his hand, and he grabbed her by the throat, straining to keep her away. He could feel the strain in every muscle. He kicked his legs and bucked his body, trying, desperately to dislodge her.

His left arm buckled under her ferocity, and her teeth sank into his wrist. A glow of triumph lit her eyes. Her mouth opened for another bite just as he heard a man's voice say, "Thank you, Estelle. That will be all for this session."

The quality of the light from the screen changed, and he heard the hiss of static.

And she ... it ... was gone.

Grant lay on his back, panting, his muscles shaking from exertion. His wrist throbbed. Blood ran down his forearm and into his sleeve. He pulled himself up and onto the arm of his chair. He glanced at the electronic snow on the screen just as it flickered and cleared. The face of a middle-aged man in a white lab coat appeared. He was sitting at a desk with a file folder open in front of him.

"Immediately following the taping of the session you have just watched, Estelle Campbell made a recovery that was nothing short of miraculous. There were no more sessions, no more hallucinations, no more wounds. Estelle told us that the little girl who had been tormenting her had disappeared. Those were her words, 'she disappeared'. The existing wounds healed and no more appeared. Estelle Campbell calmed and resumed normal relationships with those around her. She was released two weeks later. I am at a loss to explain her affliction or her recovery."

His face disappeared to be replaced by electronic snow again.

Grant reached out and pushed the "Stop" lever. Then he pushed "Eject." The tape carrier rose from the machine with its cargo of electronic impulses stored on spools of magnetic tape. He removed it from the carrier and looked it over in the glow from the TV.

He heard something splat onto the coffee table and looked down to see a drop of his own blood. Pushing up his sleeve he examined the deep teeth marks in the flesh of his arm, just above the wrist. Blood welled from the wound. His eyes widened with curiosity. So much for it being a hallucination. Getting up from the chair, he picked up the fallen lamp and plugged it in. Light flooded the room.

Down the hall, in the bathroom, he stripped of the bloody shirt and cleaned his wound. Opening his first aid kit, he applied an antibiotic ointment and a bandage. He would stop at a clinic tomorrow and have a doctor look at it. He had heard that human bites always get infected. Not that whatever it was that bit him was human.

Back in the living room he picked up the tape and padded out to the garage. Grant glanced around and noted a red can of gas for the lawn mower. Picking it up, he sloshed it around to find about a pint still at the bottom. He grabbed an empty five-gallon metal can from under the work bench and dragged it to the center of the room, glad he hadn't parked in the garage tonight.

Tossing in the tape cassette he poured the gasoline in after it and followed with a lit match. A "whoompf" made him glad he hadn't leaned over the can. As it burned merrily, he walked over and opened the garage door. After a few minutes, the flames subsided, and he looked in to see the ash and melted plastic at the bottom of the tin. Giving it a kick out to the driveway, he closed the door and went inside to finish his takeout.

Huber

BY LANCE LOOT

"**D**ude, look! It's a freaking Huber! I haven't seen one in ages!"

Jimmy dashed over to the object he was fired up about to take a closer look.

"Hold up ... you say 'Huber?'" Eddie replied, glancing up from a yellowed stack of '70s porno mags he was rifling through.

Jimmy and Eddie were checking out a yard sale at a house so average, it could have been plucked straight out of a Norman Rockwell painting. Their browsing had proven fruitless overall—most of the advertised inventory fell into an undesirable category of obsolete appliances, hideously outdated furniture and clothing, or desiccated books and magazines that would molder to dust if the wind blew the wrong way.

This latest discovery, however, was a breath of fresh air.

"'Huber as in that old-ass vacuum perverts used on themselves?" Eddie asked, jogging up.

Jimmy scrunched his face in disgust. "Yup, the very same. Jesus, you *would* remember it for that!"

The Huber was a bulky contraption, twice the size of an average vacuum cleaner, its body composed of boxy contours. Everything was gun-metal gray, save for an ebony wooden handle at its top. It had an extendable wand attached to its side for cleaning nooks and crannies. The front bumper had a subtle U shape to it, as if slightly bent in a sneer; perched just above were two spheres on short stalks, resembling teed-up golf balls.

"Hey, what d'ya think those are for?" Eddie asked as he studied the curious circles.

"Vacuums of yesteryear used to have headlights, yeah?" Jimmy replied with a shrug. "Prolly that."

Eddie cocked an eyebrow. "Sorta look like closed eyes though, don't they?"

"Sure, Eddie," Jimmy chuckled. "Cuz it needs to be able to see so it doesn't ram into shit, right? My mistake, they *must* be eyes ..."

"Well, I mean ... why not? These Hubers were supposed to be like the first smart vacuums, right? Like primitive Roombas?"

"That'd be pretty sweet, I could use a smart vacuum!" Jimmy snagged the ebony handle of the Huber and began wheeling it toward the makeshift checkout area. "Long as the thing works I'm good, cuz that shitty vacuum my parents gave me is about on its last legs, and we've got a lot of cleaning to do before the party later."

"Uh ... 'we?' Who's 'we?' You mean *you've* got a lot of cleaning to do while I pre-game and provide moral support, right?" Eddie shot him a grin.

"You're a real prick, you know that?"

They laughed as they reached the cashier, and Jimmy purchased the Huber.

True to his word, Eddie had his lackadaisical ass plopped on the sofa, sipping a beer, while Jimmy feverishly cleaned his ranch-style house in preparation for the night's festivities, vacuuming the carpet with his new Huber. The machine's drone was surprisingly placid, sounding more like a purring cat rather than a mechanized wailing.

"Man, I'm really liking this thing!" Jimmy said as he vacuumed in fluid up-and-down patterns. "And its cord is like five times longer than my other vacuum. I can do the whole house off the living room outlet!"

"Mhm," Eddie replied listlessly, scrolling through his phone.

Jimmy side-eyed his recalcitrant friend. "Alright, dude! That's enough friggin' beer, save some for later! Why don't ya gimme a hand for Christ's sake, there's still plenty to do!"

"Hey, I'm supervising!" Eddie snickered. "Besides, you're doin' just fine on your own!"

A flash of red near the floor caught Eddie's eye, and his gaze darted toward it. His snickering swiftly ceased.

The Huber's stalked spheres were wide open, revealing crimson orbs; the blood-like pigment danced about like licking flames.

They were most definitely not headlights.

No.

They looked like enraged, hate-filled eyes.

The motor's whirring amplified several decibels, the purr mutating to a deep growl. Puzzled, Jimmy stopped cleaning to glance upon the machine. "Huh? What's up with this thing?" He couldn't see the eyes from his vantage point.

But Eddie could see them plain as day from the couch. The unblinking scarlet eyes drilled into him like a demon's horn, blazing with intensity. Terrified, he yelped and sprang up, dropping his beer—the ale sluiced out of the felled can, soaking the carpet.

"Dude, what the fuck!" Jimmy cried, powering off the Huber. "I asked you to help, not fuck shit up!"

"But ... the fucking *vacuum*! I was right about the eyes, man! They—" Eddie gestured to the Huber but saw that the eyes were closed, the spheres now gray like the rest of its chassis. Bewildered, he blinked several times, but they remained unchanged.

Jimmy studied the front of the vacuum, frowning. "What the hell are you talking about, dude?"

"The eyes! They were just there a second ago, man!" Eddie exclaimed.

Jimmy crouched and ran a few fingers along the gray circles. "I dunno, these definitely aren't freaking *eyes*, dude." He toyed with them, thinking they could possibly be covers concealing something, yet they were unmovable. "Hell, I don't even think they're headlights."

"I know what I saw, man ..." Eddie muttered, a chill capering his spine.

Jimmy rose with a smirk. "That's it ... you're cut off on the beer, at least till the party. No more hallucinating eyes on the goddamn vacuum for you." He chuckled, gesturing to the frothy stain in the carpet. "However ... now's your time to shine, dude! Pretty please, get this out. I've got cleaner and towels in the kitchen."

Eddie nodded and went to retrieve the supplies. As he passed the Huber, he could have sworn he saw a glint of crimson, as if the vacuum had winked at him.

Eddie's heart skipped a beat.

Maybe I do *need to give it a rest on the beers ...* he thought with a shudder.

The remainder of the cleaning progressed without a hitch.

Jimmy finished the vacuuming, sweetened up the living room, then assembled an alluring smorgasbord of alcohol. Shockingly, Eddie provided dutiful assistance by scrubbing down the bathroom. He didn't mind either—anything to put some distance between him and that freaky vacuum.

He was wiping down the toilet bowl when Jimmy appeared in the doorway, mopping his sweaty brow. "The crew should be showing up any minute. Look, thanks a ton for your help, dude. No way I could have done all this in time without ya!"

Eddie cracked a crooked grin. "So does that mean I've earned a beer ... or three?"

"Hell yeah, Eddie!" Jimmy held out his arm, helping him to his feet. "Have as much as your heart desires!"

"Oh man, you're gonna be ruing those words by the night's end, watch and see!" Eddie sniggered as he went to grab a brew from the fridge.

The front door burst open, and a trio of guests swooped into the house, guffawing over a shared joke.

A tall, blonde wrestler-looking guy was the first to appear, and he immediately sashayed about the living room like he owned the place, his eyes appraising everything. "Cute place, Jimbo," he said.

"Gee thanks, glad it gets your seal of approval, Don," Jimmy replied, rolling his eyes.

Another guy—short and stocky with shoulder-length dark hair—roamed the room like he was searching for something, checking on top of and behind every piece of furniture as if on an Easter egg hunt. "Yo, Jimmy!" he said in a baritone timbre. "Got any beer in your new place or what? Where ya hidin' it?"

"Maybe try the fridge, Chad," Eddie said, cheersing with his can. "Ya know, where you'd normally find it."

"Thanks, smartass," Chad retorted as he sauntered toward the kitchen, making sure to ram his broad shoulder into Eddie as he passed; his beer wobbled precariously for a moment, but he steadied himself, making sure not to have another spilt-ale mishap like before.

"Hey, see if there's any Three Floyds in there for me!" Don said to Chad, following him into the kitchen.

"Hey Jimmy, congratulations on the new place!" a curvy, black-and-blue haired girl beamed as she strode into the room, extending a wrapped present his way. "I gotcha a little house-warming gift! It's not much, just thought it was something you'd like!"

"Thanks Amber! Jeez, you didn't have to get me anything!" He plunked onto the sofa and opened the present, exhuming a bulky, gray knitted blanket, promptly tossing it over himself. "This thing's as soft as a cloud! A friggin' *heavy*-ass cloud, but still, it's amazing! I appreciate it!"

"No problem, glad ya like it!" Her gaze shifted to Eddie, standing like a statue in the corner, quietly draining his beer. "Hi there, Eddie! How's it goin'?"

Eddie's hazel eyes dilated, flitted to meet Amber's emerald eyes for a spell, then dropped to his feet as his cheeks flushed scarlet. "Oh, hi, Amber! Yeah, I'm good." He paused to swig his beer, but realized it was empty—his face turned a shade darker, thinking how dumb he must look slurping an empty can. "Hey, uh ... I'm gonna grab a beer, would ya want one?" he asked her, then swiveled to Jimmy. "You want one too, man?"

Before either of them could respond, Don and Chad emerged from the kitchen, chortling and clapping one another on the back. And rather than beers, they each clasped their own bottle of Captain Morgan, taking generous gulps in between chummy claps.

"Yo, what the hell, Jimmy!" Chad bellowed. "It's silent as a grave in this shithole! Put on some music or something, man!"

"Oh sure, anything for you, *Chud* ..." Jimmy murmured, lifting the remote and putting on a '90s Alt Rock playlist via the TV; Chris Cornell's howling tenor echoed throughout the room.

"Who else ya got comin' to this house-warming party, Jimbo?" Don asked.

"Just you guys. Wanted to keep it kinda lowkey, ya know?" he replied.

"Well shit, that's lame. At least ya got plenty of booze though, cuz I'm gonna need it!" Don took a fervent pull from his bottle, then turned to Amber; his macho demeanor immediately melted away like quicksilver, replaced with a forced, hammy smile. "Hey babe, ya want anything? Want me to getcha a beer?" he asked, adopting a fake, sickly sweet tone to his voice.

Amber's pretty face hardened. "Don, I told you a hundred times, *stop* calling me 'babe.' And anyway ..." She glanced over to Eddie and smiled. "Eddie already said he was gonna grab me one."

Eddie immediately sprung into action as if someone had inserted a quarter into him. "Yeah! Yeah, that's right, I did! Be right back!" He raced for the kitchen.

"Hey, don't forget about me!" Jimmy called out.

"I got you, man!" Eddie hollered amidst clanging glass bottles.

Don grunted and sank into a brown armchair. "Lamest party ever," he muttered as he slugged his rum.

Chad followed suit, opting for a faux leather chair on the other side of the coffee table. "Got that right," he added, mirroring Don as he glugged his bottle.

"Hey, don't be a bunch of killjoys!" Amber said as she plopped next to Jimmy on the couch, patting him on the back. "This guy just bought his first house, be happy for him!"

"Yeah, that is pretty cool," Chad conceded; he grinned at Jimmy, raising his rum high. "'Grats, man! You're a big boy now!"

"Congrats," Don mumbled, still sulking from his rejection.

Eddie bustled into the room, juggling three open bottles of beer. "Here ya go, Amber!" he said, handing her a flaxen-hued ale. "Got you a Corona, I know you like light beer!"

"Aww, thanks, Eddie!" she replied with a warm smile, prompting butterflies to hurtle about his gut.

"And for you ..." Eddie passed Jimmy a drink. "Your fave: Zombie Dust! Don't ever say I don't know ya, man!"

"Hell yeah! Cheers, dude!" Jimmy exclaimed as he clinked beers with his pal.

With each guest in possession of an alcoholic beverage and the initial awkward exchanges out of the way, the house-warming party proceeded full steam ahead. Mirthful, raucous laughter erupted and countless jokes at other people's expenses were cracked as everyone steadily acquired a respectable buzz. Don and Chad were beginning to feel especially warm and fuzzy inside, both of their Captain Morgan bottles three-quarters consumed, as they swayed in their seats like concussed prizefighters, giggling stupidly.

Jimmy couldn't help but giggle stupidly himself as he noticed Eddie and Amber scooting closer to one another on the sofa as the night progressed. They'd been entertaining the same flirtatious song and dance with one another for years—perhaps something would finally blossom from it.

About goddamn time ... Jimmy thought as he watched his friends with a loopy smile, four Zombie Dusts deep. The two were conversing about horror films.

"How the hell have you never seen *House by the Cemetery*, dude?!" Amber exclaimed to Eddie. "It's an underrated masterpiece!"

He shrugged. "Just haven't gotten around to much on the Italian side of things, ya know?"

"No, as a matter of fact I don't know, because that's criminal AF! In fact, we're gonna change that *stat*!" She shot him a coy grin. "How about you come to my apartment tomorrow and we'll watch it?"

Eddie sputtered on his mouthful of beer. "Oh damn, really? Sure ... yeah! I'd really like—"

"Yo, the fuck is that shit?" Chad slurred suddenly, pointing a wobbly finger at the Huber propped in the corner.

"That's my new Huber!" Jimmy replied brightly. "Just got it today. Runs like a champ too, I cleaned the whole house with it!"

Don's glossy eyes staggered from Jimmy, to the Huber, then back to Jimmy. "Some kinda vacuum or summat?" he warbled, his mouth slack-jawed.

"Not just *any* vacuum, Donny boy," Jimmy said, leaping and moseying to the machine. "This, my friends ... is a *Huber*!"

Don and Chad continued to stare blankly.

"C'mon, you guys ... it's a Huber, a classic!" Eddie added, rising and coming to his friend's aid. "You *gotta* remember those commercials we saw all the time as kids!" He scrunched his face and pitched his voice up an octave. "'*If your mess has got you in distress*' ... then the little cartoon Huber vacuum scooted into the scene ..." He suddenly thrusted a finger into the air and grinned like the Cheshire cat. "'*SUCK-tacular!*'" he declared in a James Earl Jones-esque voice. "Then Huber sucked up all the trash Kirby-style. C'mon, you guys don't recall that shit?! And remember the myth about lonely creeps using the wand's lowest suck setting on themselves?"

"Um ... *what*?" Amber said.

"I'm likin' the sounds of that right now," Don said with a hazy grin as he polished off his Captain.

"Ol' Huber here is *infamous* to say the least!" Eddie said with a smirk. "Come to think of it, I wonder why they stopped making 'em ..."

Chad was about to tease Eddie, that is, until he caught a flash of red out of his periphery. He swung his beady eyes to the corner: the Huber opened and closed one of its eyes rapidly, revealing a gleam of red for a split second. It took a few moments for Chad's sloshed brain to process what he saw, but he got there eventually.

"'Ey, the fucker just winked at me!"

"Nah, bro!" Don garbled as he teetered to his feet. He lurched toward his friend like a brain-dead zombie. "Nah, she's winkin' at *me*, bro! You ain't stealin' *my* date!"

He spun and stumbled toward Amber, seated on the couch—his muddled mind thought Chad was referring to her. In his haste, Don's shin caught the coffee table, and he toppled over it, landing on top of her.

"C'mere babe, gimme a kiss," he slurred.

Amber gagged as his rancid, boozy breath assailed her. "What the fuck Don, *no!*"

Don struck and planted a wet, sloppy kiss on her mouth. She broke free and turned her head sideways as he came back for more.

"Get the fuck off me!" Amber shrieked, trying to escape from under him, but he was too heavy.

Jimmy and Eddie immediately leapt into action, manhandling Don and tossing him away like a sack of potatoes. He tumbled to the carpet, cackling. Meanwhile, Chad just sat there and watched the whole spectacle, swigging his rum.

Eddie looked like he wanted to murder Don. "The fuck was that, you piece of shit?!" He advanced, but Jimmy held him back.

"Dude, don't!"

"I'm gonna kick his fucking ass!" Eddie snarled.

"Eddie, stop!" Amber cried. "He's a piece of shit, but it's not worth it!" She glanced at Don's slumped form with pure contempt. "Please, just get him the fuck away from me."

Jimmy and Eddie obliged, dragging Don—his eyes rolling in his skull while jabbering incoherently—to one of the bedrooms, flinging him onto the covered mattress. They closed the door as they left.

"This some wild-ass party, huh?" Chad chuckled as they reentered the living room.

And on that vile note, the party was over.

Fortunately, the house had four bedrooms: Don was already sequestered away in his, Chad took the one across the hall from him, Jimmy was in the master, and Eddie and Amber shared the final room. Eddie wanted to stay with her—much to Amber's delight—in case Don decided to try anything else, opting to sleep on the floor while she took the bed.

As they all settled in for the night, a large, boxy shadow from the living room began to slowly wheel into the hallway, a cord slithering behind in its wake like an inky serpent.

As Don's eyelids fluttered open, the first thing to register with his alcohol-addled consciousness was a pounding headache.

"Ugh ..." he moaned, caressing his forehead.

The second thing was a pair of ruby-red eyes glaring at him through the darkness.

" ...the fuck?" He rubbed his peepers aggressively, but when he reopened them, the eyes were gone.

That's the last time I drink a whole goddamn bottle of rum! he thought hazily.

But then, a rustling sound, like small wheels trundling across the carpet.

Approaching the bed.

Closer.

Don froze, his heart vaulting to his throat.

Closer.

His eyes roved the blackness, but he couldn't discern anything.

Then it stopped.

Fearful, Don retrieved his phone and activated the flashlight app, revealing a huge form looming over him.

"Shit!" he squealed, flailing about the mattress.

But after a few seconds of nothing, he realized it was only the Huber, still as stone, its gray exterior glittering in the glow of the flashlight.

Those bastards must be fuckin' with me ... he thought angrily. Then he grinned as a horrible idea struck him. *But I know just how to get back at those cocksuckers!*

He eyed the vacuum's wand, recalling what Eddie had mentioned earlier about what perverts had famously used it for, then pushed the Huber's power button. He was surprised by the machine's soft, purr-like whirring, quiet enough not to wake anyone. With a sly sneer, he dropped his drawers and seized the wand, making sure its suction setting was at its lowest.

Prior to waking, he had been enjoying a smutty dream starring Amber, and his member still stood at full-mast. He brought the wand closer, the Huber's purring sounding almost sultry as if eager to please, then swallowed his cock entirely with it. The sensation was like a carnal ecstasy he had never experienced before, and he moaned as his mind began to pick up right where the dirty dream had left off.

He was mere seconds away from climax when it happened.

First, the Huber's purr distorted into something more like a snarl.

Then, its red eyes flew open, their hellish glow bathing the dark room in a sanguinary radiance. The wand's tender inhaling magnified to a tornado-like vacuuming, but as if the maelstrom were swirling with blender blades. White-hot pain ripped up and down Don's shaft as he screamed, trying to yank the thing off his anguished manhood, but the suction was too powerful. He felt himself getting repeatedly sliced and flayed from tip to base, and his cries devolved to primal, agonized screeches.

Suddenly, the Huber powered off, going silent as death, and Don tore the wand off. The pain was debilitating as he dared a glimpse at his ruined rod: it more so resembled a butchered worm of some kind, riddled with gashes and missing chunks of flesh. Blood was pumping from every affliction and streaming down his sides.

Don could only lean his head back as his eyeballs rolled up into their sockets and everything went black.

Chad awoke, bolting upright in bed from all the screaming.

It sounded like it came from across the hall.

Don's room, he thought, wondering with dread what could be going on in there. His head still felt woozy from all the rum, but cold terror was swiftly sobering him up. He strained his ears for additional noises, but there was nothing.

Silence.

"Fuck me, I don't like this ..." he muttered aloud, goosebumps blooming along his thick forearms. He swung both legs over the side of the bed, about to rise, but then,

Creaaaaaaak.

The door groaned open, and a narrow column of light crept in.

Chad glanced over in time to see a shadow slide into the room and vanish within the darkness.

"Yo, man ..." he called out in a weak, quivering voice. "Whichever of you's there, come out now or I swear I'm gonna break your fucking nose, okay? I'm serious."

The intruder obliged, slinking into the swath of light; Chad's eyes bugged out in surprise.

It was the Huber.

"... the goddamn *vacuum*?!" He broke out into relieved laughter. "Alright, you guys got me good!"

If he had been paying closer attention, he would have seen that the wand attached to its side was saturated with blood. Don's blood.

The scarlet eyes blasted open as the machine sprang to life, the resulting roar like a chainsaw.

Chad stopped laughing. "What in the fuc—"

The Huber launched forward with alarming speed. Chad howled in pain as the bumper bit down on his feet, mincing them as if it had a revolving grinder under its guard.

The Huber plowed up the front of his body like a rock climber on wheels by utilizing its powerful suction, shredding and mangling all flesh in its path. Chad fell back onto the bed from the machine's weight, shrieking like a skinned banshee as he felt hundreds of tiny spinning razor blades slash his skin to ribbons, until the Huber mowed over his face, quickly reducing Chad's anguished wails to choked gurgles.

Holy shit, that was some nightmare ... Eddie thought as he rubbed his eyes.

He glanced up at the bed and saw Amber, safely sleeping. He smiled as he stood and stretched his limbs, granting his body a reprieve from the stiff floor.

What the hell time is it? Eddie checked his phone—three thirty in the morning. His mouth felt dry as cotton from the beers, so he tiptoed out of the room for a drink of water. As he tread into the hallway, he noticed the doors to Don's and Chad's rooms were open. He frowned and closed his door behind him, still leery of Don's abhorrent behavior earlier.

Eddie got water from the kitchen sink, swilling it down in two gulps. Leaning against the counter, he couldn't help but grin as he thought of Amber. After all the years of guarded emotions, missed signals, and awkward exchanges, it finally looked like he had a chance with her.

Can't believe it's gonna happen! he thought. *And with an old-school Italian splatterfest viewing, no less—best first date ever!*

He entered the living room, heading for the hallway.

Something was off.

Eddie halted.

There was a black electrical cord snaking along the room's perimeter, creating oblong shapes and patterns; it looked like the world's longest strand of black licorice. Furrowing his brow, Eddie assessed where the cord was plugged into the outlet; his eyes tracked its winding trajectory until it ended behind the faux leather armchair.

But how did this—

A motorized roar shook the room as the Huber turned on and tilted upright, bringing it into view from behind the chair. The red eyes flashed to life and the vacuum surged toward him.

"*Holy God!*" Eddie yelled.

He spun to escape, but the Huber was too fast, slamming into his heels and careening him back into the kitchen. He fell to the linoleum and scampered to the sink cabinet. The vacuum was already on him again, its bumper chomping on Eddie's ankle.

"*Fuck!*" he wailed as several blades mauled his leg.

He yanked open the cabinet doors, grabbed the first container he touched, and hurled it at the machine. Upon contact, the cleaner bottle split open, drenching the Huber in bleach. It groaned and slackened its hold slightly, but that was all Eddie needed as he ripped free and scrambled inside the cabinet, overturning buckets and cleaners.

The Huber regained its bearings and charged, inadvertently slamming the cabinet doors closed. Enraged, it repeatedly rammed the cabinet, each time splintering the wood further, as Eddie curled into a ball, fearfully awaiting the inevitable.

"What the hell's goin' on?!" Jimmy shouted, marching down the hallway.

Noticing the open bedroom doors, he peeked inside: Don's exposed, bloody corpse was splayed on the mattress.

"*Oh fuck ...*" he said, his face going white.

Chad's room was no better.

He stumbled into the living room and retched onto the floor.

"Jimmy!" Amber said, racing into the room. "Are you alright? I heard screaming!"

"It's Don and Chad ..." he mumbled. "Murdered ... fucking *murdered*. We need to leave. There's some—"

An ear-splitting screech blared from the kitchen, and the Huber zipped into the living room, its eyes glowing like red coals. Amber was closer, and it crashed into her; she cried out, instinctively outstretching her arms for protection, and the vacuum attacked, chewing up her arm like hamburger meat. She screeched like a shrill siren.

"What the *fuck!*" Jimmy hollered in shock. He spotted the gray knit blanket—Amber's house-warming gift—nearby, half on the sofa and half spilt on the floor. As Amber's screams crescendoed, he snatched the bulky blanket and launched it at the Huber's deadly maw—a quarter was swiftly inhaled, but the majority of the heavy fabric bunched up, clogging and stymying the vacuum.

Amber wrenched herself free and rolled away, clutching her ragged arm as she wailed in agony. Jimmy rushed over, gingerly helping her up.

The Huber coughed and sputtered as its gears struggled with the afghan, but then, its eyes flared with a blinding brilliance like twin suns; its mechanical bellows amplified tenfold, like an airplane engine, and the rest of the blanket was shredded to bits.

It turned its wrathful gaze on Jimmy and Amber, creeping forward. Amber, blood spurting from her grievous injury, was in no condition for a quick escape; she slumped to the floor, moaning. Jimmy stepped in front of his friend—the thing would have to get through him first—stared the hellish vacuum directly in the eyes and—

"*Hey, shit-guzzler!*" a voice shouted from the kitchen.

The vacuum wheeled around, and its eyes dimmed slightly as if confused.

It was Eddie. He was gripping a bottle of Captain Morgan with a torn-off piece of his shirt sleeve stuffed in the open neck. He was standing next to the stove and ignited one of the burners, promptly alighting the shirt sleeve off of it.

"Suck on *this!*" he barked, chucking the bottle.

It pirouetted through the air like a glass ballerina, then smashed directly into the Huber's "face." A fireball flashed, and the machine was set ablaze. Its roaring morphed into high-pitched squalling, and it began zooming back and forth like a flaming chicken with its head cut off, the lengthy power cord flapping in its wake.

Eddie dashed into the room, nimbly evading the panicked vacuum, and reached his friends. The roiling flames leeched to the carpet and furniture, setting the whole room on fire.

"C'mon, we gotta go!"

Jimmy nodded as they both took hold of Amber, assisting her and careful to not touch her mangled arm.

"Don and Chad ...?" Eddie asked.

Jimmy shook his head. "Gone, dude ..."

"Fuck ..."

They stumbled out the door and into the night, lumbering through the front yard to the sidewalk. They turned to watch the house burn, the blaze rapidly consuming the wooden structure.

"Guys …" Amber finally said in a strained voice. "What the fuck was that? Am I crazy? Did that really just fucking happen?"

"Yup …" Jimmy said.

"No more fucking yard sales, man!" Eddie exclaimed. "And I hope I never—"

The front bay window of the house shattered into a million pieces as the Huber soared through the air toward them like a blazing, mechanized demon, its crimson eyes erupting with hellfire.

"*Man, fuck this vacuum!*" Eddie screamed.

The trio spun to flee. The machine collided with Eddie's backside, but as it did, it had gone beyond the limit of its power cable, unplugging it from the outlet in the burning living room. The Huber's ruby eyes faded to black, its life extinguished, as it powered off, landing on top of Eddie in a harmless heap.

He scuttled out from under it, his friends pulling him to his feet. Bewildered, they all stared at the vacuum. Then, at the same time, they all rushed to one another and embraced, burying their faces in each other's shoulders, tears flowing freely.

Eddie lifted his head to glance at the lifeless Huber; the hair on the back of his neck stood up like quills. "You know what, I can see why these fuckers were discontinued."

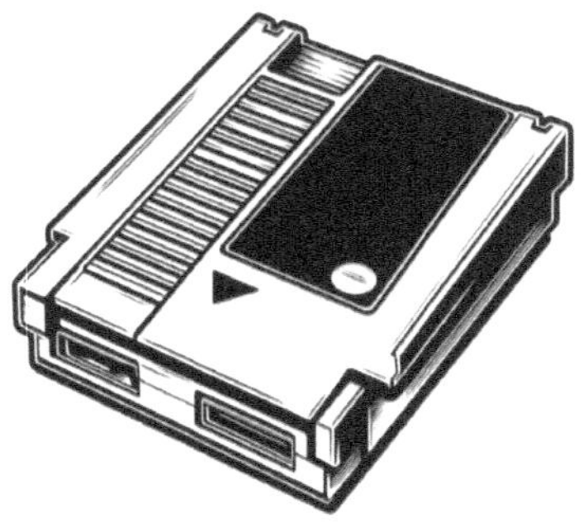

The Blank Cartridge

BY ROBB BASHAM

This spring break had been a bust overall. Not a horrible vacation, just underwhelming. Billy and Kenan had squandered it with the usual activities and time-wasting pursuits: $2 days at the matinee (lots of campy sci-fi "classics" that guaranteed they would be the only ones in the theater), treks far and wide on their bikes and lots of couch co-op, beat-'em-up action on Kenan's Super Nintendo when the spring showers were pouring down torrentially. All Billy had was a Nintendo, the 8-bit one that no one wanted to play anymore. But that didn't stop Billy from hitting up gaming shops to secure the NES carts that were slowly being phased out for their evolved counterparts. Billy and Kenan were the president and vice-president (respectively) of their school's Retro Appreciation Society. Kenan even coined their motto: "Yesterday's technology is today's adventure."

Ryu Hayabusa was bouncing off walls and slicing down enemies with his katana in the *Ninja Gaiden* game Billy got a month ago at the End of Winter Sale that his local mom-and-pop video store held when his mother knocked at his door. The jarring noise caused Billy to cast Ryu into a pit, triggering the dreaded GAME OVER screen.

"MAN! I was *soooo* close to the end!" Billy grumbled as Mom stated her purpose.

"Hey, hon. Kenan's here and wants you to come out to play," she said.

Billy walked over to the console and powered it off and took out the grey cartridge, placing it on his shelf with the others that lacked their boxes. He exited his room and walked to the front door, where Kenan was waiting with an almost urgent fervor. He yawned, looked at his watch and realized it was 9:30. It felt later than that. He yawned again and addressed his friend.

"What's up, Kee?" Billy asked.

"Dude! The yard sales are calling! *LESSGOLESSGOLESSGO!*"

Every spring, just before school let out for the summer, his neighborhood hosted yard sales around the block. It was a community spring cleaning event. They were hit-or-miss, unless you knew where to look for your desired quarry. The Thompsons, an elderly couple, would have nothing but dusty books and dinnerware. The boys would politely, but fervently pass their lot by in the quest for the ultimate secondhand haul. For the last two years, the Davis clan had lots of what they sought: budget-title sci-fi movies and vintage pulp paperbacks that featured scantily-clad vixens and hardboiled gumshoes armed with tommy guns. Those books were true contraband, secreted away from the eyes and probing hands of their parents. It was time to see what prospective treasures awaited them this year. Billy and Kenan walked out into the brisk, but sunny April morning.

Noon came by quickly and the boys had done well for themselves. Kenan had a grocery sack full of back issues of his favorite comics (*Tales of the Unexpected* was totally bitchin' and he found some obscure issues he had been missing in his collection). The Murrays were loading them off and gave him a heck of a deal, not realizing how rare some of these truly were. That didn't matter to Kenan, who just wanted more brain-rotting comics to read. The artwork from that time period was unrivaled, for sure. Billy grabbed some Signet noir paperbacks and a couple of *Dick Tracy* comics from the Davis lot. He had placed them in Kenan's bag, and they took turns holding the loot since it was getting heavier with every yard.

The boys were getting hungry, realizing they hadn't eaten since leaving Billy's house. There was one more yard sale to hit before they went to grab lunch. They traveled to the outskirts of the neighborhood and worked their way back to Billy's. The house two doors down from Billy was their final stop. This yard wasn't bustling with commerce and activity, so the boys had the whole lot to themselves to pick through at their leisure. Three weeks prior, the elderly couple had passed away in their home. The husband went first, and a broken heart claimed his beloved a day later. Billy realized he never even knew the couple's names. The man who was at the table with the change box and the woman who was putting out some jackets and hats must have been their children, since both looked just like the deceased patriarch. They must be here to help clear out the estate.

On a table sat a box of records. The front half was a collection of 7" EPs and singles. Billy thumbed through these and didn't see much of anything. He almost picked up a single, but decided against it because he didn't have a record player. That Randall and the Revenants 7" (their big single, "She Drove Me to It," with the instrumental as a b-side) was cool but it would have to sit amongst its vinyl brethren collecting dust for now. The myth behind that record was far more interesting to Billy than the actual song on it. He was looking through a box of country and western cassettes when Kenan called his name. He looked up and saw his friend squatted over a cardboard box filled with unseen treasures.

There were seven Nintendo cartridges stacked in the box: *Galaga, Ikari Warriors, Super Mario Bros./Duck Hunt,* three sports games, and a cartridge without a proper label.

Billy had those three decent games, and he didn't care whatsoever about the sports games. It was the unlabeled one that held his attention. What could be within that plastic shell? A tech demo of some sort, a rare promo cart, who could say? His curiosity gripped him like a snake from *Pitfall* and he asked the man what it could be.

"Uh ... y'know. I'm not entirely sure. My son had so many of these damn things and he's not here to give you any clue. He left them when he went off to college, so out they go," he answered.

Billy gave Kenan a glance, his buddy reciprocating a head tilt that signified *why not, man*. They broke eye contact and Billy turned back to the mysterious cartridge in his hand. That was all the affirmation he needed to make his decision. He went for his wallet, attempting to pay, when the man shook his head. When he spoke again to the boy, his demeanor had softened some.

"Nah. You can have it. This plastic junk is just gonna sit and collect mold in my house. Danny ain't comin' back for these, so take it. *IF* you take the rest of them," the man offered.

What kid could say no to that? Sure, he already had these, but it doesn't hurt to have spares in case he needed to trade for something later. He held out his hand for a shake, which Simmons took and shook genially. Billy beamed and lifted his box of games to his chest. The boys left the yard and walked back to Billy's house.

This was quite a fruitful day. Both boys touted a bevy of goodies, and they shuffled off to Billy's room to divide the loot.

After testing the games that had labels (all of them worked, though *Double Dribble* had a lot of dust inside of it), Billy grabbed the mysterious cart and blew into it, wiping the inside with his shirt before inserting it into the console. The boys looked at each other and their unspoken "telepathy" came to the agreement that it was time.

"Since you found the games, I think you should have the honor of pressing the power button," Billy declared.

Though he maintained his silence, the excitement on Kenan's face was transparent. He took a deep breath to collect himself, though he wasn't sure why he did that. After that moment of whatever, he pressed the button and the indicator flashed red. The boys sat on the floor in front of the game and waited for the title screen. There was a tune coming from the television that the 8-bit system had *no* way of producing. It had a creepy, almost ethereal lilt. The screen began flashing in gold, silver, white, and red along with the default black. The image throbbed in rhythm with the music, which was beginning to make the boys a bit uncomfortable. Billy got up to turn off the console but stopped with his finger hovering over the button. The music had stopped so abruptly that he had to look at the screen. The image that rested there was unsettling.

On the screen was a skull surrounded by letters and symbols in gold. Neither boy had ever seen these characters, but both felt dread drop into their stomachs like a brick. The skull had that distinct 8-bit pixelation, but the redness emanating from its sockets was far too bright. Billy was afraid it was going to damage his television, but he was compelled just like Kenan to keep staring. The skull began to speak: a raspy, witchy voice that raised the light-colored hairs on their arms.

> WHO DARES TO AWAKEN ME?! THOU MUST BE COMPELLED BY VIM AND VITALITY TO SUMMON ME FROM THE INFERNAL DEPTHS! REVEAL THY INTENT!

An alpha-numerical array appeared on the screen under the skull, the numbers 0-9 sitting above the letters which were splayed out like a computer keyboard. A box flashed on the Q, signaling the chance to answer the inquiry from this horrific, disembodied being.

Billy picked up the controller and used the directional pad to scroll through the letters, noting that it moved with ease and finesse like a computer mouse (or the SNES peripheral Billy was so jealous of when they played around on *Mario Paint*). He knew what to ask first.

What is your name?

The skull moved around the screen for a moment, clearing the characters. It recentered itself on the screen and gave its reply. The tone was a bit calmer, but nonetheless larger than life.

> SOME CALL ME A GOD...OTHERS CALL ME A PLAGUE UPON MAN. I HAVE EXISTED FAR BEYOND TIME AND REALITY. FLITTING BETWEEN REALMS HAS GIVEN ME MANY MONIKERS, MANY OF WHICH WERE BEQUEATHED UNTO ME BY DENIZENS OF WORLDS I HAVE CONSUMED AND VOMITED FORTH INTO THE VOID. IF YOU REQUIRE AN ANSWER FROM ME, THEN YOU SHALL ADDRESS ME AS THE WATCHER OF THE DARK. I AM THE END OF ALL LIFE, THE HERALD OF OBLIVION TO COME. WHAT IS YOUR NEXT QUERY?

The letters and numbers appeared once again, the cursor on the Q key.

"Well, that was pretty damn unsettling, huh?" asked Kenan.

Billy nodded. Did they dare ask this *thing*, this Watcher of the Dark, any more questions? He wanted to press reset or turn the power off, anything to end this terrifying nonsense. He went to press the reset, but it wouldn't budge. He hammered it harder with his finger, which caused him pain due to it not moving. He went to press the power next, only to be met with a similar immovability. The red light became a beacon of their torture.

"Dude, it won't turn off! What the hell is this," Billy was stricken dumb by fear. What were they going to do? And, more importantly, would this be the end of his Nintendo? Surely not, right?

Kenan went to the A/V cord to remove it from the set. He was subsequently fed a jolt of electricity that immediately sent his body crumpling to the floor. Smoke seemed to be floating off his skin. Billy went over to Kenan and shook him, his friend not showing any signs of life.

Fuck! Is he dead? Oh, this is bad, he thought. This "game" just possibly killed his best friend. This was not the way their summer was supposed to end! In his panic, his thoughts seemed to completely fail him. Unsure of what to do next, he picked up the controller to ask another question.

Is he dead?

```
   INDEED. HE ATTEMPTED...AND FAILED...TO BANISH ME BACK
TO THE INFERNAL DEPTHS. HIS MORTAL HANDS BETRAYED
HIM UNTIL THE BITTER END. I SHALL NOT BE EXILED ANY
FURTHER.
```

What could that mean? Could the Watcher be planning to escape from the console into this world? Billy didn't want to entertain the notion anymore. Hell, he didn't want to do any of *this* anymore. He weighed his options: the buttons and the A/V were out, and he didn't dare to turn off the television itself. He didn't want to have a dialogue or stroke this being's ego. But, for now, he didn't have much of a choice.

What do you want?

```
   YOUR WORLD WILL BE YET ANOTHER TERRITORY TO CONQUER!
YOU SHALL AID ME IN MY CONQUEST OF CARNAGE, WHETHER
OR NOT YOU ARE WILLING...SUBSERVIENCE WILL BE THE PATH
OF LEAST RESISTANCE FOR YOU.
```

This horror needed to be stopped. If it had already destroyed countless worlds before it arrived here, then this could prove more of a difficult undertaking than Billy wagered. He gulped and took a deep breath. He grabbed the controller to converse with the demon.

I challenge you!

There was an uncomfortable, heavy silence that seemed to linger in the room. It was almost deafening. But this silence was soon replaced by a cackle only a power-hungry conqueror of life could laugh. Something about the heartiness of that laugh seemed unnatural. Then again, wasn't this whole damn thing a bit unnatural?

```
WHAT IS YOUR NAME, MORTAL? IT MAKES EACH CONQUEST
MORE PERSONAL WHEN I KNOW THE NAME OF THE REALM'S
HERO!
```

Billy.

The sockets in the skull began to glow with that dangerous, harsh red light again. The Watcher moved up and down as if it was sizing up the child that stood before him. Seemingly satisfied with the prospective challenger, the Watcher nodded and spoke one last time through the television.

```
VERY WELL, BILLY. WE SHALL DUEL AND SEE WHICH OF
US POSSESSES THE TRUE METTLE TO RULE YOUR REALM.
ENTER INTO THIS ARENA OF EQUIVALENCE AND FACE YOUR
DESTROYER!
```

The red light surged forth from the television and completely swallowed Billy. His vision was obscured, and his world felt like it was spinning way too fast. It made him slightly nauseous. He was starting to feel sick when he suddenly dropped onto what felt like solid ground. He instinctively patted himself down to see if he broke or sprained anything on the way to the ground. Not a fracture whatsoever, thankfully.

Billy looked around and took in the sight. He was in the middle of what looked like an arena floor. Surrounding him was an audience of at least 1,000 spectators. Their faces were pallid, ashen, and forlorn. These were the faces of the conquered, the tormented, and the indentured. *Very likely the same people he claimed to conquer*, he thought with a touch of contempt. Seeing these emaciated visages filled him with a rage, one that burned clean within him. His courage came rushing out of his mouth before he even had time to control his words.

"Come out and face me, coward! You cannot even show yourself amongst your mangled flock?"

Near the other end of the arena floor, a shape cloaked in darkness began to materialize. It was a darkness even more cold and all-consuming than space. This being stood equal in height to Billy, looking like a malevolent silhouette. It marched into the center, just a few feet away from him. It addressed Billy and his taunt.

```
   WELCOME TO YOUR DEMISE, BILLY. HERE YOU SHALL DO
BATTLE AND HERE YOU SHALL FALL. I APPEARED TO YOU AS
A SKULL, THE MEMENTO MORI. I HAVE NO TRUE FORM FOR I
AM THE WATCHER OF THE DARK, THE ASPECT OF OBLIVION.
THIS FORM SHALL DO FOR OUR DUEL. NOW, CHILD. CHOOSE
YOUR WEAPON AND BEG FOR YOUR MERCIFUL END.
```

Out of nowhere, a rack of archaic weaponry was willed into existence. It had the standard warrior fare: maces, swords, cudgels, and an axe. One sword looked like a katana, such as one that Ryu from *Ninja Gaiden* would have wielded. He almost grabbed that one, but another weapon caught his eye. It was a broadsword. The blade was freshly sharpened and free of nicks. The hilt was coppery and looked recently shined. Affixed upon the bottom of the handle was a black skull with rubies in the eye sockets. It was made of the same absence of light as the Watcher. This was the weapon that Billy would use to save his world! When he had made his choice, the rest of the rack lost its composure and seemed to melt back into oblivion.

He cast his gaze onto his opponent, who was wielding a mace. It looked like it was made of some sort of obsidian. Not quite as life-sucking as the darkness of which the Watcher was composed, but it still looked dangerous.

```
   SHALL WE BEGIN, BILLY? THERE ARE OTHER WORLDS THAN
THESE TO CONSUME.
```

He lifted the broadsword and took a duelist's stance. The Watcher did the same. Within the gap between the fighters, a creature whose very life echoed with pain and fractured agony appeared. It looked human in theory, but the mangled form in front of them was no longer a living being. Merely a mocking gesture toward mankind. When it made the announcement, it came out in a voice that validated its agony.

"These two fighters have gathered here to duel for the challenger's realm. May the strongest pugilist be victorious, or may the gods take pity upon us ... FIGHT!"

The "mediator" melted into a pool of viscera, which soaked into the floor. Billy looked at the Watcher and proceeded to hurl himself forward with intent to unleash hell. He swung down, hoping to cut into his opponent. However, the mace blocked the blow. A couple more attempts at landing a strike upon the monster proved just as futile.

He was beginning to feel winded and yet the Watcher hadn't even gone on the offensive. What was its strategy? Was it to wear the boy down before delivering a killing blow? As if giving the boy an answer, the berserker was upon him, mace in both hands and raised skyward. Billy noticed an opening that was so apparent that he didn't even think twice. He thrust his broadsword into the Watcher, driving it deep into its chest. A blood-like, coagulated substance erupted from the mortal cavity and sprayed all over Billy's face. Some got into his mouth, and he spat it back out immediately. It left a bittersweet taste on his tongue: acidic and saccharine, yet not completely disgusting. The Watcher collapsed onto the ground, onto its back and facing Billy. It began to seemingly fade out of existence. As it began to lose opacity, the Watcher gazed upon the boy one last time. What met Billy's eyes was something that would live with him until his dying day:

They were Billy's eyes, right down to the sky-blue color.

The image disappeared within a fraction of a second. Had he just seen that, or had this ordeal cracked his mind? He wasn't so sure anymore. Billy looked upon the faces of tormented souls, then his knees buckled under him. He fainted, with his last thought being that he had died after all. His suspicions were rebuked when he woke up on his floor in the same crumpled position from the arena.

He rose up from the floor slowly and took in the scene all at once. The Nintendo was charred, and the wires were spliced. The television screen was cracked, with two red dots emblazoned on the glass. His door was opened, looking like it was off the hinges. There were three cops, an EMT, and his parents. It was dark outside, and he could see the red-and-blue spinning lights of sirens. He looked over at his still-dead friend and began to cry. His mother ran to him and began to comfort him in her arms. The EMT put Kenan's body on the stretcher and hauled it out of the room, just previously given the go-ahead by the coroner. The officers gave Billy their condolences and went to deliver the horrible news to Kenan's folks. Billy's parents made sure he was okay before they left the room, leaving him alone with his thoughts.

The next morning, Billy woke up to the sound of someone knocking on his door. His father's voice rang from the other side.

"Hey, son! Come out to the living room, will ya? Your mom and I want to talk to you," he beckoned.

"Be right out, Dad!" he replied.

Billy rose up and realized he had been sweating profusely while he slept like a corpse granted its slumber. That ordeal had taken a lot out of him, it seemed. His pillow was drenched, and it was so cold it almost burned his fingers. He looked outside at the new sunny day and then up at the sun itself.

What a wonderful star. It would look even better shattered, cast into nothingness.

WHAT?! Had he really had that thought? That was so unlike Billy, who craved summer like a fiend. He shook his head and looked into the mirror on his closet door. Two sockets filled with a dread darkness were housed in his skull where his eyes once were.

The Watcher left Billy's room and stepped into the world he would devour next.

Homo Follicular

BY DAVID-JACK FLETCHER

"Do you ever ponder?"

"Do I *ponder*?" I raised my eyebrows and returned a small Mother Mary to a table.

"Yeah," Jack said, picking up a ratty book, "like, do you ever ponder about the nature of existence?"

I laughed. He was always asking the weirdest shit. "Uh, no, I can't say—"

"You're telling me,"—he threw the book down and kept walking, picked up an old pair of rusted scissors—"that you've never wondered what it would be like to be a blade of grass?"

"Put the scissors down," I said.

Jack did, wiping rust on his faded jeans, and sniffed. The yard was dusty, considering it was outside in the full view of the blistering sun. I was only in that yard because of Jack, his taste for old stuff. Antiques, sure. I could understand that. But the remnants of some old fart who'd just died ... No thanks.

"Like, what if you had to stand next to the same people your whole life, just growing and getting shit on by some dog, and every now and then, this crazy loud machine comes just to cut you down again." Jack turned to look at me, as if this scenario was the most important thing in the world.

I avoided his eyes as I sometimes did when his level of insanity—philosophy, he called it—got a bit much. I moved past him, pretending to look at the tables of junk, touching objects at random to sell the act.

He tugged at my shirt sleeve, the image of a poop emoji pulling to the left. "What about this?" he asked, holding up a worn painting of Mother Theresa.

"What about it?" I grimaced.

Putting it back, Jack smiled. "Or this?" *The Last Supper* greeted me.

Releasing air through tight lips, I sounded a little like a tired camel.

"Or—"

"Jack," I cut him off, "enough of the religious shit." It took everything in me to keep smiling in that moment.

He knew I'd grown up in the Bible Belt, but he didn't know the specifics. The way my father would bash thick tomes of religion across my palms for using the 'S' word—science. Or how my mum would kiss the cross dangling around her neck and pray in silence when she found gay bear mags under my mattress. She never looked at me again, not properly. Just polite nods and reminders that Jesus still loves me. I once replied, "Sure, Mom, but does he love you?"

That was the last thing I said to her before she died.

"Sorry, Mark," Jack said, cutting my memories away. He could see in my eyes I'd gone somewhere, and threw an arm around me, drew me close, and kissed me. His beard scratched at my shaven face, and I giggled.

"That's the best feeling in the world," I said softly, and he kissed me again.

"Can I help you, gentlemen?" A voice broke our moment and we turned. A thin, older lady with deep-set eyes and sunken cheeks stared at us. Her lips were turned up in what I thought was intended as a smile. But on her it looked odd, her yellowed and blackened teeth chipped. Some missing.

"We're just, uh, having a look," I said, pushing away from Jack, and picking up an old hairbrush.

"Oh, isn't that a *lovely* piece?" the woman asked.

I nodded and passed it to Jack, the antique aficionado. He studied it for a few seconds, eyebrows creasing. Holding it away from his eyes, he stared into the silver brush, turning it over in his hands.

"It belonged to my late sister." The woman frowned and made the symbol of the cross. "She's in Hell now, but I still pray for her."

The fuck?

Jack pursed his lips and scratched at his beard. "Well, maybe she went the other way, you never know."

"Oh no," the woman said, shaking her head, "she was a whore. She's definitely riding the Devil's cock right now. And whoever else is down there."

I laughed despite myself, unsure what else to do. Jack giggled, too, though his was more of a *Get me the hell away from her* type. She lifted a small, wrinkled hand, and pointed at me. Her eyes were piercing, grey, and her lips spread thin across her face.

"There's nothing funny about Hell," she said.

I waited for her to continue disciplining me like an old nun, cracking the whip on my hands like my own mother used to do. Instead, she lowered her hand, relaxed her shoulders, and tapped the hairbrush.

"That's only forty dollars," she said, her voice small and fragile. She was selling the sweet old lady bit, but needed some more work on consistency.

"For a brush?" I asked. "At a yard sale?"

She cleared her throat and eyed me again. "It was my *late sister's*. It's priceless. And you're inheriting something *very* special."

I raised an eyebrow and touched Jack's elbow. *Time to go.*

Before she could speak again, Jack pulled out a fifty and passed it to her. "Keep the change, and uh, have a ... good day?"

When we got back to the car, Jack threw the brush over his shoulder, into the back seat, and looked at me. "What the fuck was that? Dementia?"

I shook my head. "More like an old religious nutjob."

I carried plates of lasagna and steamed vegetables to the dinner table, Jack rubbing his thick belly to say he was hungry.

"Smells amazing," he said, sucking airfuls of steam through his nose. Once I'd put the plates down, he drew me in—he loved doing that—until I was seated on his lap. "Thank you for dinner, Marky. And for today. I know yard sales aren't your thing."

I smiled, nuzzled into his beard, and kissed him on the lips. "It was worth it to meet that old lady," I said, standing up, and hunching my back. Adopting an old woman's voice, I said, "There's nothing funny about Hell!"

We laughed at the memory and Jack tucked his chair in, poured some pinot noir for himself. Water for me, as usual—since four years earlier and several anonymous meetings. Still, we clinked glasses, stared at each other for a moment, and took a sip. Turning to his food, Jack stabbed at the pasta sheets with his fork, ignoring the knife next to his plate.

Classic.

My own lasagna steamed into my eyes, and I rotated the plate to get the vegetables first. Mother's rules were hard to break. Stuffing peas into my mouth and chewing, they felt odd—they weren't mushy, they didn't taste right. I looked over at Jack, eating away and sipping pinot like nothing was wrong.

"Duh theeese peac tayst off?" I said, followed by a *gak.*

"I dunt undastand ya, matey." Jack mocked me with a smile.

I swallowed the peas, which scratched against my throat, and forced them down through a few closed-mouth splutters. "Ugh, those peas are disgusting."

"Mine are fine." Jack shrugged.

I coughed again, rubbing at my throat, which felt strange. Like I hadn't swallowed properly. Reaching into my mouth with two fingers, I felt around, shifting my tongue left and right. Stretching all the way to the back—*Gak gak*—I felt it.

My eyes widened as I realized what it was and started pulling. Jack grimaced as he watched me, but still managed another sip of pinot. I pulled slowly at first, could feel something in my stomach, untangling.

Pulled again.

My fingers came loose, covered in green mush and saliva.

Pulled again.

Looking down to my mouth, I saw it. Thick, black strands, like tendrils.

Hair.

Jack put down his wine glass—*Finally*—and stared with a hand over his mouth. "Mark, what the ..."

I choked up more hair, pulling strand after strand to the dinner table and fighting the urge to vomit. A small, wet pile was forming on my plate. I could feel it uncurling in my stomach, sinking into the acids down there, mixing with my dinner.

Pushing my chair back, I stood, now unable to breathe as a clump started its way through my esophagus. Choking and gasping for air, eyes watering, I glared at Jack to do something—anything. To help me get the hair out of my body.

"What do I do?" Jack was up now, pacing in front of me as I fell back against a wall.

The clump of hair was lodged in my throat.

"Swallow it back down," Jack yelled at me, his own eyes tearing up. "Push it down, please!"

I tried. I forced my throat to swallow. No good. My lungs were burning, seizing. I took in air through the nose, but it was closing up.

"Here." Jack reached for my glass of water. "Drink it, it might help the hairball soften up!" He moved my hands from my throat and mouth and poured the water into me. It gurgled for a moment, like circling a drain, and then spilled down inside me.

The clump dislodged, sunk back into my stomach, and I gasped for air.

Jack kneeled before me, gripped the sides of my face, and looked at me, his lips trembling. "Are you okay? I thought ... I thought ..."

I nodded, gripped his torso, and he wrapped me in a hug. My breathing started to slow down, my passageways opened again. "I thought I was going to die."

"Me too, Marky, me too." Jack breathed hard. "Oh god, I thought you were gone."

We stayed like that for a few minutes, just grateful I was still alive.

"Where did all that hair come from?" I asked.

Standing together, we looked at the lasagna, now cold and looking completely uninviting with the wet, gluey hair piled on top. We moved closer to the food, and I scraped the pile of black hair aside. We inspected my plate first, and then Jack's. Nothing. No hair. Just vegetables, pasta, and coagulating sauce.

Somehow, in the center of the table, the hairbrush.

"How did *that* get there?" I asked.

Jack shrugged and moved to it. Picking it up, careful like it was a rare object, he looked between the brush and me, and back to the brush. "I left it in the car. I only bought it to get that old lady off our case."

"Then how did it get there?" My voice was as high as it could go, and I coughed again at the effort to speak.

"I don't know, Marky," he said.

We stared at each other silence for a few seconds, then I said, "Get rid of it. I don't like it."

While Jack was out at the garbage bins, I tipped our dinner into the kitchen bin, inspecting it once more. Just to see. Just to make sure.

Still no hair, and what I'd thrown up at the table was still there, in a mess.

I heard the front door click shut, followed by Jack's heavy footfalls trotting down the hallway towards me. We had one of those long homes, where each room was behind the other, and a wide hallway that gave access to several bedrooms, finally ending in an open living, kitchen, and dining area. It was our dream home, something we'd worked so hard for, and had achieved despite all the setbacks—family, laws, the usual homophobia that saw us rejected for home loan and home loan.

"How are you feeling?" Jack leaned on the kitchen bench with both arms, sizing me up.

I nodded. "Better. It just ... It's so *strange*, don't you think?"

"It is," Jack said, biting his lower lip. Then, easing off the bench, he stretched and yawned. "The brush is gone, in the bin."

How did it get from the car to the dining table? I nodded again and returned to cleaning up, as Jack plodded off to the bedroom to get changed. He usually wore footy shorts in the evenings, exposing his thick, meaty legs and the thousands of curly black hairs. I loved Jack's legs, loved how he gave a heavy growl when I caressed the backs of his knees. But tonight, with the taste of wet, sloppy hair on my tongue, it made my stomach flip.

Once the benches were sprayed and wiped down, I returned to the dinner table. To the clump of hair splattered there, with peas and pasta sauce strewn throughout. I covered my mouth with one hand and picked up the hair with the other, listening to the soft squelch of trails of thick, black strands between my fingers. An unchewed pea fell loose and splatted to the table.

For some reason, I thought of Jack's question earlier that day. *Do you ponder?* The nature of existence and all that. With my own recent brush—I shuddered at the word—with death, his words somehow seemed profound. I realized I hadn't heard him shuffling about in the bedroom, even though the door was open, and it was adjacent to the kitchen.

"Jack?" I called.

Moving from the table to the kitchen bin once more, I dropped the clump of hair with a *plop*, and breathed the last of my anxiety away.

"Jack, my little teddy bear?" I invoked the rarely spoken nickname I gave to Jack after our first date. The one he hated, and the one which always garnered a groan in response.

Nothing.

Peering around the corner, I saw his clothes in a heap on the bedroom floor, as usual. *Philosophy professors, always something more important than being tidy.* Jack was on his back, his big belly rising and falling through quiet snores. Smiling, I hurried to get undressed so I could join him.

For once, I adopted his habit of leaving clothes on the floor and sunk deep into the king mattress to cuddle my husband. He turned to his side, so I was the big spoon, and mumbled how much he loved me as he used the remnants of his consciousness to squeeze my hand.

"Love you, too, teddy bear," I said, and kissed his back. He was a hirsute kind of guy, which I loved, and despite the incident earlier, I found comfort in the hairs sprouting from his back. They felt like home.

As I snuggled deeper, my stomach knotted, harsh cramps seizing across my belly. I breathed through it, tried to relax, sure that it was just a symptom of swallowing the hair. It would digest in the night, and tomorrow would be better.

Another cramp, like a knife to my spleen, and I contained a groan so as not to wake Jack. Something was moving inside me, and I imagined hair sloshing around in my guts, grabbing at my organs. When a third cramp struck, I shuffled out of bed and staggered to the living room, shutting the bedroom door behind me.

Reaching the chaise lounge, I buckled at the knees as my stomach spasmed again. It didn't feel like I was going to be sick, not like food poisoning. Not like swallowing a chicken bone. It was like a fist thrashing around inside me, punching its way through my stomach.

I fell back to the lounge, hands tight around my belly, and held back another groan. Through the darkness, in the corner of my eye, a glint of light. Looking towards it, I saw the object on the kitchen counter. Glinted again, like a wink. Like saying, "Hey fucker, I'm back!"

The hairbrush.

"What ... ngh ... do you want?" I knew it was insane—everyone knows it's insane—to talk to a hairbrush. In that moment, sitting alone in the dark with my guts about to explode, I had no choice. I had no choice but to believe the hairbrush was alive. Or at least harbored some life-like quality.

Do you ponder?

The real question was why it wanted to murder me. Why choke me and make me swallow clumps of hair?

Lurching to the kitchen bench, I held up the hairbrush and shook it, hoping it might achieve something. I threw it across the kitchen, listened to the dull clang of silver against the wall, and the slap against tile as it fell.

"What is happening to me?" I asked through gritted teeth, as if the object could speak. As if it could answer me.

One unsteady foot after the other, I hobbled to where I'd thrown the brush. Flicked on a light and blinked through the intensity. It just sat there, on the tiles, as any hairbrush might. It wasn't alive, it wasn't doing anything.

But how did it get here?

As I looked down at the brush, the silver reflecting back at me in the yellow light, I saw the kitchen bin. The lid was open. Still clutching my stomach, the spasms getting stronger and more intense, I stared at the bin.

At the wet trail of black snaking from inside.

"It can't be ..."

The tendrils of hair moved from the bin, sliding across the tiles towards me. I stepped back, hit the wall, and moved to the right. Stumbled through the dining area and back to the lounge, calling for Jack, calling for help.

The bedroom door burst open, Jack holding a cricket bat and blinking sleep from his eyes. "What's happening?" he asked. His eyes dropped to the ground and widened as he saw what was following me. "The fuck is that?"

"Hair ..." was all I could stutter as I collapsed to the ground. Another spasm was building, I could feel it. I braced for the pain.

As Jack raced towards the hair, swiping at it with the cricket bat, I crawled into the corner, just to get away. Just to keep moving. But the pain was intense now, reaching through my body to the tips of my fingers and toes. It wasn't going away this time, and

I felt the hair—the tendrils—I'd swallowed moving through me. No more punching, no more spasming. It had figured me out. Knew where it was, had mapped a way out.

I felt it reaching through me, pushing at the edges, and as I finally let go of my stomach, I saw the tendrils snaking through under my fingernails. I screamed and watched my nails fall to the floor, one by one, as the hair wound its way out of me.

Looking at Jack—thinking he was the last thing I would ever see—I watched him battle the hair-monster. It flung itself at his face. He dodged. It coiled around his leg and squeezed like a viper, and he fell to the ground with a thud.

"J-Jack ..." I stuttered. "Ja-ck ..."

My fingers were not my own now, the tendrils bleeding from me, splitting the skin on my hands. I looked down at my naked body, saw the skin on my legs and ankles split open. Tendrils gushed out like tentacles, searching for their lost kin. Snaking towards Jack. I tried to hold them back, but my fingers were just bone now, and the pain in my stomach had me seizing.

"Jack ... R-run!"

He couldn't. The hair-monster on his leg had squeezed so tight it had snapped his fibula in half—jagged, bloodied bone jutting from his skin. He still fought the creature, tugging and pulling and thrashing.

As the tendrils seeped towards him—towards their lost tentacle—my stomach trembled again. The skin finally tore apart, more tendrils spilling out, wrapped around my guts. As my intestines spooled on the floor, wet gunky hair entombing them, I tried to collect what I could. Tried, with bony fingers, to put them back in.

"Mark!" I heard Jack calling my name as he crawled towards me, the tendril no longer on him—it had joined the others. Behind him, around him, all I saw was red, and black. Hair everywhere, stretching out across the tiles and the furniture, and crawling up the walls.

It started forming something, a shape. A figure.

The tendrils collapsed in on one another, strands of hair pulling themselves tight, and coalescing into something new. From one of the walls, the hair thickened, stretched out, formed fingers. A hand.

As it grew, I felt more hair spew from my body as I clutched to life. I knew it was too late for me, but that's the nature of existence—the fight to survive. Even in the last moments, I still thought about Jack's stupid philosophical bullshit.

Jack.

The hand grew into an arm and I watched the rest of the tendrils form the shape of a woman.

"Who are you?" Jack screamed through his tears. "What the fuck do you want?"

I wanted Jack to run, wanted him to be free of whatever this was, but as his voice came closer, I knew he would never leave me. I felt his fingers on my face, heard the tremble in his voice as he begged for this to stop.

"Jack ..."

The tendril-woman coalesced further, the figure taking a more human shape. I struggled to keep my eyes open as Jack fumbled with my internal organs. He grabbed at my intestines, my spleen, my kidneys, and rushed to shove them back inside my split stomach.

They just plopped back out.

"Leave us alone!" Jack cried, as the tendrils formed a face.

The shape, almost complete, smiled at me. Teeth I recognized—yellow, black, a few missing—started to form.

"You ..."

She pointed at me, as she had earlier in her front yard, and I felt the tendrils wrap around my lungs and tug.

"My late sister," she said, her tongue formed through thick, matted hair, "definitely went to Hell. Just like me."

As my breathing stopped and consciousness began to fade, I felt the last of the tendrils wrap around my heart.

"Please ..." Jack begged.

"Oh, come now." The woman laughed. "He's just a little ...broken."

Jack's whole body shook as he wailed, holding the remains of Mark's body and spaghettied organs in his arms. The woman, now fully formed and stark naked, kneeled next to him. She examined Mark's form and sighed.

"W-why?" Jack stammered, unable to look away from his dead husband.

She sighed again. "Because you picked up the hairbrush." Dipping her finger into the pool of Mark's blood, she sucked on it and moaned. "Ah, I've missed that."

"Who are you?" Jack asked.

"I *used* to be a woman," she said. "Now, I guess I'm something else. *Homo Follicular*, I suppose. It's hard to explain or even to comprehend, really. But I ... exist ... inside the hairbrush. I come out when I sense the right people are nearby." She chuckled and scooped more blood onto her finger, like sopping up sauce with bread.

"Right people?"

"You," she said. "Your philosophies about existence. Blades of grass and all that, remember? Life can be anywhere, isn't that right?"

"This is impossible," Jack muttered, repeating the words again and again. He hugged Mark's body, rocking back and forth, ignoring the pain in his broken leg.

"Don't worry, he's not gone forever. Just ... traded places."

"Traded places?" Jack pulled Mark's body closer, in a tight bear hug.

The woman nodded. "I offered a sacrifice. Took him in exchange for her."

"Her?"

"Yes." She turned to face Jack, sucked the blood off her finger, and smiled. "He's gone to Hell. My sister will be arriving soon, it's just ... Well, how are *you* feeling, Jack?"

In the next instant, the woman was gone, and Jack was left to clutch at Mark's body until the stench was too much. Crawling away, hating himself for leaving Mark alone like that, he sobbed. He sobbed and wailed as he reached for his phone, plugged into the wall, and resting on his nightstand.

His hands shook as he dialed 911.

My sister will be arriving soon.

His stomach trembled as he waited for an answer, and he held his belly to stow the pain.

His whole body ached when he saw the hairbrush, sitting at the edge of the bed. He tasted something on his tongue, and pulled out a strand of wet, black hair.

How are you feeling, Jack?

The Screams Were Coming From the Fanny Pack

BY JOEY POWELL

A muffled hum vibrated through Kayla's room, similar to a buzzsaw behind a wall but faint enough that she questioned whether she had heard it all. Faint like a ring in her ear. Faint like an itch lingering on her skin post-scratch.

No ... She *definitely* heard something. She craved the quiet of these fall evenings when the sun would disappear behind the trees surrounding her trailer much earlier than it had in the months prior, signaling to the rest of the humble residents of the trailer park that it was time to wind down for the night. The quiet allowed her anxious fifteen-year-old mind to freely channel her thoughts onto the pages of her journal. But that dang buzzsaw-like sound was ruining her peace and quiet. It had gotten louder since she first sat on her bed, sounding less like a hum and more like a series of shrieks.

But where was it coming from?

She swung her legs off her bed, driven toward the sound, and slowly approached her dresser, eyeing the vintage fanny pack she had placed on top of it earlier that day. The closer she came to the fanny pack, the louder the screams became.

Kayla didn't know a single thing about the fanny pack she'd bought for five dollars at a yard sale around the city limits. Though she could tell it was beat to all heck she knew that underneath the scratches lining the exterior was a layer of once-beautiful leather that, if cleaned and buffed properly, would look close enough to new. It seemed like a fateful moment when she brought her bike to a skidding stop in the middle of a suburban neighborhood street with her eyes locked on the fanny pack surrounded by an assortment of old junk.

She *needed* that fanny pack desperately.

Three weeks ago, Kayla walked through the doors of her new high school for the first time. For reasons her parents wouldn't tell her, they needed a "fresh start" in a new city. The move didn't make much difference to Kayla—she didn't have many friends to begin with.

When she stepped out of her first period classroom that day, Kayla was greeted by a tall, slender girl with curly black hair and skin so flawless she questioned whether it was natural or the result of extremely well-applied makeup. The girl introduced herself as Jubilee Summerton and offered to walk her to class. Kayla didn't know it at the time, but Jubilee Summerton was, like, a *really* big deal. She was quickly climbing her way to a hundred thousand followers on social media, and her engagement was stellar. Kayla should have guessed, though, since walking by Jubilee's side made her feel like the most seen girl in the entire school.

Since that day, Jubilee all but ignored Kayla, smiling passively on the off chance that they saw each other in the hallways. Kayla couldn't resist this uncontrollable urge to impress Jubilee—to *make* Jubilee notice her again like she had on Kaya's first days of school.

When she came upon the fanny pack, it seemed meant to be.

The entire school year, Jubilee had deemed every Monday "Fanny Pack Monday".

Today was Saturday, and Kayla had just enough time to refurbish this vintage fanny pack and return it to its original glory.

Kayla eyed the fanny pack curiously. The zipper was splayed wide open.

Too wide open.

Wide enough that either end of the zipper formed a near-perfect diamond. Whereas the teeth of the zipper should have been rounded, they now appeared angular and sharp.

She stared into the space between the teeth, expecting to see the stitched lining of the bottom, but there was no bottom. The interior of the fanny pack was pitch black. A vast, dark void with no bottom that she could see. As the shrieks became more pronounced, Kayla began to wonder if there was a surface far beyond the mouth, stretching past what her bedroom lamp could illuminate, and whether deep down upon that surface was a person screaming.

She tugged on the zipper, but it wouldn't budge. Any ounce of strength between her thumb and index fingers couldn't move it.

Tap tap tap.

Kayla's eyes shot over to her bedroom window, behind which the buck-toothed grin of Randall Dodson taunted her. One eye stared directly at her, while his other lazy eye looked down to her bedroom floor at nothing. Randall was two years younger than Kayla, and his unfortunate appearance was off-putting to most. He spent much of his free time shooting squirrels and rabbits with his BB gun, bragging to anyone who would listen if he maimed one.

Lately, she'd wake up in the middle of the night and catch him outside her window, watching her sleep. She'd told her parents, who told *his* parents, but the late-night visits hadn't stopped.

It was getting late, and all she wanted to do was investigate this strange yard sale trinket, which she'd spent the day refurbishing and now was opened wide and softly screaming.

"What is it, Randall?" she called out to the window.

He simply laughed in response.

"Go to bed, Randall," she called out again.

"I got you something," he said with a squeaky crack in his voice, softened by the glass in front of him. "A present."

It occurred to Kayla that Randall could actually be useful in that moment. The fanny pack wasn't *actually* screaming, was it? That was impossible. It had to be her anxiety playing tricks, her anticipation that tomorrow she'd wear the fanny pack across her body, just like Jubilee Summerton. When Jubilee saw her, how would she react? Would she approve? Would she think the fanny pack was lame?

Kayla ventured to the window, holding the open fanny pack by one strap. With her free hand, she unlatched the window and slid it up, removing the barrier between her, the boy, and whatever oddity the boy wished to give her.

She spoke before he had a chance to. "Do you hear that?" she asked, holding one strap of the leather fanny pack high enough that he could see.

Randall fixed his one good eye on the bag and grinned as if Kayla was playing a game. "Hear what?" he asked.

She brought the bag closer to his face, gripping the strap tightly in case he made a move to snatch it. "Do you hear anything? Anything at all?"

He turned his ear to the fanny pack, then chuckled. "Are you pullin' my leg?"

How could he not hear it? The screams were even *louder* now.

"Screaming," Kayla said.

"Nah," Randall answered, leaning away from the bag. "I got somethin' for you that might fit inside it, though."

As soon as the words came out of his mouth, Kayla noticed two things: Randall's arm behind his back and a thick, pungent stench wafting in from his side of the window.

Dead animal, Kayla thought. And, judging by the smell, likely not something he killed, but rather scraped up off the sidewalk.

"Go home, Randall," Kayla said. She slid the window down and dropped the blinds before he could expose the "present" he'd gotten just for her.

She placed the fanny pack on her dresser, then put one shirt, a second shirt, and a third shirt over it until the bundle suppressed the screaming enough for her to sleep that night. Maybe she was losing it.

But the day after tomorrow was Monday, and she couldn't *not* wear the fanny pack.

Eventually, she drifted off to sleep.

Kayla shivered as soon as she awoke, a wave of icy air stinging her backside. She could have only been this cold if she slept outside, but the rough fabric of her hand-me-down sheets and pilling comforter told her otherwise.

Her bedroom window was wide open.

Shoot. She forgot to lock it. Her mind did a dreadful dance wondering what that creepy kid Randall had done. Had he stolen something? Had he left a dead rodent on her carpet?

She sat up, and immediately her eyes locked onto the fanny pack. The shirts she had used to smother it were now on the ground in front of the dresser.

Kayla wrapped her comforter around her body, taking it with her as she got out of bed to have a closer look at the fanny pack. The zipper of the object was closed, the teeth now tightly connected, and a trail of dark red smudges like tacks on a corkboard began at the corner of the zipper and down the dresser.

He actually did it, she thought. *He put a dead animal inside the fanny pack.*

Whatever rotting carcass was in that thing would surely ruin it. But tomorrow was Monday, and she *had* to wear the fanny pack. Would she be able to get the smell out before then?

She unzipped the fanny pack, and, unlike the night before, the zipper glided with ease. To her surprise, it didn't release the stench of death. Instead, there was nothing. Only darkness.

She lowered her head to the bag, turning her ear to see if the screams would come. An acidic *churning, sloshing,* carved through the bag's interior and into Kayla's ear, like a stomach digesting a meal. And if she listened very closely, she could swear she heard the wailing cries of a young boy with a cracking voice.

Randall's parents stopped by later that day asking whether Kayla or her parents had seen their son. Given Randall's refusal to stop spying on their daughter, Kayla's parents expressed no concern that the boy had seemingly vanished in the middle of the night. Kayla could have told them that Randall tapped on her window the night before. She could have told them that her window was open when she woke up this morning. And she could have told them that a young boy's screams were coming from the fanny pack.

But that would be ridiculous. Fanny packs don't eat little boys, no matter how creepy and gross they are.

Besides, tomorrow was Monday, and she couldn't *not* wear the fanny pack.

Kayla always wondered how long it took Jubilee Summerton to get ready in the morning. On Mondays, she live-streamed her makeup routine, but any time she started the live feed, her hair was already curled, she was already perfectly dressed, and her skin was already glowing. Was it even possible that she had makeup on *before* applying makeup?

No—that would be silly.

Kayla gave up following along with Jubilee's contouring routine almost as soon as she started. Jubilee's entire vanity was lined with brushes and tubes and powders, a sight that would make a Renaissance painter squeal in delight. Kayla couldn't afford all that makeup. But she *could* afford a five-dollar, not-so-gently-used leather fanny. And she *could* restore it to near-perfect condition.

As Kayla stepped into the kitchen Monday morning, her mom turned around and asked, "What's that?"

"What's what?" Kayla said back.

"Across your body."

"It's a fanny pack."

Her mom giggled. "Why are you wearing it like that?"

"This is how you wear fanny packs, Mom."

"No ..." her mom giggled again. "Fanny packs go on your—well ... *fanny*. You know in Australia they call them bum bags?"

"People wear them like this now, Mom," Kayla said, waving her arm across her body.

Her mother grinned. "If you say so."

Kayla knew her mom didn't mean anything by it. She knew her mother was thinking in a very *kids these days* kind of way, but she couldn't help but think she was being mocked, and that was not the way she wanted to start the day.

Whatever. Her mom didn't get it.

But Jubilee Summerton *would*.

ZZZZZIP ... A vibration bubbled on Kayla's chest. She looked down, catching the zipper of the fanny pack lowering itself. Blood drained from her face. She knew what might be coming next.

With the bag a quarter of the way unzipped, a muffled cry sprang faintly from Kayla's bony rib cage. She clutched the bag tightly, effectively suppressing the sound.

The sudden movement prompted her mom to whip her head around, no longer grinning. "Everything okay?"

"Um ... Did you hear that?"

"Hear what?"

Another squeal erupted from inside the bag. When her mom didn't react, Kayla understood that only she could hear it.

And that was a good thing because she *had* to wear it to school that day.

Walking toward the front entrance steps of the school grounds, Kayla went nearly as unnoticed as she normally did. Some spotted the leather bag bouncing on her chest and gave her a validating nod. Some spotted it and rolled their eyes.

Assimilation: Cool to many, lame to others.

But Jubilee's opinion was the only one she cared about, and it bothered her how much she cared.

Kayla sauntered awkwardly to the flagpole, where Jubilee and her crew of perfectly-dressed girls stood and chatted every morning before the first period bell rang. Instead of walking past them, hoping for some form of acknowledgment, Kayla walked toward them, making sure Jubilee could see the fanny pack.

All of the girls were wearing their fanny packs across their chests. Jubilee's looked like a disco ball sparkling in the early morning sunlight. Instead of greeting them with a confident, "Hey, ladies," like Kayla had planned on doing, her nerves got the best of her, and the only thing that came out of her mouth was air.

"Nice fanny pack," Jubilee said to Kayla with a twisted grin that she couldn't read.

Kayla, happy to be noticed at all, softened. "Thanks, Ju-wibee—" *Oh, god ...* Did she just mispronounce Jubilee's name? Did she say it fast enough that nobody noticed?

The girls snickered. Was it because of how she said Jubilee? Did she look funny with her fanny pack?

"I just got it," Kayla said. "It's genuine leather."

"I can see that," Jubilee said. "Where did you get it?"

This was a question Kayla was absolutely not prepared for. She was never able to shop for expensive brands, specifically because her family couldn't afford them. Even the idea of window shopping at fancy shops or perusing boutiques was alien to her. Why obsess over something she could never have?

But she now understood this was a part of the assignment—an assignment that Kayla and Kayla alone had thrust upon herself. And a task that she had failed to complete. Without a single brand name to dangle from her lips, her jaw stayed open, hoping to form a response that would never come.

"Is it vintage?" Jubilee asked.

It most certainly *was* vintage, but Jubilee's idea of vintage was much different from Kayla's.

"Yeah, it's vintage," Kayla said.

"You didn't, like, get it at a thrift store, did you?"

This time, an answer came quickly. "No."

Jubilee squinted her eyes. "Are you sure?"

ZZZIP.

That sound again, cutting through the chatter of the courtyard, the zipper creating a small opening between two rows of teeth.

Kayla's eyes darted to the bag, but the rest of her was frozen in place.

Jubilee giggled, "Did that zipper just ... fall down?"

The rest of her crew laughed as well.

"Come on," Jubilee said. "Is it legit real leather? It's okay, I have some pleather stuff in my closet."

The fanny pack unzipped itself slightly wider, now a third of the way open as if reacting to Jubilee's taunts.

Jubilee made a pouty face. "The zipper won't stay up. I think maybe the bag's a little ... worn out."

Kayla couldn't speak. This was an absolute disaster. She had to leave now, skip class, toss the fanny pack in the nearest dumpster, and let herself go back to being a loser for the rest of the year.

She clutched the zipper and pulled it upward. Thankfully, the zipper didn't give her any resistance. Kayla nearly said, "See?" If only her ability to zip up the bag proved anything at this point. Instead, she said nothing.

Jubilee addressed her friends. "I have to go to the bathroom, ladies." Then, she turned to Kayla. "You wanna come with?"

Maybe Kayla was misreading this situation all along.

She followed closely behind Jubilee, watching her hair bob with every step. On social media, Jubilee swore time and time again that her hair was naturally wavy and voluminous, but that made about as much sense as a pro wrestler being "naturally" muscular. Either she was some freak of nature, gifted with perfect hair by some generous deity, or she was doing something that she wasn't telling everyone.

Whether or not she was lying about her hair didn't matter to Kayla. She simply wished her hair could be that perfect.

The bathroom was empty when they stepped inside. Instead of going into one of the vacant stalls, Jubilee turned and faced Kayla.

"So, like … I don't want to make you feel awkward or uncomfortable or anything, but …" Jubilee crossed her arms. "Why are you so obsessed with me?

The word "obsessed" stabbed Kayla through the stomach.

"I'm not … obsessed with you," Kayla replied.

"I see you staring at me all the time, liking my posts, and now … the fanny pack … What's next, are you gonna, like, cut my face off and wear it or something?"

"What? No, I wouldn't cut off your—that's crazy. Why would you think—"

"Look, maybe you got the wrong idea when I said hi to you after class that one day. So, I had just recently gotten detention for being 'disruptive' in class or whatever, and Mrs. Tabert said that if I walked the new student from her first period to second period classes, she'd shave some time off of my detention hours."

"I … thought you were just being nice."

"Oh, I was. But nice in the way you, like … hand out meals to homeless people, you know?"

"Are you saying I'm … charity?"

Jubilee sighed and pursed her lips. "Listen, honey, I know you live in a trailer park, and I really feel for you and your family, but associating with you would ... kinda be bad for my brand. I hope you understand. No hard feelings?"

ZZZZIP.

The fanny pack was coming undone again.

Kayla's embarrassment turned to rage. Suddenly, a dark thought came to her, accompanied by a fancy brand name. "Versace," she said.

"What?" Jubilee grunted.

"Versace. That's the brand of this bag. My family lives in a trailer now, but that's only because we're having a home built nearby," she lied. "Three stories ... and a pool."

"A pool?" Jubilee repeated. She had a nice backyard that she loved to show off on social media—an amazing lounge area and a guest house that could rival Kayla's entire double-wide—but one thing she didn't have was a pool.

"Oh, yeah. It's gonna be really nice. I could invite you and your friends over when it's done. That is ... if it doesn't hurt your brand."

Jubilee eyed the fanny pack hard. "That's not Versace."

Kayla lifted the fanny pack over her arm and head and unfastened the buckle, letting the straps dangle downward. She held the bag out for Jubilee to take. "Tag's on the inside." Kayla put her hand to the zipper and slowly pulled it sideways. "Don't believe me? Have a look."

She tossed the fanny pack to Jubilee, who caught it awkwardly.

"What's wrong with this zipper?" Jubilee asked.

"What do you mean?"

"It's, like ... sharp."

"It only *looks* sharp. Go ahead. Look inside."

"Why is it so dark?" Curiously, Jubilee lowered her hand to the opening of the fanny pack.

Had she heard the screams as Kayla had, Jubilee would have never thought to bring her hand anywhere close to its interior. The straps of the bag dangled freely on either side, the separated plastic buckles beginning to look like claws more than two pieces to be conjoined.

No … they didn't just *look* like claws … the buckles were transforming *into* claws. Each end expanded into three jagged fingers, and since they were right below the bag, Jubilee couldn't see them grow.

The claws twitched.

The fanny pack unzipped itself, spreading its sharpened teeth wide, forming that same diamond shape Kayla had seen before Randall tapped on her window two nights ago.

Before the bag ate Randall.

Jubilee gasped. "What the—"

The claws shot up from below the fanny pack, the flimsy straps following with them, and clutched Jubilee's arms just above the elbow, the thin points digging deep into her skin.

A roar escaped from deep within Jubilee's throat, infusing shock and pain and utter confusion all at once, a prolonged scream that surely someone would hear. Kayla knew at any moment someone would burst through the door and wonder just *what the heck* was going on. And what would they see? Kayla wasn't even sure what she was seeing was real, and if it was, how would she explain it?

Luckily, she didn't have to wonder for too long.

The fanny pack pulled itself toward Jubilee's hand, devouring it instantly. The claws quickly climbed up Jubilee's arm, and as the fanny pack ascended, making a sickening gurgling sound on its way up, so too did Jubilee's arm vanish within the fanny pack. When the fanny pack got to Jubilee's shoulder, one claw dug into her chest, the other into her back, and the mouth widened, expanding past what the leather material could allow without tearing. But it didn't tear. The bag remained intact as it consumed her screaming head, then slid down the entirety of her body, swallowing her whole.

Laying on the tile surface of the bathroom floor, the fanny pack returned to its normal size. The mouth closed itself, with a sharp *zip*. The claws retracted, forming the ends of a buckle once again.

There was nothing left of Jubilee Summerton but the echo of her screams ringing in Kayla's ear.

In The Attic Lives The Corn Husk Girl

BY JASON A. JONES

I could see myself in the reflective glass. The portrait of the corn husk girl stood on a hand-crafted pedestal with clawed feet made by a local woodcutter. The glass was encased within a wooden frame with hand carved, human fingers which seemed to slither around the portrait from top to bottom and around the sides. It was an exquisite piece of antiquity. I was mesmerized by it. I couldn't believe something like this was in an everyday, run of the mill yard sale.

But it was, and I bought it.

I brought it home much to the chagrin of my husband, Richard, who insisted on putting it upstairs in our attic. It seemed to unsettle him, I guess. I agreed to the proposal because I had recently made the attic space into my own personal refuge—a refuge where I could get away and just be by myself. I set the painting into a dark corner on the far wall by an old window that was in need of repair. My husband said he was going to replace it with a new one, a promise he has yet to fulfill.

Here lately, when my husband goes to work, I take the long walk up the spiral staircase with a key that was only made for the door to the attic. I open it and enter, the strong smell of mildew and dust invading my nostrils. I've set an old rocking chair next to the portrait and opened the old window to let the summer breeze flow through it, making the stale air bearable and breathable. I usually bring a book to read, but today I decided that I just needed to be still and quiet, letting the silence infiltrate my ears like the sweet harmonies of a song sung acapella. It was just me and the small girl behind the glass, the sun shining brightly, exposing the true colors, hand painted on the worn canvas. That's how I wanted it. She looked like me somehow, and through those weeping blue eyes, there was an understanding that my heart was breaking. But the silence was short-lived and shattered by the horrible sound coming from my husband downstairs.

"Have you been up there all damn day?! Get the fuck down here!" he shouted. I put my hands to my ears, not because of the yelling but because his voice sounds like nails on a chalkboard. I peer into the little girl's eyes, closely, put on a smile for my husband, and say,

I'll be back soon.

As soon as I hit the floor landing, he is waiting for me with a slap to my face immediately causing me to fall on the bottom stair step. I shudder and look at his eyes—eyes blank and black. He picks me up from where I'm laying and throws me into the kitchen table, the left side of my torso hitting the sharp corner of it. I instantly see red underneath my shirt. I'm bleeding and he is snickering. Tears begin to flow down my cheeks. I'm usually not a weak person, but every once in a while, the abuse gets the best of me.

"Are you gonna cry, now?" He hovers over me like one of those helium monstrosities at a Thanksgiving Day Parade.

"I'm gonna give you something to cry about," he says as I struggle to my feet. I feel bruised and ultimately defeated.

What a classic line, you fucking bastard, never heard that one before.

"Fix my dinner. I work too damn hard and I'm tired of coming home to a wrecked house and my wife constantly up in that god forsaken attic. Why are you up there all day long anyway?" He insists on slamming the refrigerator door shut after he reaches for a beer. He shuffles his feet and my head aches from his soles scraping the floor. I hear him breath heavily as he sits down in his recliner in front of the television set, a god awful voice emanating from it, talking about the current scores of basketball games. A dull ache penetrates as I reach in the pantry for a box of instant potatoes to go along with supper. Not too long after he has his fill of food, he has his fill of me. While he's on top of me, my mind drifts to the attic and to the painting, wishing I was there instead of underneath his sweaty body. The thought of the small child imprisoned on the wall makes me sick.

 Before he left for work this morning, I received the gift of a black eye because I had forgotten to prepare his lunch. In the attic, I moved my rocking chair directly in front of the portrait surrounded by glass and stared into my own reflection, taking sharp breaths, and coughing because of my side. I spit a little bit of blood into my hands and felt the stinging rush of tears. I got up from the chair and headed towards the door when I heard a small gravelly chuckle from behind me. I turned, and my stomach knotted inside of me.

 Looking into the glass, I could see a hunchback creature standing on the other side smiling hideously at me, its long, stringy, gray hair swaying in an imaginary breeze. With its long fingered claws it clutched the doll made from dried corn husks. The little girl was gone and was replaced by this awful grotesque thing. I slowly backed away to the attic door all the while staring into the white eyes of the entity in the portrait. It began to speak to me.

 "I can see your pain, my dear, and I want to help you," it whispered, the voice sinister and menacing. A giggle came out of the throat as it wiped blood from its mouth. I reached for the door knob, and it was locked. I fumbled inside my pants pocket, pulled out the key, and tried to use it to no avail. Whatever this was had me where it wanted me.

 "Sit down, my child." Its voice sounded far away. I sat down and felt my skin prickle. It stared at me, finally lifting a bony finger and pointing it.

 "You want him dead, don't you?"

 "Who are you?" I asked.

 "Your savior," it said, slowly.

"I can give you the freedom you want and I know you want nothing more than to stay here in this attic alone. I can feel it radiating from your bones."

"I want to spend every moment here," I whispered, my mouth quivering.

"You shall have it." The thing smiled, bearing fangs and laughing, drool running down its chin. It slowly backed away into a void within the painting, finally disappearing into nothing. I'm transfixed on the tattered canvas, thinking perhaps, it would reveal itself again. It didn't and now I have to reluctantly leave the confines of my sanctuary. Richard would be home in a bit, and I knew it would be another horrendous evening trying to appease his every whim.

As Richard delved into his usual evening routine of sports and beer and beatings, I knew I had to try and get him up to the attic. Somehow I had to get him near the portrait.

"Would you like another beer, honey?" I asked. He'd already drank his fourth, and he never was the type to hold it down. In his relaxed state, I knew the time would be right to ask him a question.

"Honey, could you please replace the window in the attic? You've promised me it would get done." I could feel my body tremble like an earthquake as I spoke. He looked away from the TV and glared at me.

"I'll get it done soon."

"You keep saying that."

"Don't bother me with it now. I'm trying to relax and secure this buzz I've got started." Even in his somewhat inebriated speech, I could tell the rage was threatening to sober him up.

I persisted, "I've never asked you for anything other than this one thing. It's important to me. Please!" I started to beg like a sniveling child, feeling disgusted with myself.

"Really, Mary, you need it done, now?" he asked, soberly. I could sense the tension, veins reaching the surface of the skin on his forehead. I was surprised, when after a few minutes, he sighed heavily, scratched his head, and slowly looked up at me. With a slight grin, he said, "Okay. If it'll get you to shut up. I'll need to look at it so I can assess what needs to be done."

As we approached the attic door, Richard, suddenly, slammed his shoulder into my bruised side, knocking me through the attic door. I fell to the floor with a thud, ripping my jeans on a protruding nail. He hovered over me with the blackest eyes I'd ever seen up to this point. I saw that look before, and I knew it wasn't going to end well for me. Staggering, I got up to my knees only to be kicked in the stomach by his steel toed boot. I gasped for air and curled up in a ball. His attention wavered as he looked toward the corner of the room.

The painting! No!

With a sinister smile upon his face, he pounded his way to the painting, looking intently into the reflective glass, an evil smile lingering on his face as he stared into the face of the corn husk girl.

"I'm going to destroy this!" he shouted.

"Please ... Richard ... don't!" I tried to scream but it fell on deaf ears.

As he placed his hands on either side of the wooden frame, ugly, deformed fingers broke through tearing into his chest. The hand twisted and turned as Richard's eyes rolled into the back of his head, his screams piercing the still air in the attic space. Suddenly the grotesque form of the hunchback appeared on the canvas and smiled. It pulled its hand out of Richard's chest, holding his bleeding heart. The hand and the heart returned to the other side, the horrid creature licking it with its maggot covered tongue. Richard's knees cracked as he fell upon them, his chest opened and bloody like a festering wound. I writhed in agony as I began to crawl to the corner of the room, heaving to the sight of the crimson pool surrounding my dead husband.

"Come to me." The creature gurgled, pieces of organ meat hanging from its open hole. I crawled at a snail's pace and finally reached the edge of the rocking chair. It stepped out of the glass and stood over me like an ugly flesh covered tower.

"What's done is done. Welcome to your forever bliss," it said as strings of red saliva fell from its lips. The horrid figure loomed over me and reached for my cheek, its hot breath fragrant with the smell of decay. It finally walked away from me, corn husk doll in hand, and leered at me while slowly stepping behind the attic door. My eyes began to close slowly as I heard the thing laugh, its footsteps bounding down the staircase with wet thuds until they disappeared entirely.

It's been a few years since then, and all of my time is spent in this attic now. I've heard yelling and screaming down below for the last few months. Every so often I hear feet falling on the staircase, and I wonder if something or someone will eventually destroy my solitude. Yesterday, I heard a key in the lock and the door opened and a woman I didn't recognize walked into the room. She went to the broken window and opened it, the chilled air of winter sweeping through. She turned to sit in the dusty rocking chair, looking into the corn husk girl's eyes—my eyes—the woman's face was bruised and swollen. Upon seeing her reflection in the shattered glass, she shuddered. She lifted a hand to an exposed part of the canvas and gently caressed the face of the corn husk girl. Her lips parted and she mouthed the word, "Hello." A small smile began to form on the face of the girl in the portrait, long, skeletal, fingers bleeding as she squeezed the doll tightly. After a few minutes, *I* whispered ... *hello.*

That Old Charm

BY DAVID WASHBURN

HGTV is not ready for what I'm cookin' up next, lemme tell you. People like to ask me "Maria, why would you take on such a big renovation like that? Don't you want to take time to rest?" and I'm like *unh uh honey, Maria can rest, relax, and whatever later. But for now, we ain't slowin' down. Ria's Rehabs* is taking off and we're doing big things and I finally have a solid crew and I really believe in this team and this next project. In the meantime, make sure y'all are following me on all of my socials, you can find them in the description below, and if you aren't already, make sure you comment, like, share, and subscribe. Until next time, love you guys, let's build something! Byeeee.

That's another video ready to publish for YouTube, I am so grateful for the success that is coming quickly from these jobs and what we're doing on YouTube lately. The house over on Southdale Boulevard was a big undertaking and when it went viral, I felt that fire in me turn to a blaze. It's time to strike while the iron is hot and that's what we're doing now. I mean it when I say that I have no time to chill. I can vacation or do whatever once the whole world of renovation and DIY knows my name. Maria Wallace will be the next big thing in the YouTube and home improvement cable television world. I'm not afraid to believe in myself and I'm okay with my mouth writing that check because I already told the bank I'm on my way.

Right now I'm driving to an estate sale that I was told about that's said to have quite the array of items available. Not sure what to expect going in, but I am looking for accent pieces or older fixtures that are still in good shape. Always open to refinishing a piece as well.

The project my team and I are working on now is still getting started. We are getting in there to come up with a game plan first before we start filming. It is a big deal because an executive from HGTV is flying in to see what we're working on, and they want to use *my* name to elevate their platform. I couldn't be more excited for this opportunity either. The contractors I've been working with deserve this spotlight, and my assistant who is a big part of interior design and decor will benefit too. I know my name is on the YouTube channel and the brand looks like it is all about me, but this is truly a team effort.

I was tipped off about this old craftsman-style house that was in need of a serious makeover. The porch is falling apart, needs new windows, new doors, new flooring, maybe has a wall or two too many; I imagine the bathroom will need to be gutted and redone entirely too. The kitchen might as well be done also to keep up. It is a big job. New roof, the whole shebang. This is the perfect investment to flip and also highlight what we're all about at *Ria's Rehabs*.

This is the house on Butler Lane.

I pull up to the Butler house and Giancarlo and Ant are there waiting for me in the yard. They've been here the last few days doing some of the dirty prep work that goes in before we turn the cameras on. We've got enough B-roll footage of the *before* portion of the property to do what we need to do moving forward. I called Giancarlo and gave him a heads up that I picked up this gorgeous antique mirror from an estate sale and that I will need help getting it out of my car.

"Let's see it!" Ant says, as I step out.

"You guys, this sale wasn't much, but wait until you see this thing. It's stunning!"

Giancarlo goes to the back and opens the hatch. "Let's get it into the house."

I rush to stand in front of the guys before they see it. "Wai-wai-wai-wai-wait!" I spurt. "We need a little drama. Drum roll please."

Ant begins pantomiming the drums with his index fingers, waving them quickly while making the fast snare noises with his mouth. Giancarlo stands on his tippy toes to try and look over me, and I put a hand up playfully to block his view. "No no! Wait!" He wrestles my arm down and we all laugh before I give in. "Fine! Fine! You ready?"

Giancarlo and Ant stand back. "Show us!" Giancarlo says with a playful bravado in his voice.

I tug on the blanket I have covering it to protect the glass and reveal my purchase. "Tada!"

Unveiled is an antique mirror with a mercury-coated frame, deterioration around the bevels and etchings. Something I envision being perfect for the bathroom, as it is a work of art and will only be that much more magnificent once it is restored. The glass is foggy, with a yellow hue that no amount of Windex can fix, but that is part of the charm.

The men proceed to admire it and make comments about the aged finish and that it will need some work. Giancarlo comments on how much he loves the etching designs. As they lift it to slide it to the lip of the vehicle Ant comments on how much heavier it is than it looks.

"Bend with your knees," I tell him with a laugh.

"So, we were able to tear down the wall that separates the bathroom and the kitchen on the main floor," Giancarlo reports as they hoist the mirror out carefully.

"Any problems?" I ask.

"We had to replace a lot of the pipes. Went ahead and cut out all of the rotting galvanized pipes and put in all new PVC pipes," Ant explains, side-stepping through the front yard, keeping pace with Giancarlo as they carry the mirror.

"Yeah. That took us a little longer than we would have liked but we are waiting for the walls to dry after rebuilding the drywall. Once the mud dries, we will sand and paint and we can start moving quickly I think," Giancarlo adds.

"Sounds great you guys! I don't know what I would do without you two!" I tell them this as genuinely as I can.

Giancarlo is my rock. Being the head foreman and contractor of choice for many of my past renovations, he has become somewhat of a partner to me, and it is a relationship I try to harness with fairness and respect. He does fantastic work and good help is hard to find.

And reliable contractors who know how to communicate effectively can be even harder nowadays.

Ant, or Anthony ... he is a good guy too. I met him through Giancarlo. He's a recovering alcoholic who just needed something to keep himself busy while he was in recovery and attending AA meetings. Giancarlo personally vouched for him, and I believe in second chances so everything just came together organically. So far it has been a great partnership, and he is a lot of fun to have around. We've had a lot of laughs together, and his energy keeps us young.

We get the mirror into the house and the men get it into the bathroom safely, leaning it against the tub. As they catch their breath I compliment the walls and the work they've done and we talk about what's next for this bathroom. I explain to them that I plan to touch up the mirror in the bathroom today and what we will need to do after. They offer their insight and together come up with a game plan to have this mirror mounted over the sink by this time tomorrow. The men leave for lunch, and I set up my camera to begin filming the time-lapse of me bringing this mirror back to life. Everything is going great!

So, this morning we showed up early to get a head start on the day. The floors need attention, and there is a staircase needing some serious care. The to-do list before the people from HGTV get here is long and per usual, the list grows with new problems as they present themselves.

The first thing I do is eat breakfast with the guys. There are more helping hands on site today as we attempt to knock out our list of projects. I also have Vera here today and for the next couple weeks to assist with filming for the YouTube channel. She also edits eighty percent of these videos nowadays. She is a key player on this team.

As the work moves right along, my focus starts with the mirror and getting it mounted. Ant and I go into the bathroom. He checks the stability of the walls and gives his approval. He and I install the hardware to safely hang the mirror and it is relatively pain-free. I take a step back and look at it and it truly is a game-changer. This thing was a perfect choice.

The whole tone of the bathroom is full of character. The stories this old mirror can tell really is something to ponder.

"Good job on restoring it, Maria," Ant compliments, "you really outdid yourself on this one. It looks brand new, but original at the same time. Just ... wow!"

"Thanks Ant. It really does look great, huh?"

We end the moment and Vera stops recording, "that was great, you guys. Anything else here?"

"No, I think we should move onto other things, and you can just get some more passive footage of everyone working," I suggest.

Later in the evening, we take a break in one of the bedrooms, just chatting. Some of the new guys are recapping their day, and I am taking notes of their progress. As we're going over these details for the last twenty minutes one of the men is unable to provide any details about some of the electrical work, as Giancarlo had been the point man for all things electric. Which makes sense, him being the only licensed electrician and all.

"Gian has been in the bathroom for a while," one of the new guys says.

"Yeah, homie is in there taking a dump," another guy jokes.

"I'll look for him," I say to the group as I go into the hallway, making my way through the house. "Giancarlo," I sing-song aloud, "where are you?"

"He's prolly hiding somewhere sleeping!" someone shouts from the other room.

I walk slowly through the hallway, "come out, come out, wherever you are." I pass through the kitchen and step around the tools on the floor of this very active construction zone. Danger lurks with every step. I walk into the open area outside of the kitchen and see the bathroom door is shut. I knock three times, rapping my knuckles against the hollow door. "Giancarlo, you okay in there?"

My voice is met with silence. I knock again. "Giancarlo. Answer me, please," I say more assertively. Now I'm worried. Something might be wrong. If he needs help, I need to go in there. I knock again, louder than the two times before. "If you don't answer me, I'm coming in there."

I hear footsteps coming toward me through the kitchen. It's Ant and Vera. The concern is valid now.

"I'm coming in. You were warned!" I say as I turn the knob. I am met by a sunset peeking in through the blinds as I cover my eyes with my hand and see Giancarlo just standing there. "Hey!" I shout as I walk over to him. He stands there, non-responsive, staring into the mirror that Ant and I hung earlier this morning. I snap my finger in his ear and wave a hand in his face. "Hellooooo," I sing as the others file into the bathroom behind me.

"What the–" Vera asks, "Gian, what's the matter with you?"

Ant storms over and stands in front of him and puts his hands on his shoulders and jostles him. "Hey, big dog," he says, jostling him more, "hey, you good?"

Giancarlo snaps out of it after Ant shakes him and he pulls his eyes away from the mirror and looks around at the entire team standing in the bathroom with him. I can tell you this. That bathroom is very spacious but cramming seven people in there, not so much. "I'm sorry guys. I guess I just spaced out for a second," he says to everyone. He looks at me with an uncomfortable grin. "Nice work on the frame. It looks amazing Maria."

I am still a little stunned at his behavior. That wasn't any normal *spacing out* right there. "Uh ... thanks," I say as we all step out of the bathroom. Weird, right?

Today, I am arriving a little later. The team has already been working several hours, and I can't wait to see where we are with today's workload. I walk past Vera who is shooting a testimonial style interview with one of the younger guys about repairs he has been making to the porch. I wave at them, and they smile back, eyeballing the two boxes of donuts I'm carrying into the house, letting them know they're welcome to them when they are done with their video.

No sooner than I walk in, Ant sees me and makes his way to me quickly. "Maria, I have to show you something."

I set the donuts down on a folding table in the entryway. "Is it bad? What is it?"

He leads me to the bathroom and holds out his arm to go inside. "See for yourself."

I walk in and I tell you, if this were *Looney Toons*, my jaw would be on the floor right now. "What the fuck!?" I growl as I try to make sense of what I'm seeing. I storm over to the mirror and see that the frame is deteriorated again, almost like I never restored it. The glass is all foggy again like someone breathed on it. But that isn't the weirdest part. Across from the mirror, the wall that the mirror would be reflecting, there was black mold growing there, in the perfect oval shape. "Seriously though? What in the hell–"

"We can't clean this ourselves. We need to call in a professional," Ant says in a tone that suggests that he hates to be the bearer of bad news.

"Yeah, yes. Okay. I will get on that now," I say as I pace back and forth. How the hell does that happen? I've never in my life seen this before. "Do you know where Giancarlo is?"

"He is upstairs fixing the ceiling I think." Ant follows me up the stairs continuing,

I hear a drill sound and follow the noise into one of the bedrooms and find Giancarlo on a step ladder holding a power drill. "Hey! Did you see the mold issue in the bathroom?"

"Maria," he says, stepping down from the ladder, "Yeah, Ant showed me. Gonna need to call in someone to take care of it."

"Why didn't you call me?" I ask him, genuinely upset that something this big would be treated so cavalier.

Giancarlo folds the ladder and carries it past Ant and I, heading out of the room. "You were on your way. It seemed like something that wouldn't make a difference either way."

We discuss the plan for the day and things are largely on track still, despite how odd this is. I am so pissed. I spent hours finishing that coating and—Uggh!

I made the call to a service that specializes in mold remediation and setup for someone to come out today. They should be at the house between noon and four and hopefully we get good news that will keep us on track. I really don't want them here when the peeps from HGTV show up later this week.

For the last two days the restoration crew had been taking care of the mold issue. This limited how much we were able to do proactively *inside* of the Butler house, but we

managed to take the kitchen counters outside and stain them. Ant was able to clean the tools while some of the other guys switched their focus to the landscaping.

As I arrive this morning, I see the others waiting on me. We all make our way inside and everything is dry and seems normal. The walls need to be cleaned up and done again in the bathroom but hopefully one of the new guys can knock it out today. Things aren't great but they could certainly be worse. We're two days behind but have worked miracles before.

It's getting late, and we've all been at it since before eight this morning. It is almost nine right now, and everyone is getting a little irritable. I've already gotten in between two of the younger guys and stopped a shouting match that might have escalated. I think it is time I call it a night. I tell everyone to wrap up and come back tomorrow with fresh eyes and rested spirits. It is Wednesday night and HGTV has one of their big wigs flying in on Friday morning. We need to be at our best and be ready to show him footage of where we started and where we are at as he sees the Butler house in person.

This is ridiculous! Not sure what is going on, but I just got a call from the police asking if I was the owner of the house on Butler Lane. I tell them *yes,* and they proceed to tell me that they received reports from a passerby earlier in the morning that they were walking their dog and heard screaming coming out of the house. Being members of the Neighborhood Watch, they called the cops. It must be a slower night I guess because as I am arriving at the house at three in the morning there are four police cruisers parked in front of the house.

I get out and speak to the lead officer who explains to me that when they arrived, they had to break through the front door and promptly apologized for the damage. The officer then explained that two of them arrived on the scene and heard the screaming as well and that is cause for them to enter.

I ask the officer what was in there, and he walks me to one of the squad cars where Giancarlo was in the back of the car. Not handcuffed, but just sitting, staring ahead with no expression.

"Giancarlo!" I shout, assuming he hears me through the glass. He does not.

"Listen, he attacked our officers but they were able to calm him down. We don't know what was going on in there but he apologized and no one got hurt."

I stare at Giancarlo the entire time as the officer's words become mud in my ears and I am not even listening now. "Thank you, officer, for your help. Is he free to go?" I ask.

The officer tells me they must write a report but eventually releases Giancarlo, and as they leave, I take Giancarlo home. On the drive I ask him where his car is and why he was there in the first place, and he doesn't respond. We arrive at his house, and he steps out of the car and walks into his home without a word. I am worried now and wonder if it is a good idea for him to be working now. Of course, without him though, this whole thing slows way down. Ant is great, but he is half the contractor that Giancarlo is.

"Get some rest! We have a big day tomorrow; I need you well-rested!" I call out to him as he shuts the door to his house.

It is almost eight. I yawn big as I order my coffee at a Dunkin Donuts drive-thru and order two dozen assorted donuts for the team. I'm super tired and need to get this renovation back on track but last night was a headache to say the least. I got home, and it took me a while to get back to sleep. *Sleep?* More like a *nap*. But I can sleep when I'm dead I suppose.

"Hey everybody, good morning," I say, pretending to be more upbeat than I feel, "I got donuts, enjoy."

Two of the guys come for the top box and pull out a donut and Giancarlo comes out of the kitchen and saunters over. "Good morning," I say.

He looks at me. "Morning Ria."

His eyes carry heavy bags underneath like he has not slept. Dark circles. "Hey, if you need to, you can take off and come back later. Get some rest. You look like–"

"I'm fine," he interrupts.

We talk about what needs to be done before the big day tomorrow, and he assures me he is good and can sleep after. Which doesn't seem too out of the norm from his expected attitude about work. The same attitude that we've bonded over as partners since the beginning. If we ever clicked on one thing, it was always work ethic.

I walk into the bathroom to get a look, and would you believe that? That damn mold! I look closely at it and the reflection on the wall is growing again, the same oval shape as before. Worse than before. And it looks like the wall around the mirror is growing mold much faster now and spores are spreading out like roots, almost reaching the ceiling. The freshly painted wall, for a second time, is covered in fresh mold. I stand here for a moment, burying my face in my hands as I resist screaming. I lean against the door and slide my ass to the floor and wallow in defeat, if only for a moment.

Fuck.

I call the restoration people. They agree to come back out and are just as confused about the mold as I am. They get to work and assure me that we can work it out in the end once the mold is gone for good.

It is Friday. Today is the day. I am here, seven A.M. to have things as show-ready as possible, all things considered. As I pull up, I see everyone is here already. I am pleased to have such a punctual team. That wasn't always the case before. I also notice the restoration service van parked outside with their sliding door open. I get out with my trademark donuts in one hand and coffee in the other and see the front door is wide-open. I step inside and drop the donuts and my coffee as I see Vera.

"Vera!" She is in the living room, sitting, slouched against the wall with her head slumped forward. I cover my mouth with wide-eyed horror, a sickening amount of blood soaks the front of her shirt. I see one of the other guys sprawled out on the floor with a screwdriver in his eye lying on the floor, still as a stone. I back into the hallway, nearly tripping on the box of donuts I dropped as I fumble for my phone. I dial 9-1-1 as I walk through the hallway. "Hello!" I cry out. The phone rings once and someone answers.

"Nine one one, what is your emergency?"

"Um, yes. There is, uh" Ugh, great! I can't talk now. "I–I need an—"

"Ma'am. Just breathe. What is the matter?"

"Fucking ambulance. I need an ambulance."

"Address?"

"There are two people dead. There was a struggle." I'm pacing the hallway on the call.

"What is your address?"

"Sorry, um, 1959 Butler Lane."

I walk down the hallway to discover even worse things waiting for me in the kitchen.

Ant! No!

"Oh my God! No! Ant is dead!" I cry into the phone with tears streaming down my face.

"Ma'am. Responders are enroute. Please remain on the line until they arrive."

I am unable to speak. My voice breaks with my heart. One of the other young guys is also dead. Ant lays on the floor bloodied. His face looks swollen and one of his eyes is black and purple. Blood pooling on the floor around his head as his face bleeds from what looks like several blows to his head.

The other guy is on the fresh stained countertop with a Sawzall on his chest and his jaw and throat shredded. The countertops are stained in his blood now.

"Ma'am, are you still with me?"

I sniffle and fight through the tears and the words stick in my throat. "Yes."

I open the bathroom door and see two of the restoration service men on the floor in the bathroom. Their white button up uniforms are stained in blood as they lie motionless on the tile at Giancarlo's feet. He stands there with a nail gun in his hand staring into that fucking mirror again. The mold seems to have overtaken a majority of the wall and has begun crawling along the ceiling.

"Please hurry!" I say to the operator.

"ETA three minutes."

"Gian ..." I say to him, softly, "Gian, please ..."

I take slow steps into the bathroom, shaking, unsure exactly what happened. Giancarlo jerks his head and looks at me with deep black eyes that grip my soul at first glance. I freeze,

"Ma'am"

"What happened here, Gian?" I asked him.

"Ma'am, stay with me. You need to leave. Wait for the police."

"Gian ..."

He lunges at me quickly, and I run away screaming. I drop the phone as a result and as I turn the corner into the hallway, I hear him fire the nail gun multiple times. The popping sound of each shot breaks the silence and makes me shriek each time. I am thankful he misses. I go through the kitchen and into the other hallway and another two shots miss. I go into the living room and hide behind a sawhorse draped with plastic sheets. I try to control my breathing because I feel like he can hear my heartbeat and ragged exhales from any room in the house.

I hear a knock at the door just outside of the living room. The wide-open front door. "Hello," a man calls out.

I hear Giancarlo's footsteps coming down the hall.

"Hi there, I'm Edward McCain and I am looking for Miss Maria for–" *Pop! Pop! Pop! Pop! Pop!* That was the executive from HGTV, falling to the floor after five shots interrupted him, that *must* have hit him. He hits the floor, and I see his face staring right at me. He sees me and reaches, struggling, unable to speak. Every nail is in his face as blood trickles down and his eyes flutter. Giancarlo's shadow looms over Edward as he stands on top of him. *Pop!* A final shot into the temple puts an end to his suffering.

"Come out, come out, wherever you are," Giancarlo sings to me. He steps into the living room, and I am sure I'm next. He rips the sheet off of the sawhorse that I hide behind, and he sees me. I scream as I stand quickly, facing him. He raises the nail gun and pulls the trigger. *Pop!* I flinch as he fires again with another *pop!* He stares at it, empty. I see my opportunity and I push the sawhorse into him hoping that it distracts him or at the very least blocks him for a second. I rush past him and out of the living room. He drops the nail gun and chases after me. I race outside, onto the porch, down the stairs and hear his heavy work boots stomping behind me.

I turn back and see him with a claw hammer and those pits of black in his eyes and murderous expression. I run as fast as I can up Butler Lane and as I am screaming for help, the police turn onto the street with their lights flashing and sirens wailing as an ambulance and fire truck follow. The police stop in the middle of the street when I guess they see me and one of the officers gets out with his gun drawn, aiming at Giancarlo.

"Freeze! Drop the weapon and get the fuck on the ground!"

I keep running and never look back. A second later I hear three gunshots in succession, and they are loud enough to stop me, and I am forced to turn back. That is when I see Giancarlo on the pavement. Two officers and a paramedic rush to him, and a firefighter startles me from behind.

I don't understand completely what happened at the house on Butler. But that mold problem didn't exist before I brought that mirror inside. And my friend Giancarlo wasn't a bad guy before he got lost inside of that mirror. I am the lone survivor of the massacre on Butler, but only at the cost of my friends. My shot at commercial success, and my livelihood. I was striving to be a female-driven independent success story. Now I worry that my legacy will be me just being another statistic telling a survivor story as people view me as a woman playing the victim.

Dollusions

By Caleb J. Pecue

Before the accident, Winnie had always found her room to be cozy. The pale blues and pinks—an odd combination for some, but just right for her—surrounded her and the collection of stuffed animals and porcelain dolls. Some of them lived with her on her entrapment, barred in by the draped, striped fabric that flowed down from the canopy. They were, however, happy she was stuck in the bed with them—or so she fabricated in her mind.

"I won't leave for long," she explained to Toad, the pastel green and tattered stuffed frog at the foot of her bed. "I just need to go outside."

That won't do, the frog spoke back to her.

Winnie, don't you love us? a gray bunny with one eye missing asked from the corner of the room. He was propped up on a neatly folded quilt on top of the back of an armchair. *Don't you—*

"Now, now, Carrot," she started to explain for what felt like the millionth time that the rotation was in effect so that each animal had a chance to sleep with her on the bed and that tonight was Mr. Toad's night. Then, and only then, would she consider him and that was only if Olly the Elephant would allow him to take his night.

That just won't do, Toad attempted to regain control of the conversation. *Outside is where the Bad happened.*

A collective *yes* echoed from the other animals, along with a few grunts.

Inside, much safer.

Yes, safer.

"Come on, guys," Winnie said, untucking her arms from beneath the blanket. Winnie never understood why her mother always tucked the blanket in so high around her collar; she wasn't sick.

It's too cold out there. You'll catch a cold, a neurotic raccoon stated from the top of the chest of drawers, next to Petunia whose shiny porcelain face bounced a ray of morning light across the room.

Petunia wasn't hers, really. She was a relic of someone else's and happened to be plucked up from a yard sale or estate sale or something like that by her grandmother as a sort of get-well-soon gift. Winnie was content to leave Petunia on the dresser along with all the rest of the porcelain dolls her mother had given to her. And as it were, Petunia never said anything to her anyway.

"It's already sixty-five degrees outside, Roger, and I have my coat."

The weather had finally let up from its late spring raininess and Winnie just wanted to play. It wasn't fair that she had spent nearly the whole year in bed. It wasn't fair that the car—

"Winnie!" her mother called up from downstairs.

Oh, lord. That woman, a grumpy, oversized bear grumbled from the floor of her closet. He was put there when her mother was vacuuming one day and hadn't been moved back to his rightful spot in the corner, next to the hamper. This upset everyone and Winnie knew that Ben wouldn't soon forgive her. *Good graciou—*

"I'm stepping out for a bit, do you need anything?"

"I'm fine, Mother," Winnie yelled back down.

Good. Good. That settles it.

No outside time while Mom's away, Kitty stated with a purr.

All day inside! All day with me! Olly said with a trumpet from his trunk, already cozied up next to her under the blankets.

While it wasn't yet Olly's turn, Winnie did have a fondness for him and allowed him, more than the others, to sit next to her in bed throughout the day. At night, he'd go back to his home next to Carrot on the back of the chair if it wasn't his turn.

I wish you'd all go outside, Ben said, sulking. She could only just see his feet sticking out from around the louvered bifold doors. *Give us some quiet.*

"I won't be long darling! You have your alert button?"

Winnie rolled her eyes with the question that needed not be answered. She hadn't taken the darn button off from around her neck since it was strung there after they got home from the hospital. And in all this time, she had only needed to use it once when she fell out of the bed during a nightmare, her legs doing little to help her back in.

Can I push the button? asked Tabs the Tiger who had a penchant for anything that could be clicked. This especially annoyed Winnie whenever she needed to use her laptop and Tabs was always there to make the little light of the caps lock button go off. *Can I, can I, canIcanIcanI?*

"No Tabs, we don't need to right now. I'm fine," Winnie said, pushing Tabs off of the bed. He landed with a soft *thump* on the mahogany floorboards. And she swore she saw him frown as he went over the edge.

She almost apologized to him, feeling a sudden urge of panic that she may have hurt him, when his voice came up from below, *Did you know you have bunnies under your bed?*

Ha, ha ..., Carrot sarcastically laughed while Roger cackled, bouncing a little—or so Winnie imagined—too much until Winnie thought she heard the *clink-clink* of Petunia's porcelain hitting itself. *Careful,* Winnie heard her grandmother say to her in her mind as she remembered the day Petunia moved into her collection. *Porcelain breaks, darling.*

She never understood why someone would willingly make a child's toy out of such easy-to-break materials. Perhaps that was one reason she didn't gravitate toward them. Or, perhaps it was the scary makeup that they all seemed to wear.

"Winnie," her mother said from the doorway. "I asked you if you had your alert button."

Winnie assured her that she did, untucking it from her nightgown and shaking it while her mother moved around the room and picked up a few paper drawings and pencils that had fallen off of her nightstand.

"That's good, darling. Please be sure to try and stay in bed. Your recovery depends on a lot of rest. We don't want you to get another infection."

And although Winnie knew her mother couldn't hear them, she heard the animals make a shrieking sound as they remembered the torment they all went through while she was away in the hospital.

"But Mom, I want to go outside," Winnie stated, her voice warbling, yet determined.

"Absolutely not. Maybe later, we can take you downstairs for a movie, if you'd like."

Her mother sat at the edge of the bed, stroked Winnie's hair, and kissed her cheek. Winnie kept her gaze at Petunia who she swore was smiling at her pain.

"Will I ever walk again?" Winnie asked the question that had been asked many times before. Her mother moved her hand to her bottom lip to steady her quivering.

"In time, we hope," she lied, the medicinal nature to her response did little to reassure her. Winnie knew that the *we* was a reference to the onslaught of doctors and physical therapists, all of whom she'd rather forget.

As her mother stood, she scooted Winnie's wheelchair up to the edge of the bed and adjusted Walter the Alligator who had been playing on it since her last bathroom break earlier that morning. It was a lot of work to move into it, and she had spent months perfecting the motions she needed to do to get out of the bed—albeit, *perfect* was far from what most would have called it.

"If you need anything, press the button and Mr.—"

"Mr. Haskell from across the street will pop in. Mom, I know."

Her mother shook her head and kissed her cheek once more and then left the room, mostly closing the door behind her.

Thunder roared and rain pelted the metal roofing as she and Olly snuggled in the bed, watching a video on her laptop as the afternoon light faded. The lights flickered, and Winnie knew that it was only a matter of time before the connection got so bad that the quality would suffer so much that the faces in the video would become indistinguishable. So, she closed the laptop and slid it back under the side of the bed.

Tell us a story, Winnie the Pooh said, unseen. Winnie didn't actually know where he was, except for thinking that the last time she saw him, he was in the closet with Ben. Her dad thought it was cute for her to come home from the hospital at birth with a stuffed animal christened with her namesake. Winnie didn't really like it, though. Yet, she couldn't find it in her heart to let Pooh go after all the years together, to let the memory of her father fade. And so, she allowed Pooh to move from place to place within the room until forgotten and lost. Every now and then, she'd hear him though, and she'd smile remembering her father.

A *crack* of thunder roared, shaking the old glass panes in the windows on the opposite wall that bookended the chest of drawers. A few of the animals let out a scream, along with her own.

She brought Olly in closer to her and stared across the room at the pink wall. There she noticed a small, black dot, high up, just at the edge of her view, where the canopy started to obstruct, and she wrinkled her nose, squinting.

The room had grown dark as the storm clouds moved in and so she jostled herself to the side, reaching for the lamp's cord. As she pulled it, a flood of dim light filled the room. She repositioned herself in the bed and squinted in the direction of the dot. A shadow from the canopy of her bed cascaded up the wall, still partially obscuring the dot, which she assumed was a beetle or spider or ant.

Her room was prone to getting insects—a hazard of leaving her windows ajar con-stantly—and this always upset her as her mind would race thinking about all the unseen bugs that must have been there if there was one so out in the open.

What's she looking at? asked Carrot.

What are you looking at? Olly mimicked asking without any real thought, his trunk tapping her arm, but she ignored him. *Huh?*

She adjusted herself, pulling herself toward the middle of the bed, while her lower half stayed put, almost creating a *V*-shape. She could make out the dot on the pink floral wallpaper, although it didn't quite look like a dot anymore. From there, she could see a line that snaked up to the moulding at the ceiling, disappearing under.

A leak? she wondered, and became immediately irrational, thinking that her animals were all doomed. If they became moldy, she knew her mother would not let her keep them.

"Is that water?" she asked, hoping that it wasn't.

Where?! screamed the neurotic raccoon. *Help me!* he continued to yell as Winnie scooted herself even closer to the foot of the bed. She huffed as a bead of sweat collected on her forehead. No matter how hard she willed it, her bottom half would not respond to any command her brain sent out.

Water, water, every where; nor any drop to drink, Orville the Owl cooed from high up in the netting that held a few of the animals in the corner of the room. Winnie paid him no attention as he recited *The Rime of the Ancient Mariner*.

She squinted more and just as lightning flashed and the lamp flickered, she noticed something that made the hairs on the back of her neck stand. *That can't be*, she thought to herself, but her eyes told her a different truth than her brain.

What's going on? Ben called from within the closet.

I hate storms! Olly shouted, and Winnie felt his fur grace her toe—or she thought she did; phantom feelings were confusing to her as each time it happened she thought she was regaining her feeling and that would signal a true start to recovery. Never mind how often her mother ignored her question of whether she'd ever walk again, a part of her knew she wouldn't.

Another flash of lightning and now Winnie was sure that her eyes had not deceived her.

The line on the wall was much wider and had spread down farther. It appeared fuzzy like a caterpillar that had been stretched too far. It appeared to wiggle like one too. Each time the ripple reached its end, the thing stretched farther and farther, closer to Roger who grew increasingly worried by the stares. Petunia, though, seemed to not mind; her cold face, still stiff.

What is it?! Roger shouted.

"I ... don't know," Winnie admitted, never removing her eye from the fuzzy thing crawling down her wall, expanding and growing. It moved rather slowly but with each passing moment she could tell that it inched closer and closer to the top of the chest of drawers.

I don't want to die! Roger continued to shout. *Get me! Help me!*

Winnie wanted to laugh because although she didn't want to lose any of her animals, she found it interesting that a stuffed animal was contemplating death. And although the foreign entity was cause for alarm, she felt as though Roger's real motive was to get a spot in the bed.

The thing crept down farther, widening at its base as it did so. From Winnie's vantage point, it appeared to be at the top of Petunia's head, although she knew it was simply on the wall behind her. So, she was safe for now.

Still, with Roger's cries, Winnie moved to get into her wheelchair. *Help me!* he shouted once more. And while a part of Winnie knew this conversation was a fabrication in her mind, it felt as real as any other conversation. She couldn't help but be worried for him and wished that he could actually move on his own.

"I'm coming!"

She grabbed the left edge of the bed and pulled her body across it. Her muscles in her arms ached as she had already pulled herself in a near-full circle on the mattress, which was more movement than she had done alone in quite some time.

Her mother was usually there to help with the transfers.

My chair! Walter cried as he flopped onto his side.

She grabbed the arm of the wheelchair and immediately it scooted back. *Shoot! The breaks aren't locked.*

Careful, Winnie, Olly said from behind her. She looked back at him, the light from the lamp silhouetting him somewhat. His big ears were spread wide across the pillows. *Don't want to go back to the hospital.*

Winnie didn't really understand why Olly was considered her favorite but they had grown even closer after her extensive stay in the hospital, as he was the only animal that she allowed in the bed there. "*You should've seen the car … You're lucky to be alive …*"

She moved her attention back to the chest of drawers. There she could see the thing had begun to creep and spread down around the sides, which assuredly meant that it was on the top surface as well.

Ah! Please! Roger cried out.

She pulled the brake on the wheelchair and attempted to pull herself from the bed. For a moment she bridged the gap between the bed and the wheelchair. Her alert button hung from her neck, stretching down toward the floor that felt farther than it actually was.

Winnie grabbed for the other side of the wheelchair with her free hand and attempted to twist herself into the seat just as—*Help! It's on me! It burns!* Roger shouted.

My chair! Walter exclaimed. *Don't sit on me!*

"My heavens," Petunia said, but something was different. The voice actually felt as if it were coming from that side of the room. Never did Winnie really consider that the make-believe voices came from within her own head and not from them, at her own location. Yet, Petunia's voice felt like it occupied actual space.

Clink-clink.

With a huff, Winnie righted herself in her chair, wedging Walter between her and the sidewall. *Grr, I'll bite you.*

"Wait, Roger. I'm coming," she said, unlocking the brake.

Hurry!

She could see the black, fuzzy thing enveloping him, as it crawled up Petunia's side. The light flickered and—

Clink-clink.

I fear thee, ancient Mariner! I fear thy skinny hand! Orville continued, unaware of the horror below that started to stretch its way toward him.

Winnie, momentarily stunned by the lightning, began to move toward the chest of drawers. As she stretched and reached up to grab Roger, the bulb flickered and suddenly the room went dark. She pulled back. A flash lit up Petunia's face.

She was staring right at her. *Wasn't she facing the other way before?* Winnie wondered. Extending her hand again, she pulled Roger from the shelf.

Thank you! he whispered as a cracking sound started.

Clink. Clink. Crack.

Winnie pulled the thing—*the fungus?*—from Roger's fur with a ripping sound. It was slimy, and she swore it wriggled and pinched the flesh on her palm. She tossed the disconnected blob across the room. It landed next to the hamper and slowly began to crawl up it, growing.

She looked back at Petunia, whose porcelain had started to crack under the fungus's pressure. Her right arm had already shattered into a sharp point. Her face was partially covered with the fungus and it appeared to be crawling into a small hole at her mouth.

"My heavens," Petunia said, although the voice was nothing that Winnie had ever imagined for her. Like speaking into a conch shell, it echoed and was tinny. "Finally."

No amount of make-believe would have prepared Winnie for what she saw next.

Petunia's shattered hand raised upwards. Attached, the black fungus looked like the strings of a marionette's puppet.

"Oh my god!"

Winnie! A collective scream came from all of the animals. Yet, Petunia's gaze was strictly on Winnie.

"The amount of time I've watched you, Winnie," the fungus said. "I was there when you first came outside. Oh, how I've missed your touch! And what a perfect vessel! None of the others would have done. Already so lifelike."

"What are you? What do you want?" Winnie shouted at the doll.

A part of her wondered if it were all but a nightmare and that at any moment she'd fall out of her bed and wake up.

"I want to help you. I want you to play with me, again."

Petunia stood, her movement somewhat unfamiliar and inhuman.

Clink-clink.

Out of instinct, Winnie let out a scream. She feverishly pressed the alert button as the doll began to slide down the front of the chest of drawers, the fungus spreading.

Ouch! screamed Carrot. *It's got me!*

She glanced over to see that the fungus had spread along the windowsill and leaped across to the chair where it was burrowing into Carrot's missing eye socket. Stuffing protruded from the wound.

Petunia's feet landed onto the mahogany flooring with a *clink* and she began to move toward Winnie slowly. *Go!* shouted Roger as Olly started to toot. From the floorboards Winnie heard Tabs scream and she knew it was upon him too.

She could not save them all and the fungus appeared to be moving quicker and quicker.

Winnie grabbed the tops of the wheels and moved over to the bed. She plucked Olly from the pillow and went to turn the wheelchair around. Yet, she found herself impossibly stuck, like on a rainy day in the mud.

But what about me? Toad exclaimed from the foot of the bed.

Petunia appeared to be moving even quicker now as tendrils of fungi reached the bottom of her foot.

"Stop!" shouted Winnie, attempting to move her foot to no avail.

"My heavens, we just want to help you, Winnie!" Petunia said. "Don't move."

The fungus pulled at Petunia's arm, raising it, almost like a knife. And just as Winnie thought it, the fungus slammed the arm down into her foot. Blood spewed out from a hole left behind, although Winnie couldn't feel it.

As the room spun in her head, Winnie heard the hiss of Kitty.

"We can fix you, Winnie," the fungus pleaded, discarding Petunia to the floor. She flew across the room, shattering against a bookcase and Winnie thought she heard Petunia let out an audible sigh. The snakelike fungus skittered up the metal of the wheelchair. It coiled around the wheel and up the arm rail until it crossed her body just as Winnie attempted to pull herself into the bed, tugging on the draping from the canopy.

She flopped halfway onto the bed as the fungus coiled around her legs. Toad flew off and hit the floor with a muffled *thud*.

Winnie let out a scream as she felt a burning in her foot. *Pain*, she thought.

Real pain.

Burning. Real. Pain.

She felt the fungus crawl into her wound. She felt the tendrils wither their way up through her thigh. Up, up, up, pressing down on her muscles, paralyzing her in its own way. Her breathing became faint as she felt her heart slow. A tickling, burning sensation moved in her chest and now higher a choking in her throat.

She squeezed her eyes shut as it hoisted her lower half into the bed. When she reopened her eyes, she watched as Olly, illuminated only by flashes of light and a few rays of late afternoon sunlight that had started to reappear, disappeared under the blackness. She screamed again, a guttural cry cut short by the pressure.

And again.

And again.

She closed her eyes, picturing all of her animals—now silenced—and her world grew black.

When she reopened them, a man was over top of her, and the pressure had subsided.

She recognized him immediately: Mr. Haskell.

"What a mess! Honey, are you alright?" he asked, shaking her, sitting down at the foot of the bed. Stuffing and porcelain lay everywhere as if a tornado had come through, but no sign of the fungus was left.

"My heavens, Mr. Haskell, I'm fine. I just had a bad dream. But can you please not sit on my feet. They hurt."

With a smile, Winnie felt her little toes wiggle from underneath the sheet and knew that her recovery had only just begun.

A New Gimmick

BY DR. STUART KNOTT

You're gonna need a new gimmick, kid, Jamison's voice still echoed in my head. My meaty hands tightened around the steering wheel as I saw that bronzed, mustachioed hard ass sitting behind his desk, barely acknowledging me as he flicked through a stack of papers. *It's just not workin'.*

The worst part was that the curmudgeonly old bastard was right! I've been busting my ass for ten years trying to get myself over as a plucky, underdog challenger. Ring announcers introduced me as "The Man That Can," and matches were structured where I'd look like a fighter, even in defeat...even when stretchered from the ring by a couple of the boys dressed up as orderlies.

Ten fuckin' years staring up at the lights! Oh, sure, there was the odd standing ovation, and some old-school fans who remembered me from my days down South still popped when my music hit. Jamison might hand me a pity low-tier championship if someone got hurt or toss me into multi-man matches or as a veteran challenger for his latest despicable heel, but Lawrence Marcus (AKA: Lawrence King, AKA: The Man That Can) wasn't getting the main event any time soon.

Still ... A new gimmick? The times I've seen guys go to the expense and effort of repackaging themselves only to crash and burn made my head spin, so I tried pitching some alternatives to salvage my career.

"What if I snapped? Turned on the fans and started mowin' guys down?"

"You could put me in a tag team? Me and Bret Barański could be a good fit?"

"What about some squash matches?"

"Has Sean got a challenger for next week? I could go the distance?"

No each time.

No, no, no.

You're played out, Marcus, Jamison said, lighting a cigar. *People want somethin' new and fresh. Old school don't cut it no more.*

Man, I was pissed! Twenty years in the wrestling business, losing days and years, lovers and children, to life on the road, struggling to entertain everything from sweaty gym halls to small arenas to a loud, loyal, but by no means minuscule crowd, and all I had to show for it was a beaten-up body, a ringing in my left ear, and a mangled knee. Sure, the boys in the back shook my hand and I had a lifetime of memories and memorabilia that would maybe one day be seen as a steady, relatively influential career, but what did that matter when these up-and-comers were spinning end over end off the top rope and flipping all over the ring?

A new gimmick? Christ alive!

When Jamison had suggested I *take a few days t'think about it,* I wasn't gonna question the old goat. Real Pro Wrestling was scheduled to be in town for the next week, so I holed up in a hotel with a big bag of ice on my knee, a well-done steak, and flicked through endless crap on the television rather than endure the arduous trip home to Tennessee just to then drive halfway across the country a few days later.

I spent the first day sketching out gimmick ideas, but my mind was a blank. I'd taken a nasty bump three nights ago when McIntosh (who went by the name Fachan, wrestled in a kilt, and had Celtic symbols tattooed all over his torso despite having never set foot in Scotland) had gotten a little overzealous with a gutwrench suplex and accidentally bashed the back of my head off the railing that separated the fans from the ringside area and I'd been a little out of it ever since.

There's some mild swelling, nothing serious, the doc had said, tossing me a useless Z-Pak before walking away.

Still, by this point, my head felt ready to split so I staggered out for a wander around town. I always liked to tour the local area, check out the food and sights, but I wasn't really looking for the hustle and bustle of the crowds, so I hopped in my rental and settled for a relaxed drive with the window down, the radio playing softly, and just letting my aches and woes fade to a dull throb.

That was when I'd spied the sign advertising the yard sale, and memories of my family taking me round the block every other Sunday, greeting neighbors and browsing their wares, caused me to pull over and check it out. My mind had been a million miles away, lost in the fog of these memories, the worry about my career, and what I was sure was probably a mild concussion, when I spied it hidden at the bottom of a battered, soggy box full of clothes.

Before I knew it, I was back in my hotel room. I barely remembered the drive back, much less paying for the item or talking to the seller, and my food sat forgotten on the bedside table as I stared at my purchase.

The mask that sat on the pillows of my hotel bed appeared like a leering, disembodied head. It was exactly like a traditional *luchador* mask—beautifully crafted Lycra with shining patterns emblazed into it—but wore a demonic scowl that transfixed me. It was a dark maroon red, the color of dried blood, with black and silver accents, glaring eye holes, and flame-like decals that gave it a monstrous appearance.

I stared at it for hours, my aching hands doodling and jotting notes. I tore sheet after sheet from my notebook. My eyes locked onto the mask's vacant eye holes, until the sun set and the inky darkness of night crept in, the moonlight glittering off the mask's shining accents.

I blinked, as if waking from a daze, and stared at my notebook. I was never much of an artist, but my crude sketch stared back at me, like a faceless mannequin silently judging me. Its head was covered by the mask, the torso bare but for scribbled elbow pads (a necessity these days, Father Time casts a cold shadow, after all) and leather clasps around the wrists. The bottom was a deviation for me: tights rather than my traditional trunks, with flames to match the masks' aesthetic, finished off by buckled boots.

I had scribbled a name beneath the sketch and underlined it three times for emphasis: *El Chernobog*

"The fuck is that?" I wondered aloud to the empty room—empty, but for me and the leering mask, its drawstrings dangling like entrails. "Did that come from you?"

I was expecting silence. I felt ludicrous, but the throbbing buzz in my bruised head flared. I grasped the back of my head in pain, my notepad dropped to the floor, and my eyes watered, blurring my vision. The mask doubled and swam before me, seeming to grin at me, almost floating, bathed in shadows, a sneering visage that burned into my very veins.

"You wanna wear a mask?" Jamison had seemed surprised when I walked into his office in my new getup. I won't deny it, I relished seeing him startled for a change. It was nice to see him speechless for a change since he was always so high and mighty. "A 'roided up *luchador* ..." he mulled it over, sucking on his cigar. "It's new, at least!"

His attitude offended me. I wanted to reach over the desk and throttle the life out of him until his eyes burst, but I kept my cool. He was the boss, after all. The meeting lasted a couple of hours. In it, we mapped out the next six weeks, which would see Marcus King written out of RPW in suitably dramatic fashion. It meant taking another loss (and letting the guys beat me with chairs and drive me through sugar-glass) but it'd all be worth it once I came back under the mask.

Essentially given six weeks of vacation time, I threw myself into the gym: weight training, cardio (definitely the cardio, as forty rushes towards me like a freight train, I can't afford to get gassed in the ring), and working on my in-ring mannerisms with Barański, running the ropes and testing out a few new moves.

"You gots t'be slower, meffodikal," he lisps as we trade lock ups. "You ain't a fall guy now, dig? You's dis demon fing. Nuffin' hurts you, nuffin' slows you, nuffin' bodders you."

I have to say, I felt myself reinvigorated by it all. The mask was a little tight and seemed to dig into my flesh, but my hesitation about taking on a new persona, altering my in-ring style, evaporated when I first stepped between the ropes in my gear and locked up with Barański. I'd always been one of the bigger guys—6'2, 320lbs (325 on a bad day)—but my style had always been very grounded, very technical, and very (as Jamison put it) "old school". I would target limbs—the wrists or ankles—and tie my opponents up, wearing them down and fighting from beneath. Jamison seemed to miss that this could allow the younger, more athletic guys to learn a little something about psychology, building towards their bigger moves, and working the crowd rather than just popping them with glorified stunts. He'd also missed the opportunity to show a contrast of styles. All he saw was a big guy, a veteran, the young talent could score a win over to make them look good.

I was confident that El Chernobog would change all of that. I found myself keeping the mask on, even while showering, almost afraid to remove it lest I lose the character—a rage-filled brute who shrugged off every attack and tossed guys around like they were nothing. I practiced my body movements in the mirror, clenching my hands, rolling my shoulders, and stomping around with a stalker's hunch. No longer did I greet the boys backstage. I simply brushed past them, my focus squarely ahead, and glared at my reflection, sure that the mask was as alive as the gnashing teeth behind it.

It was a *faux pas*, of course. I was the one who insisted that the guys greet each other, shake their hands, and show the proper respect, even if they hated one another. *It's not about your ego*, I'd say. *It's about trustin' the man opposite you in the ring.*

If any of them were brave enough, they'd've challenged me on my rudeness, but I was essentially untouchable. They might have pinned me time again in the ring, but backstage was an entirely different story. Experience trumped everything. Backstage, *I* was judge, jury, and (when necessary) executioner, settling disputes and keeping the boys in line, so no one was going to talk down to me. Even Jamison held his tongue when he noticed my change of attitude in the nightly huddles, with the sounds of the crowd shuffling in echoing to eager ears.

"Smart," I growled at my reflection. "He's a leech, but he knows his place."

I was in the back, palms pressed to the bare stone wall behind the mirror, fully dressed and psyching myself up for my big in-ring debut as El Chernobog.

"This is fuckin' *it*," I whispered. "This is our time."

Our time? I frowned.

The mask shifted.

Did it feel tighter?

No, stupid, I rolled my eyes. *It's just loose.*

I reached behind it and tugged on the strings, tightening the mask, pulling it close to my flesh.

"*My* time," I corrected, and stormed out of the locker room.

The rush from the crowd as I step through the curtain fills me with a warm fire that makes all my nagging doubts and pains a distant memory. I hate being away from the ring. Not only does it cost me money, but it's hard to find a high as euphoric as the chanting of a crowd. Whether it's a handful a hundred, or a little over a thousand like tonight, the thrill is more than addictive, it's elemental, and it takes everything I have not to bask in their awe as I stalk my way to the ring, lights flickering, a sinister dirge—an electric guitar riff on "Night on Bald Mountain"—accompanying my every step.

"And!" the ring announcer shouts into a microphone producing a flare of feedback, "From Parts Unknown: *Ellllll Cherrrrnobog!*"

I clambered into the ring and stood, slightly hunched, hands balling in and out of fists, mentally repeating my newfound mantra over and over:

It's your time. It's your time. It's your time!

Fittingly, Bret Barański stood across the ring. Toned, his skin slick from a pre-match dousing, he paced in his black and pink tights with the nervousness of a caged animal. It was just as we'd talked about, he had come out all full of pep and pazazz, playing to the crowd, slapping hands, even handing his sunglasses to a kid in the front row, but his bravado faltered in the face of his monstrous new opponent.

The referee made a signal, and the bell rang. Barański charged me, flying in with a crossbody, and I snatched him out of the air with my burly arms, driving him to the mat with a slam to audible gasps. Barański nipped up to his feet, quick as a cat as always, and ran off the ropes with a clothesline. I simply shrugged it off and dared him to do it again. He took the bait and ended up stretched over my thigh in a backbreaker, his face the perfect theatrical mask of anguish. Beat for beat, we hit out marks with few flaws. Barański and I had worked together for years and had meticulously gone through the match beforehand, with only one aspect being a concern for him.

"My ankle, Big Man," he'd said, "she is tender, so don't blow yah load tossin' me over dem ropes!"

Barański swung at me for the spot, and I pivoted, grabbed the back of his long, curled hair, and hefted him at the ring ropes. He tumbled awkwardly over, bashing his shoulder on the ring apron, and favoring his left arm as he sold the fall, his snarls of pain lost as the referee began a ten count.

The crowd counted along, purposely out of synch, which irked me. I hate it when they did shit like that. It messed up the flow of a match. Barański rolled into the ring and baited me into a lock up.

"Waddafuck wuz dat?" he hissed in my ear.

"You said to watch your ankle," I replied, shoving him away.

"Just feckin' slow it down!" he hissed as I swatted away a dropkick.

"Two minutes, fellas," the referee said as he moved to check on Barański.

Irritated, I shoved the referee aside, ignoring his protests, and hauled Barański roughly to his feet.

Slow it down? We'll fuckin' slow him down! I shoved Barański's head between my legs and hoisted him up from the gut, instinctively, he rolled with the move, preparing to distribute his weight for the inevitable powerbomb.

Thinks he's so fuckin' smart! I shifted somewhat before the drop, unbalancing him ever so slightly, then fell to my knees as I drove his back and neck to the mat with everything I had.

Three slaps of the referee's hand and my arm was raised in victory.

Finally!

For the first time in what felt like forever, I'd scored the pin fall. The crowd was a chorus of boos, but not out of disinterest or boredom, they hated seeing their charming hero so readily defeated by my hands. I basked in their jeers, soaking them up, and snatched my arm away from the referee as he told me to clear the ring for the main event.

Buzzing, joyous, I headed to the back, sure that Jamison would congratulate me on a successful redebut. Instead, I was met by Barański, who awkwardly clutched the back of his neck and his side.

"I sed t'slow th' feck down!" he shouted, quickly attracting a crowd. "Yah cudda killed me, yah big twat!"

"Oh, don't be such a bitch," I barked, pushing past him. The adrenaline was wearing off, and I could feel the throbbing of a dozen aches and pains coursing through me. I just wanted to shower and get a good steak.

"Bitch me?" Barański replied, insulted, and blocked my path. "Bitch *you*, is more like!"

Barański's palm was on my chest as if holding back a mewling child. I glared down at it and wrapped my meaty left hand around it, removing it from my person and squeezing so hard that Barański's face contorted into an agonized yawn. "Don't you fuckin' touch me, you Polish ingrate!"

"Hey, *hey!*" Jamison called, rushing over, his headset still around his neck. "What's all this, eh? C'mon, guys, we've got a show t'run!"

"Tell it to *him*," Barański nodded towards me, rubbing his bruised wrist. "Takin' liberties, feckin' nearly killt me out there! And take that feckin' fink off!"

Barański swatted at my mask, and my vision turned blood red. I swung a right-hook without thinking, colliding with Barański's jaw, and sending him sprawling to the cold concrete floor. He was out like a light, his eyelids fluttered, and his left leg twitched involuntarily.

Two hours later and I still needed that shower, still hadn't had my steak, and my body cried out for rest. Jamison had quickly hurried me into his office so Barański could be taken to the hospital. It was probably for the best as I'd seen the way the boys were glaring accusingly at me and had felt my blood boil again, to the point where I wanted to rip their judgmental eyes from their sockets!

"Okay, okay, thanks for letting me know," Jamison hung up his phone and sighed, lacing his hands together on his desk. "Barański's stable."

"Great," I shrugged. "Can I go now?"

Jamison held up a hand. God, how I wanted to tear it from his wrist with my teeth!

"Marcus ... you broke his jaw."

"He baited me."

"Fractured his orbital bone."

"You heard what he said!"

"The guy's on the shelf for at least six months, man, c'mon! I'm tryin' t'make *money* here!"

"Some of these guys need to learn the proper respect," I snarled.

"Respect, *hah!*" Jamison lit a cigar and rubbed his temples. "Okay, listen, here's what we're gonna do. We're gonna accelerate by two weeks. Since Barański's out, *you'll* take his spot in next month's title match. We'll get you in the ring, get some wins under you, but you can blow smoke about takin' out the number one contender."

"About fuckin' time!" I rose from my seat and stabbed a finger in Jamison's face. "And *I'm* goin' over, y'hear? Don't get too smart with us!"

Jamison didn't even flinch, he looked me right in the eye. "Yes," he agreed. "You'll go over. But you'll only *stay* over if you get your shit together. You fuck this up now, and you're out, y'hear me?"

"We're all ears" I scoffed.

I tossed my plate to the bedside table and burped loudly. The steak had been a little overdone, but I wasn't bothered. I'd carved a path of destruction in the ring at every show, decimating everyone and riling the crowd up with boasts about taking out their hero and therefore deserved – no, *demanded* – his title shot. By this time tomorrow, I would be the champion, and I could get the best steak in whatever Podunk town we went to.

It's all comin' up rosy, a voice whispered in my head.

I jerked, a shiver bolting down my spine, and looked around. Nothing, of course, but something had definitely whispered at my shoulder.

I yawned and chalked it up to fatigue. Wrestling took its toll—that was for damn sure—and I needed all the rest I could get if I was gonna run with Jamison's ball.

I swung my feet off the bed, wincing at a bit of cramp, and hobbled to the bathroom. My thoughts drifted to Barański, still in hospital, his jaw loose from his skull and his eye a bruised mess on his face. In all my years, I'd never lost my cool with the boys, not even when I'd accidentally had two fingers broken from an errant stomp. Accidents happened in wrestling, you had to shake it off if you wanted to keep going.

He was weak! the whisper breathed again.

I shook my head. The throbbing had gone down thanks to the compression of the mask and the bouts of nausea and greyness had passed, but maybe I was still a little out of sorts. It was nothing some Tylenol and Advil wouldn't solve. As I reached into the bathroom cabinet to grab the pills, I shrieked, spilling the bottles and their contents on the chipped tiles as I glimpsed my reflection.

The mask was tight around my head, so tight that it ate into my flesh. I could see blood stained around the hem, bruising on my neck, and my eyes were dark, empty voids with only the smallest pinprick of red winking back at me. The silver decals warped and shifted, splitting open at the mouth into a sneering, toothy smirk. The fabric stretched and rippled, resembling the scales of a snake, and rotten teeth, jagged and yellow, grinned at me in the gaping maw where my mouth should be. Blood oozed down my chest, burst from my eyes, and I clutched at the mask, desperate to remove it, only to cry out as burning pain lanced through my palms, as though the strings that held the mask in place were razor wire.

We're in this together now!

I dashed into the bedroom, frantic, tripping over my bag and crashing to the floor. I grappled with my phone with hands shaking and stained with blood and desperately tried to dial for help, only to see that demonic visage snarling at me in the phone's reflection.

Who d'you think's gonna help you, Meatbag?

Realization dawned on me. I could feel splinters in my mind, my blood boiling, my breathing labored, as the mask became tighter around my head, driving me to my hands and knees. Blood dripped slowly to the carpet. My vision became hazy and, right when I thought I was going to black out, the mask loosened, and I could breathe again. I fell onto my ass, panting, feeling the pain in my head ease as the mask's grip relaxed. For a second, I was sure it was going to burst my skull like a melon!

Just remember who's in charge! the voice whispered ominously.

I gazed down at my phone and saw my reflection was back to normal. There was some dried blood and bruising, but the mask was just a mask, and I was myself again. If I'd ever been anything else.

I swiped my thumb at the screen and prepared to call Jamison, to beg for some time off to figure things out, but faltered at the last second. I couldn't bail now, Jamison would destroy me. This was my chance—maybe my only chance—and I owed it all to El Chernobog.

"Shit," I muttered into the empty room.

By the time the next show rolled around, I had chalked the whole thing up to anxiety and nerves. Nothing had happened since: no whispering, no weird visions, and even my aches had lessened. Not even the news that Barański had slipped into a coma bothered me. I simply hit the gym from four in the morning until lunch, popped my medication, and prepared for the biggest match of my career.

When I got to the arena, the guys eyed me with frosty suspicion and gave me a wide berth.

Good, I thought, the voice in my head slightly warped. *They've been in my way long enough!*

At my insistence, Jamison had set aside a private changing room for me. It wasn't much, little more than a repurposed supply closet, but I'd told him to *Get used to it* as I would want my own locker room after tonight, when I was officially and finally the RPW Champion.

Presently, there came a knock at the door and Steve "Caveman" Andrews, the champ himself, walked in. "Hey, Marcus, you got a sec to run through the match?"

I rolled my eyes and uttered an irritated sigh. These kids, they always wanted something. They came to me with their hands cupped and said, "Please, sir, can I have some more?"

True to his ring name, Caveman was dressed in his signature tattered loincloth trunks, simple black boots, and black wrist tape, and had a freshly shaved head of hair. His body was chiseled granite, with the kind of abs I could only dream of, and his sparkling blue eyes shone against his golden complexion. Women ogled him, men envied him, and he was a machine in the ring, rarely getting gassed and never blowing a spot. But, like with all wrestlers, fate eventually steps in. Caveman's run with the RPW Championship had to come to an end so he could get surgery on a partially torn pectoral muscle before he was sidelined for months, and Jamison had already planned out his dramatic comeback, which would see him topple the monster champion, El Chernobog.

Not fuckin' likely, the dark voice chuckled at the back of my mind, and I favored Caveman with a warm smile that barely covered my glee at relinquishing him of this strap.

It took everything I had not to pound Caveman's face against the wall until his brains oozed from his fractured skull as we went over the match. It was the most agonizing thirty minutes of my life, and I was relieved to finally make my way out to the ring, the crowd on their feet and swaying to my overture, and every fiber of my body numbed as I focused myself on the task at hand.

Caveman rushed the ring, as always, in a burst of energy and the match was on. We threw hands at each other, the crowd loving every second of it. They'd been driven into a frenzy as I'd attacked Caveman over the last few weeks, forcing his normally happy-go-lucky façade to give way to a furious vengeance. However, he wasn't in the ring with Marcus King, perennial jobber to the stars, he was facing El Chernobog, a masked monster of a man who felt no pain.

"Watch the hands, Marcus!" the referee snapped as I threw a clubbing blow to Caveman's head.

"Piss off!" I snarled back. "I know what I'm doin'!"

Caveman hopped to the top rope and flew at me, his body a corkscrew of motion, but I easily sidestepped him and he crashed to the ring mat. I was on him in a heartbeat, forcing him to the outside, where the crowd let out a collective *Oooh!* when I slammed Caveman's head into the ring post and his forehead split open, blood gushing down a face that wore a mask of disbelief.

Caveman swung blindly at me, mumbling incoherently, and scrambled back into the ring. I followed, my ears filled with a rush of wind and a constant whine, drowning out all sounds, including the referee's continued warnings. I saw the blood on Caveman's face, and I smiled behind my mask and pounced on him. Unprepared for my lunge, Caveman collapsed awkwardly to the mat, screaming as my teeth bit into his earlobe. Blood gushed as I tore it off, staining the mat as I chewed on my prize.

The referee waved his arms frantically, he screamed at me, but I didn't hear him. All I could hear was the ringing of the bell, signaling that the match had been called off, Caveman's childlike cries, and the crowd's murmuring disappointment.

"Marcus, what the hell're you doin'?!" the referee screamed in my face, bringing me back to reality.

Caveman whined on the blood-stained canvas, bright red blood leaking between his fingers as he desperately tried to stop the bleeding from his mangled ear. I gawped at him, speechless, and turned away, disgusted, to stare into the crowd. One by one their faces melted, swallowed by swirling black smoke.

Finish it!

They became faceless voids of shadow with red pinpricks for eyes.

You were robbed!

Their disquieted cacophony became a murmuring whisper.

Take what's yours!

The referee rose from his knees, his pants caked in blood. In his gloved hands, he held the RPW Championship, the hunk of gold and silver that should rightfully have been mine were it not for this small man's interference. He spoke to me, probably demanded I leave the ring, but I couldn't hear him; before my eyes, his face also disintegrated into a mess of dark smog.

Feast on him!

I felt the mask constrict again. It tightened around my head, slicing into my flesh, and I felt the agony of it warped around me, its pieces slithering to life, my jaw splitting open into a gaping maw of fangs and drool. Darkness, living and broiling and buzzing, consumed my thoughts like a tornado and everything became a red haze. All I could feel was a raving hunger deep in my belly, the fire of rage, and a surge of intent so great that I heaved the referee aside, not caring a lick as he crashed into the ring corner and dislocated his arm.

Caveman looked up at me through blubbering lips and his eyes widened. He held up a useless hand in protest and begged, pleaded, at my feet, but to no avail. The mask chattered in my ear incessantly, chanting and frothing and urging me on. I grasped at Caveman's face, digging my nails into his soft flesh, and wrenching with fingers that had become gnarled talons.

The crowd roared with bloodlust as I tore at the wailing champion's skin, shredding it, tearing his face from his skull in dripping ribbons that I stuffed into my ravenous mouth, spilling ichor to the canvas, and leaving him a gaping, screaming, bloodied skull as I feasted on his flesh.

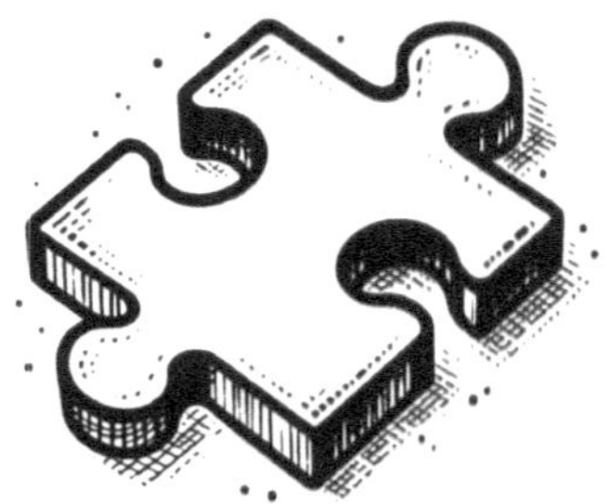

The Final Piece

By Eric Todd

"Jackson, I don't know if I can handle this puzzle. Where did you say you got it?"

"It was in a free box at the lawn sale I drove by. C'mon, it'll be fun. Just like the old days, doing puzzles together when we were dating and should have been studying."

"The difference is that those were bought at a store, were in a box, and we had a picture telling us what the puzzle was supposed to look like. This is a Ziplock bag full of pieces that look darker than your sense of humor. We don't even know if all of the pieces are here. For all we know this is multiple puzzles thrown together in one bag."

"Any other complaints, Princess Jenn, or can we get cracking on this beast?"

"Ugh, no, I guess not. Let's just get this thing started. Border pieces first and then we work our way in."

"I know how to put together a puzzle, smart-ass. We going old school with this one?"

"Duh, you know I only put together puzzles upside down. It'll maybe make this one a little fun because we won't know what the picture is until we're done."

"A woman after my own heart, I knew there was a reason I married you. Those adventurous puzzle skills. You're like a jigsaw jedi. Now we just need to get you a sexy brown robe to wear."

"How did I marry such an incredibly ridiculous dork again? What did I see in you?" she said playfully.

"It was my boyish charm and my persuasive oral arguments."

"Oh yeah, that silver tongue, I almost forgot about that."

"Maybe I'll remind you after we finish this puzzle."

"Deal! Let's get this thing put together!"

"I can't believe it took us two whole days just to get the border together. The good thing is that it looks like all of those pieces are there at least. The downside, you're going to have to wait a little longer for your reward."

"Mister, if you make me wait much longer then you're going to find that I've replaced you."

"Psh, like you could replace me. I'm not worried. Besides, it should start coming together now. We can work on it after you get home from work."

"Feel free to work on it while I'm gone."

"Not a chance, lady. You gotta earn it."

"Fine, I'll be home around seven, I'll grab Thai from that place you like. I love you," she said while bending down to give him a kiss. His hand slid around the back of her neck, holding her firmly in place as he kissed her harder, playfully biting her lip, making her gasp. She pulled away, despite how badly she wanted to continue. "Now you behave yourself sir, we can get into all of that after work."

"It would be way more exciting if you just played hookie and we got into all of that right now. Who knows, we might even finish the puzzle so you can get what you really want."

"You know I can't miss work. Now stop being a troublemaker. I'll be home later."

"Ohhh Jackson, soup's on. I'm hooooome," she called out as she walked through the door. "Please tell me you finished that damn puzzle, I've been thinking about my reward all day." She rounded the corner, and her hopes were dashed. The border was in place and only the few pieces they had placed the day before.

Jenn walked into the kitchen and put the fragrant bag of Thai food on the counter, kicking off her heels as she did so.

"Yo Jackson, come and get it before I call my boyfriend to come over for dinner and dessert."

Still no answer from Jackson. She glanced at the counter and saw Jackson's cell phone charging next to his car keys and his wallet.

He's probably upstairs playing video games, she thought as she turned toward the stairs. He was always oblivious to everything around him when he gamed, headphones on, brain off. She quickly ascended the curved staircase, her feet sinking into the plush carpeting, a welcome luxury after being trapped in heels all day.

She reached out and placed her hand on the doorknob to their bedroom. She paused and listened for the telltale sign that Jackson was gaming. Much to her surprise, she heard nothing. She slowly pushed the door open and saw the problem. Her tired boy was passed out in bed, legs tangled in the blankets, his leg hanging off the edge of the bed where the monsters could get it. She quietly walked around to his side of the bed and bent down, her lips millimeters from his ear, ready to whisper sweet nothings to awaken him and his sleeping dragon.

"Don't you fucking touch me you cunt," he screamed in his sleep as his fingers dug into her shoulders. She pulled back enough to see him looking her straight in the eye, a malevolent look of pure hatred.

"Ow, Jackson that hurts," she pleaded as she tried to get him to release his vice grip. He sat up as she struggled to get away from him. His eyes eerily looked through her, like she wasn't even there. Then, as suddenly as he grabbed her, he let go and collapsed back onto the pillow. Softly snoring like nothing happened.

Sobbing, she scrambled off the bed and slid down the wall at her back.

"Wha's wrong? When'd get home?" He mumbled, clearly still teetering on the edge of dream land.

She looked toward the sleep slurred voice and saw the confused face of the man she loved.

"I grabbed you?" The concern in his voice was genuine. Jenn didn't think that he had any idea what happened in the bedroom. Light bruises had begun forming on both of her shoulders. No shoulder baring outfits for at least a week, she noted mentally.

"You didn't know what was happening, you must have been having a nightmare and I startled you," she replied, pushing her Pad Thai around the plate, her stomach still uneasy following the scare.

"That's no excuse, babe," a tremble in his voice. "I can't be hurting the woman I love whether I'm awake or asleep."

"Give yourself a break, Jackson. It hasn't happened before and I'm sure it won't happen again. Let's just put these leftovers away so we can cuddle up with a movie and our puzzle. I'm determined to take out any frustration I have on you."

"Deal, I'll put away the food, you go pick a movie. Pick something scary, I want you extra close."

He walked into the living room with a smirk on his face. The incident upstairs all but forgotten, erased by the title screen that graced their seventy inch television, *Texas Chainsaw Massacre*, the remake from two thousand and three, starring Jessica Biel and a very nice tank top. Apparently, Jenn had other things on her mind tonight as well. She knew exactly how to get her man going.

They spent the next ninety-eight minutes side-by-side, sitting on the floor, her legs draped over him as they worked on the puzzle while the group of twenty-somethings were slaughtered on the screen one-by-one. She clung to his arm during particularly gruesome scenes and distracted him a few times with extra spicy kisses.

Surprisingly, the puzzle appeared to be progressing quicker than either of them expected. By the end of the movie nearly a third of the puzzle had come together.

"Looks like I'm going to be riding high in a couple of days at this point," she said while playfully punching Jackson's arm.

"For real, I thought this was going to be way harder, but the pieces just came together. It almost felt like as soon as I picked up a piece, I instinctively knew where it belon ..." his sentence was cut off by a massive yawn.

"Hey, none of th ..." her thought was interrupted by a yawn of her own. "Apparently there really is some truth about those things being contagious. I'm beat, are you ready for bed?"

"You're speaking my love language. I feel like I haven't slept in days."

"You ass, I just came home to you passed out like it was nap time in kindergarten. How can you be that tired now?"

"Don't you tell me my business devil woman, let's just go to bed," he said in a terrible Billy Madison voice.

"Oh my god, stop with the impressions, you know you're no good at them."

"There's something wrong with your medulla oblongata devil woman."

"Tell me why I married you again, I think I'm having second thoughts. Is it too late for an annulment?"

"You'd be lost without me babe," he said as he chased her up the stairs.

Jackson startled awake to the sound of a woman screaming, to Jenn screaming. He reached his hand to her side of the bed and found it ice cold. She hadn't laid next to him in hours.

Still digging the sleep out of the corners of his eyes, he stumbled toward the bedroom door. As he reached for the knob, he heard another scream coming from downstairs. He flung the door open and rushed down the hall. Haphazardly taking the stairs two at a time he misjudged the width of the step halfway down the staircase. He came down on his right ankle, and it buckled under his weight, rolling outward as excruciating pain shot up his leg. He called out in agony as his hand desperately grasped at the railing for support, but it was too late. He tumbled down the final five steps, landing at the bottom of the stairs, his right leg bent at an awkward angle and his ankle already swollen and bruised.

"Baby, what happened?" he heard nearby. He opened his clenched eyes and saw Jenn standing above him, eyes sunk in her head, bags the size of luggage underneath them.

"I fell down the fucking stairs, what does it look like happened," he barked.

"You don't have to bite my head off, geez. I didn't push you down the stairs."

"What the fuck were you screaming about? What are you even doing awake?"

"Screaming? I didn't even have the television on. I couldn't sleep so I decided to come down and make some chamomile tea. I came into the living room to work on the puzzle a little bit. You must have heard the kettle whistling. Do you need an ambulance?"

"No, I think it's just a sprain. Can we just go to bed?"

Jenn hooked her arms under his armpits and lifted with all of her might, straining futilely to lift her much larger husband. Her face was almost the color of a Red Delicious apple when she finally collapsed, panting and spent. She fell into his arms and all tension melted as they both rolled to the side laughing.

"My poor baby" she said as her fingers traced his jawline. "Are you okay?"

He leaned in and kissed her lightly on the tip of her nose.

"I'll be fine, love."

Her eyes opened slightly and immediately slammed shut. The sun, like a laser trying to bore into her soul through her eyes. She tried to stretch but her back was having none of it. She reached over to Jackson's side of the bed, expecting to find her slumbering klutz only to find that she wasn't in bed. She was still lying on the floor at the foot of the stairs where he fell the night before. Jackson was gone though.

She sat up, frantically looking for her husband. Then she saw him, sitting on their brown leather sofa, hunched over the nearly completed puzzle. He was motionless, sitting and staring at the table in front of him. There were five pieces left, which didn't make any sense. This puzzle was easily a thousand pieces, and they had only put together a fraction of it. There's no way that Jackson could have made so much progress, she looked at the time on her phone, in the four hours since she must have fallen asleep next to him.

"Jackson, hunny, how's your ankle?"

No response, he reached toward a puzzle piece slowly, delicately grasping it between his thumb and forefinger. Without hesitation he guided the piece into its spot perfectly. Four pieces remaining. He suddenly grabbed another piece and placed it. Three pieces left.

Jenn reached a hand out and placed it on Jackson's hunched shoulder. No reaction, it seemed as if he was almost in a trance. Another piece slid into the grooves of the puzzle. Two pieces left and there was a pit in Jenn's stomach. Something was wrong with Jackson. She slid in front of him and knelt down to his level, taking his face in her hands, gently turning his face to meet hers. She gasped as she saw only slivers of his blue eyes surrounded by bright red. The blood vessels in his sclera had burst and his pupils nearly filled the iris, eclipsing his deep ocean blue in darkness.

Even with her blocking his view, his hands still found one of the two remaining pieces and slid it into place. Tears welling in her eyes, her hand slid back onto the table as he reached for the final piece of the puzzle. She struck without warning, her teeth sinking into his throat. She could feel his pulse between her lips as clamped down, twisting her head at the same time. His only reaction, an involuntary gurgle as blood gushed from the ragged hole in his throat. She pulled her head back and stood up. He continued sitting there momentarily as his white shirt blossomed like a rose as his blood soaked it. She stood there, staring down at him as he fell forward onto the puzzle, his blood flowing along the thin lines between the upside down puzzle pieces. She grabbed the final piece from his fingers, blood oozing between the pieces as she slid it into place. It was finally time to see what was on the other side of the mystery puzzle.

She shoved the much larger Jackson to the floor, his hand trailing behind, smearing his blood across the puzzle. She covered the puzzle with a piece of cardboard and flipped it over. Grabbing the corner of the felt puzzle mat she slowly peeled the blood-soaked cloth away. A knowing smile crossed her lips as the picture was revealed. Just as she suspected, she saw Jackson's radiant blue eyes looking lovingly at ...

Her world spun. No, that wasn't right. Her head spun and suddenly she was looking behind her, like Regan in that one horror movie. Jackson's strong hand gripping her chin. The front of him was still a mess of sticky gore, blood still oozing from the wound. He peered around her shoulder and glanced at the puzzle. His jaw clenched with anger as he saw the image of Jenn kissing a man. Not just any man, she was kissing his fucking boss. He knew it, all of these years she was cheating on him. He looked at her in disgust and then back to the puzzle. Now the picture was different, he looked into his own eyes, at the smirk on his face and the waterfall of blood down the front of him. Looking down at Jenn, her head still rotated one hundred and eighty degrees, he watched as a smirk crossed her lips and his vision went dark.

Video Girl

BY DAVID E. KRUEGGER

"**I**sn't it hilarious?" Chrys asked.

"It's a doll," I said. Two fingers wrapped around the doll's torso, while their palm supported from the bottom, like a trophy.

"It's not just a doll, Ty," they said. "It's a Video Girl Barbie. There's a digital camera in the chest."

A closer inspection revealed that, yes, indeed, a camera peered out from the Barbie's chest. The lens hid among her loud clothes, a riot of Millenial bombast. Shiny pink sleeves connected to a zebra print sweatshirt and hood. Barbie's hair was gathered up to suggest volume without blocking the equipment. Turning it around, Chrys showed me the blank screen on the back.

"Is it worth something?" I asked. A frown grew on Chrys's face. Rent was due in a week, and I knew Chrys was tapped out. Sue me for letting it bubble up.

"It might have been, in the original packaging. It was just on the table though, no accessories or cables." They held it close to their face. "But, I think it takes batteries, and the cable must be standard. If I can fix it up, maybe I'll shoot a movie on it, like that guy who did moon photography with a Game Boy Camera."

"Cool," I said. "Good idea." In my mind, I made a plan to move a little cash around to prepare to cover Chrys's rent again. Once they had a little money, I had no doubt they would pay me back. Putting a damper on Chrys's enthusiasm by talking about money seemed base, no matter how much their way of doing things stressed me out.

Soon, I sat alone in the living room. Once something got into their head, Chrys was impossible to distract. Another mental note, to bring a bowl of food into their room later. Roommates who starved would never be able to pay rent. Back to my book to try to drown out the sounds of drawers opening, items clanking, and the occasional muffled curse from the bedroom down the hall.

While I watched a little TV, I finished my dinner. When no sound came from Chrys's room, nothing to indicate they would be coming out to eat any time soon, I did the right thing. I sighed and turned on the burner. Every time I do this, I promise myself I won't go above and beyond, I'll make them some ramen. But then, the water gets boiling and well, I have a little leftover chicken I can cut into slices for them, and while I'm washing a knife I might as well sprinkle some green onions on top, and they like it a little hot so I drip some La-Yu from the Asian grocery store into the bowl before I add the broth (to make sure the chili oil coats everything). Ten minutes later, I'm bringing a pretty hefty bowl into Chrys's room.

"Smells good," they said, not looking up from the screen. The monitor was awash in pink.

"It's for you," I said. "I wanted to make sure you ate."

"You didn't have to do that," they said. The speed with which they shoved the first forkful into their mouth would beg to differ. Telling them that would be a bad idea, would invite bad vibes. Instead, I said:

"What's this? You crack it yet?"

"I had to dig around but I found the proprietary editing software online. I had the right cable, in the end." A hand gestured to the Barbie, ever smiling, happy to be here. She sat on the desk, head leaning against the monitor. A gray cable wound from her back to a port in Chry's computer tower. "You need the software to access the videos."

"You're not gonna get a virus or something from this, are you?" I asked.

"Nothing I can't handle. Proprietary Barbie editing software is too niche a target to be worth it for most people trying to engineer computer viruses. It's probably being distributed by some other hobbyist."

"A Video Girl Barbie hobbyist?"

"A hobbyist in unique and obscure electronics, Ty, like me," they said.

Fixing up and selling "unique and obscure electronics" had been an interest of Chrys's for about three months. They took to it fast. They took to everything fast, but they tended to put on a hobby like an identity. Not for the first time, I considered how apt their chosen name was: Chrysalis, always on the way to becoming something else.

"What's on it? Anything?" I asked after letting the air settle.

"I actually just got it going, and," they clicked into one of the menus, "wow, there's something here. Should we see what it is?" They grinned up at me.

"It's not going to be something weird or inappropriate, is it? Did people shoot porn on these things?"

"I mean, anything is possible. Most likely, some kid filmed her other dolls and never wiped it after playing with it for the last time. The yard sale was fine. Sunny day, normal stuff. They didn't seem like weirdos."

I opened my mouth to say something else, but Chrys already clicked the file.

A black screen greeted us, but in the middle ground, something suggested movement in the darkness. Red glows hovered in the bottom corner of the image before they bobbed out of view. Bobbed. The person recording this ran in the dim murk.

"What is this?" Chrys asked.

"Your sound is off," I said, pointing to the corner of the screen that showed a speaker with an "x" next to it.

"Good call," Chrys said, and hit a button on their keyboard. A few tones increased in volume, and the sound of heavy breathing and footfalls filled the room.

A loud scream rose from the speakers, but not from the runner. From some spot in the distance, it poured like a river of misery. A chorus of screams. My palms got sweaty. My ears began to ring. My dinner grew restless in my belly.

"Chrys," I said when I could. They were glued to the screen.

A yelp and a *whumpf* barked from the speakers as the runner fell. Gray rock lit by orange glow loomed in the screen. Another scream, piercing and close. Nausea roiled through my midsection. My heart slammed in my chest. The camera lifted again. The lens obscured by a palm. The clip ended with the shot frozen. That palm, too-close and blurry, was all wrong. I stared for as long as I could manage before excusing myself to go to the bathroom in case I got sick. Chrys was already moving the cursor to restart the clip.

My sound machine was loud enough to cover the sound of whatever Chrys got up to in their room. I don't know if they were still watching the clip or if the Barbie had more clips, or what. I didn't care. When I saw the cursor move, I knew I had to leave. Chrys would want to know more. I did not.

By focusing on the whir of the machine, by using the techniques I had picked up over the years, by forcing my body to *calm down* already, I drifted off to sleep around midnight.

About an hour later, I woke up.

At first, I thought it was Chrys. The two of us had lived together for six years, since sophomore year of college, and I still didn't really understand their sleep patterns. It wasn't uncommon for them to make a little noise in the middle of the night and jar me awake. Most of the time, I drifted back to sleep, no harm, no foul. Pick your battles.

I was about to shut my eyes again when I spotted the figure in the corner. Shrouded in darkness, huddled as though afraid of being hit, I picked out the lanky hair that shrouded their face.

"Please," the figure croaked.

I didn't speak. I crawled up to a sitting position, and I reached for the lamp, but the figure whimpered.

"No," it pleaded. A hand with four fingers and one bloody stump jutted from the shadow like a diseased tree. The hand passed into a beam of light from my window. It was filthy. Wet. "Forgive me, Beth. I just need you to say you forgive me."

The voice came out in a croak, as if through a parched throat. The figure shuddered in the corner, leaned into the wall. The voice was a woman's, one I recognized. It also deadnamed me, but in the darkness of the room, I didn't sense any malice or derision. This was like getting a piece of old mail, not like talking to one of my uncles.

Leaning her head back into the corner, she breathed out. The sharp point of a chin stuck out in silhouette. She rested, leaning against the cool wall like a lizard trying to bring its temperature down.

"Forgive me," she croaked again, and blinked away.

The vanished presence left the room heavy. My body lay covered in a thin layer of clammy sweat. The sound machine kept plugging on and on.

In the constant static of the sound machine, I sometimes hear things. This is especially true if I'm agitated, which I was. The soft sound of the machine might cause me hear dripping, for example, or the sound of a door opening. This is common if the sound is something I'm worried about hearing. Depending on my state of mind, it can be easy to shut those sounds out by saying, "That's only the machine." It works for me, most of the time.

I thought Chrys was asleep. My phone read two in the morning, and they needed to sleep at some point. Still, I couldn't get over the sense that the sound from the video crept into my room even now. In the wake of the figure vanishing, I thought the scream hit about every forty seconds. It made my teeth hurt.

The sound came from the machine. Repeating this to myself allowed me to believe it. The problem was that in time, the sound from the machine took on a new shape. The rest of the night I dozed, flipping the machine off right after my alarm sang out. In the silence of the bedroom, I paused.

I strained to listen for the video still playing in Chrys's room. I unclenched my teeth when two full minutes passed and no scream, no matter how muted, drifted to me. At some point, they'd gone to bed. They probably hadn't even been watching it last night. Now I had to convince myself that I hadn't heard the other thing in the wall of sound created by the little plastic cone that carried me off each night, that it hadn't whispered "Jenny" to me from two o'clock onward.

"You look like shit, dude," Chrys told me as I sat at the table.

"How did you sleep?" I asked.

"Like a dang baby," they said. The bags under their eyes told another story, but it was hard to argue with that smile. At least someone in the apartment was in a good mood. "I did stay up a little bit though, ran into some interesting problems with the Barbie."

"Did you get a virus after all?" I asked. I took a bite of toast without tasting it.

"Not exactly, but the stuff on there is really weird, experimental stuff. There were a bunch of clips. Most are like the one I showed you: running through the dark and stuff."

"What else?" I asked. My stomach was fighting the toast sliding into it.

"Weird stuff, like horror movie stuff. They rigged up a shot of someone getting a finger bit off by a monster of some kind. I was trying to figure out how they did it when I fell asleep."

In my mind, the hand reached out, glistening and streaked with muck. The ring finger ended in a ragged stump. I clutched my stomach.

"You okay? Do you need to stay home today?" Chrys asked.

"No," I said, "Just a little tummy thing. I'm good." In truth, I was not good. The only thing that might have made me less good would have been staying home to risk listening to any other clips my roommate found on the Video Girl Barbie.

"Take care of yourself," they said. Their tone was genuine, the weak smile kind, if worried.

I thanked them and headed off to work, and all day, I thought about the chin, the long hair. I thought about Jenny. I thought about her hands on my back in the locker room, about her shrill laugh when I fell. I thought about her voice, the cruel remarks.

I even thought about the announcement on the loudspeaker, the principal calling us to an assembly. I thought about the news delivered to a room of crying teenagers. Car wreck. My face only stayed neutral because I clenched my teeth, to bite back my smile.

I ended up leaving work in the middle of the day and wandering around the mall. The worst day of a lot of people's high school career, the day they found out we could die too, was the day it turned around for me. That we could die was not news to me. I'd tried it. At the time, I thought it couldn't have come to a more deserving person. When the principal told us Jenny had been declared dead at the scene, I'd thought "rot in hell."

Now as I passed a kiosk with a guy offering me a lotion sample, I could only picture that hand. I could only grapple with the sense of pervasive filth in the room.

That night, I didn't bring food in for Chrys. After I got home, made dinner, and began to wind down for bed, they stayed in their room. I caught the sounds of the video editing software, the soft sounds of the clips they were watching over and over. More than that, the presence of the videos on their screen oozed through the air. My ears rang and my scalp prickled.

I stood on the other side of their door, my fist poised, second knuckle extended. I would rap on the door. I wanted to say hello and goodnight. It felt weird not to see my friend all night.

It was true that I had gone nights in the past without seeing Chrys, when they got deep into a project, but this dug at me, like sitting on a Lego. Swallowing, I knocked.

"Come in," they said. I did.

This was project mode for Chrys. By the wrappers that crowded the desk, it was clear that they had eaten something. Tissues balled up next to the wrappers, distinct splotches of bright red coloring them. Then I looked up and gasped.

"Chrys what the fuck? You're bleeding!"

"Oh," they said, lifting a finger to their ear. The tip came away red. They wiped it on an old tissue and then grabbed a fresh one to shove in their ear. "It's dry in here. Getting nosebleeds too. I've been meaning to buy a humidifier, but with what money, right?" They laughed, but when they turned their eyes to me, I suppressed a wince. Chrys was pale, and the bags under their eyes had only grown deeper.

"Chrysalis, we need to get rid of this thing, something's wrong with it," I said, kneeling in front of them. From the desk, Barbie smiled at me in her seated position. I grabbed my friend's hand, trying to let my warmth seep in. Chrys always had cold hands. "I saw something in my room last night, I think the videos on it are—" I stopped myself. What did I think?

"You think it's real footage?" they asked. "Of what? Hell?"

"Chrys, my high school bully appeared in my room last night. She died before gradu-ation. She was begging me for forgiveness."

"That doesn't have anything to do with the footage from the Barbie."

"She's missing a ring finger. It looks like it's been bit off."

Chrys gazed at the screen. A clip waited to play.

"We should sell it to a satanist or a museum or something," they said.

Shaking my head, I said, "Chrys, it should be destroyed. I don't know what's going on. If it has footage from hell, if it's been there, maybe it brought something back with it. If there's a connection, we have to break it."

"Yeah, *if*. And if we find the right buyer, we can get rent covered in this place for a year," they said.

I went to bed. Of all the ways to convince Chrys of something, pushing it when they had that hard set in their eyes was the worst. As I finished washing my face, I even convinced myself that they were right. If they found a buyer, it would kill two birds with one stone.

This time, she was crouched next to the bed. I smelled her before I saw her. Dirt and sweat and something like the chemical they add to natural gas woke me up, and my eyes spun over to the corner so fast, I didn't catch that she was hunched over me. To this day, I'm still proud of the fact that I didn't scream or cry out.

"Please, forgive me," she croaked. This close, I could take in her face. I spent the better part of the day before trying not to imagine it, trying not to picture what the cruel and pointed face of my high school bully would look like after almost ten years in hell. Now that I was confronted with it, I was shocked.

She looked normal.

Other than the missing finger and the long, dirty hair, she was intact. Her lips were dry and cracked. I imagined her tongue and mouth were too. She spoke like she had no moisture in her mouth at all. Dark bags, only a shade farther along than Chrys's, rested under her eyes. The eyes were the hardest thing to take. Hollow and animalistic, they scanned the room and flicked from thing to thing, watching out always for more danger, for another threat to make itself known. The spark of human thought I recognized in them was new, an ember that had been revived when she came into this world. Away from my room, away from the person she had to petition, I knew that ember would blow out and leave only suffering.

Was she here because I had told her to rot in hell when she died? Was that all it took? Is it so easy for a person to consign another to hell?

"Please, forgive me. I need you to forgive me," she begged. Five fingers clasped around four, along with a ragged stump. The knuckles were white. A cascade of hair blocked her face, and I realized she was bowing her head.

Jenny made me want to die so bad that I'd tried to. It wasn't just words. She shoved me, she spread rumors about me. Vicious rumors, rumors that sowed doubt about who I was and who I was on the way to becoming. If the circumstances were different, I'm not sure if I would have forgiven her. People make mistakes, but no one is forced to be cruel, no one is compelled to go out of their way to bully the queer kid in their math class. On a certain level, I have a sense that you make that choice and live with the results.

"Jenny," I said. I reached out a hand and closed it around hers, folded together. The grit and grime on them, the layers of dry sweat and dead skin, pricked my fingers. Her skin was clammy and feverish underneath. She raised her eyes to look into mine. The ember of her humanity grew. "Jenny, I forgive you for everything. I do not hold it against you anymore."

As she smiled, her lips bled. We stared at one another. My own lips pull into a grin.

Her smile fell away. "No," she said. "No, you said. You said if I was forgiven, I would be free."

I followed her gaze, the fire of humanity guttering out in those eyes. She stared past me, at the other end of the room. "Jenny?" I asked.

"You said I would be free! You said I just needed forgiveness from Beth. She's forgiving me, I should be free! Don't take me back! Don't take me back!" Howling in rage and agony and vanished, she left only the clammy dampness of her skin on mine and her scream echoing.

In the darkness of my room, with the sound machine going, I stared into the darkness. Turning to my right, I stared at the spot where Jenny had seen something, something that had not accepted her apology or my forgiveness. My stomach was doing flips in my belly.

I hopped out of bed. The wood where Jenny knelt was still warm with her feverish body heat. I pulled on my robe to provide a little additional armor over my shirt and boxers.

The hall was dark and full of shadows that seemed to shuffle out of my way as I stomped past them. When I touched the knob to Chrys's room, it was warm. I hesitated.

If they were awake, I would have to explain. Maybe with two instances of a person appearing, I could convince them that it had to be gotten rid of. On the other hand, if they were asleep, I could just grab it and—and what? Letting go of the knob, I padded to the kitchen and cranked the oven up to five hundred degrees. A baking sheet rested on the counter.

I stormed my best friend's bedroom. I flung the door open. Even as I burst in, they stared at the screen. "I thought I heard you," they muttered.

I tossed Chrys a glance as I marched up. A trickle of blood slid down their neck from their ear. I didn't say anything at all. I grabbed the doll, tore out the cable, and ran. The cable elicited a yell of anger. "You'll corrupt the file!" Chrys yelled. When they stood up to come after me, their feet wobbled. They seemed like they couldn't stand. Looking behind me, I saw why: blood had been trickling from their nose as well. Once the thing was melted in the oven, I might have to call an ambulance. I was down the hall when they crashed against the doorframe. "Bring it back! It's not yours!" they yelled.

I did not bring it back. In only a few strides, I made it to the kitchen, shoving my way past the shadows again, which grew deeper, and seemed to want to trip me as I passed. I slammed the doll on the baking tray and threw it into the oven. The metal tray clanged against the rack, and the doll bounced, but stayed on.

Chrys barreled in, and as soon as the oven door shut, they went down like their legs gave out. In stunned silence, I stared down at my friend, my roommate. Thin streams of blood dripped from their ears and nose, and one was starting to gather in the corner of their right eye like a tear building mass. Their back arched up into the air, and their hands bent into terrified claws. That was the moment I realized they were building steam, they were drawing in air, like a toddler who had fallen down and skinned their knee.

At the moment the stench of burning plastic reached me, they shrieked, a sound of agony so pure and so complete that I thought it would have been right at home on the footage from the Barbie. I put my hand behind me, and when it landed on the stove, which was already hot from the inside of the oven, I almost fell to the floor as well. My knees weak underneath me, I lowered myself to the ground, and allowed the backs of my thighs to rest on the cold tile. I was aware of banging on the floor below, the neighbors would need a little smoothing over in the morning if not right now.

Chrys writhed and screamed, and when I thought it would tear them apart, that whatever was happening to my friend would kill them or tear them in two, they stopped. I glanced into the oven, where the clothes of the Barbie burned weakly in a toxic puddle of foul-smelling plastic. I stood up to turn the oven off, turn the fan on, and checked on my friend. They were covered in sweat, and they breathed long and slow on the floor. The banging downstairs had stopped. When Chrys's eyes fluttered open, still narrow, and peered up at me, I was holding their hand.

"What was that?" they asked.

"Relax, dude. I'm here," I said.

"You destroyed it. You closed the door," they said. They closed their eyes, then. They only opened them to speak.

"Yeah," I said. "The door is closed. It can't hurt us anymore."

I led my friend back to their room and laid them in their bed, and the sensation never left me of being observed, stalked. I haven't gone a day since without a vague sense like I left a window open or a door unlocked. When I try to sleep, I can always see that light flicker and fade in Jenny's desperate eyes.

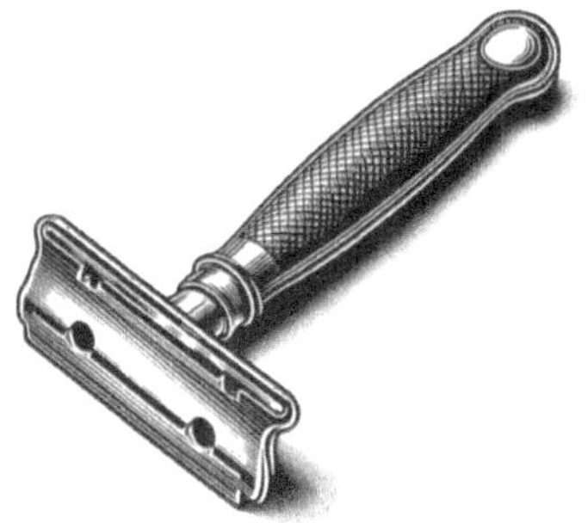

A Steady Constant

BY A.D. JONES

J osh bounded from the yard sale with a spring in his step, the mahogany box held up reverentially like the ashes of a dearly passed loved one.

The oddly localized storm clouds had already given way to the beautiful spring sun, and he felt particularly positive and optimistic for the day ahead.

"You're not seriously going to use that thing, are you?" Mike said, keeping pace at Josh's side as they walked, a look of disgust plastered on his face.

"What kind of question is that? Of course I am, it was an absolute steal."

"Dude, that's frigging gross."

"Oh, come on, I'm going to buy new blades for it. I didn't pay fifty bucks just to get AIDS or tetanus." He shook the box at Mike with a playful smile on his face.

"Same time you pick up some nice gray slacks and a big ole pot of hair pomade from the forties?"

"Yeah, something like that," he chuckled.

The pair continued along their way towards the destination coffee shop, a repeating Scooby-Doo background of pristine houses with white picket fences on their left.

Josh was forever thankful to have a best friend like Mike. A person that would accept you and all your idiosyncrasies on one hand, while viciously mocking everything about you on the other. There was nobody in Josh's life quite as abusive towards him as Mike, but he also knew that Mike would take a bullet for him without a moment's hesitation, a sentiment that he echoed with all his heart.

"I still can't believe you didn't buy anything," he said as they found their surroundings gradually being replaced with storefronts.

"I considered it," Mike sniffed. "That old wristwatch was pretty cool, but I don't know, I can't really place it, but the vibe was off."

"Dead man's watch doesn't do it for you?" Josh grinned.

"Coming from the guy who's going to be rubbing his face with that dead man's stuff, you can't really laugh."

He stared at his reflection in the steamed-up mirror, hair tied up out of the way, and a look of joy on his face ready for the upcoming ritual. The wooden box lay empty on the countertop, its contents now precisely laid out next to the sink, steam rising from the water in the bowl.

The chrome bodied Safety razor with its imitation ivory handle rested on the counter, having carefully replaced the blade inside earlier this afternoon in preparation for his first shave. The porcelain bowl beside it was filled with white foam that he had lathered up using the authentic badger hair shaving brush, the heady scent of Sandalwood, rich and spicy, filling the room.

Josh coated his face with the soap, a thick layer of white, almost clown-like greasepaint, and picked up the razor.

At twenty-six, he was no newbie when it came to shaving, but this was his first attempt at using a tool so artisanal, the weight of the razor in his hand a stark contrast to the flimsy plastic of disposable razors.

He pressed the cool metal to his cheek and carefully let the weight of the razor guide the blade down towards his jaw, a two-inch trail of pink flesh appearing in its wake. The skin tingled slightly with the menthol afterthought of the razor-sharp steel over foam.

Feeling satisfied that he hadn't sliced his face off just yet, he carried on shaving, continuing the careful, precise strokes as the foam gradually began to disappear, taking extra care as he deftly moved the razor across his throat.

Nearing the end of his debut traditional shave, he went back across the first sweep, going against the grain upwards on his cheek when the pain hit him.

"Fuck!"

He reflexively pulled the razor away from his face as he saw the small trickle of blood begin to run down his cheek, the sharp sting burning slightly.

"It's a learning curve I suppose," he said to no one as he cupped water in his hands and splashed his face, removing any remnants of foam before smoothing over a layer of aftershave balm and applying a small piece of toilet paper to the cut on his cheek.

After one final look at his smooth as a baby's butt face in the mirror he headed downstairs to begin preparing dinner.

He stepped into the front room and felt a tickle on his neck. Reaching to scratch at it, he felt the wetness immediately and upon pulling his hand away, saw the blood on his fingers.

What the fuck?

Not watching where he was going, he stubbed his toe on the corner of the coffee table, sending pain up his body that dropped him onto his ass on the sofa.

The pain was immense, reverberating through his body as he lifted his foot and shook it wildly in the air. It felt like he was stubbing his toe over and over again, the twinge of pain from his cut cheek becoming an afterthought.

This is what a broken toe feels like I guess.

Josh opened the front door, stepping aside to let Mike in.

"Evening," he said as Mike walked through into the front room.

"You know how I know we're best friends?" he said as he passed. "I actually knock on your door. I mean who does that anymore? You just text 'I'm outside' and let people come to you."

Josh hobbled in behind him and took a seat on the sofa next to Mike.

"You're not wrong I suppose. I think that comes from the anxious fear of having to deal with someone's parents or roommates though, neither of which you have to worry about here."

"Ok, way to ruin the bromance. Did you know you're bleeding by the way?"

"Oh." Josh instinctively touched the patch of dry blood on his cheek and noticed it was again running down his neck. "Yeah, it doesn't seem to want to stop. I think I've broken my big toe as well."

"He says so casually." Mike rolled his eyes. "You might want to get that looked at."

"Probably. I'll give it a couple of days and if the pain doesn't ease off, I'll go see someone."

"Well, I'm not your mother, but that sounds like a plan." He threw his keys up into the air and caught them in his fist. "Want me to drive then?"

"Please," Josh said, the conversation having focused his attention back on the pain. A rhythmic pulsing in his foot continued to beat a steady thrum of discomfort.

It was a twenty-minute drive to the gig and parking was easy thanks to Mike's wealth of knowledge on the subject of free places to park. Fifteen minutes later they were at the bar and ready for an evening of mathcore—some of the filthiest, underground metal that the city had to offer.

The next couple of hours were a sweaty blur of music and mayhem, and it was shaping up to be another excellent gig night for the pair. That was until the mosh pit for the headline act began to come alive.

Josh was in the thick of things, having such a good time that he had forgotten about the pains in his cheek and toe when he caught an elbow to the side of his face.

The burst of pain erupted as the solid elbow collided with his temple, sending him to the floor as a wave of nausea washed over him.

Mike was on him in seconds, dragging him up from the ground as the owner of the elbow, deep in a series of apologies, also helped lift Josh from the floor.

"Josh, are you ok man?" Mike asked as he gripped hold of his face and Josh felt his head being wrenched about as Mike inspected him.

"I just ..." he stammered. "It really hurts. Like it's throbbing and I feel like I'm being hit over and over." He felt completely disorientated and the lights from the stage and buzzing from the speakers were a constant annoyance.

"Come on, let's get you out of here."

Mike sat in the hospital waiting room, people-watching as he waited for Josh to return. The clinical smell assaulted his nostrils, and he was secretly disappointed not to see a child with a pan stuck on their head.

When Josh reappeared, he didn't look much better than when Mike had left him, a grimace of pain clung to his face, and he hobbled over to Mike like a defeated man.

"What did they say?"

"No lasting damage apparently. I've not broken anything, and the pain should subside. Also, my toe isn't broken either it would seem."

Mike's face soured at this.

"So they're just saying you've hurt yourself and it's normal to be in pain after? You've never really struck me as a wimp, Josh. That's really all they've got?"

"The doctor did throw out some possibilities, but they didn't seem connected as far as he thought. Hyperalgesia or even Fibromyalgia, but they're considered constant random pains, not continued pain from an actual injury. To be honest, once I heard him utter the word psychosomatic, I pretty much stopped listening to him."

"Well as long as he didn't mention concussion, let's get you home, and you can sleep it off."

The drive home was uneventful, and the constant pain striking his temple was enough to keep him occupied and so conversation was low.

After Mike saw him to the door, Josh quickly stripped off his clothes and jumped in the shower, hoping the heat would wash away some of the aches as well as the almost black, clotted blood that was now dried to the side of his neck.

Stepping from the shower, he sat on the closed toilet and felt the pulsing pain of his face and foot running in tandem. He wondered if he would even be able to get to sleep with this repeated reminder of his injuries.

Ideas were starting to circle in his mind, and he found himself caught up in a series of worst-case scenarios, trying to figure out exactly what was going on when he noticed the shaving kit laid out with military precision on the countertop.

"This is your fault, isn't it? It certainly started with you." He rubbed at the cut on his cheek, the sting still fresh and sharp, and brought away a blood-spattered hand.

"What's the deal then? Hemophilia? Or can I just not heal?" He continued out loud when an idea came to him.

Less of an idea and more of an experiment.

With all his might, he punched himself as hard as he could in the thigh, the combined thud and slap of his fist against bare flesh registering in his ears before the pain hit him.

Once again, while not an agonizing pain, it registered again and again, the feeling of impact steadily repeating—no worse, but no better over and over.

There was something seriously wrong, but he just didn't know what.

Two weeks had passed since the night of the gig, and while Josh had been in continued contact with Mike, he had consistently blown off each and every attempt made to try and hang out. Feigned interest turned into 'illness' or forgetting about plans until the last minute, something that Josh had never done previously and so alarm bells were ringing long before Mike decided to drop in on him.

"It's not locked," came the shout from inside as Mike waited patiently at the front door.

Turning the handle slowly, he pushed open the door and stepped inside.

He stifled a gasp as he took in the stark change to the familiar surroundings. The entire banister of the stairs was coated in bubble wrap and brown parcel tape, and a crude handrail had been affixed to the wall going up the stairs.

Probably most alarming was the amount of what Mike could only assume were blood stains smeared over the magnolia walls in the hallway.

It looked like something ripped straight from a horror movie.

As he stood there in the hallway trying to figure out what the hell was going on, Josh appeared at the top of the landing and began slowly hobbling his way down the stairs.

The side of his face was a pattern of yellow, green, and purple bruising, and the area around his right eye looked completely swollen shut, puffy purple eyelids bulged like a frog. His left eye was pink and bloodshot, the obvious signs of exhaustion and sleep deprivation.

The painstaking journey down the stairs, one foot down, before stepping down with the other and repeating reminded Mike of how his mother's aging Shih Tzu used to tackle the staircase in their home. The total fragility of the dance was mirrored here with a worrying similarity.

Josh finally reached the bottom step and gave Mike a weak smile, the weary grin that hid depths of pain.

"Sorry," he said as he glanced back up the stairs and shrugged. "I rolled my ankle about a week ago, and it's gotten pretty hard to get around properly."

Mike narrowed his eyes as he fully took in the person stood before him. Josh looked like he'd been attacked and beaten. A frail, injured geriatric, hobbling around the nursing home. His left hand was crudely bandaged, and the once-white fabric was soaked in blood.

"Anyway, come on through into the front room, I'm sorry I've been avoiding you, but as you can see, I'm a little worse for wear right now."

He let Josh lead the way as they moved into the other room. Another surprise waiting for him. Apart from the two sofas, all the furniture had been removed from the room, with just a beanbag chair plopped in the middle of the floor like a makeshift, malleable table.

Josh lowered himself down onto the sofa with a grunt and gestured for Mike to take a seat. "So, tell me what you've been up to, Mike. It feels like forever."

Mike watched as intermittent spasms seemed to jolt in Josh's face as he continued to force his amiable expression.

Bursts of pain, Mike assumed.

"It doesn't matter what I've been up to. Josh, what the fuck is going on with you? And what happened to your hand?"

"Stupidest thing," he said. "I caught my finger on a cardboard box and gave myself a row of papercuts. Absolute stinging bastards, as I'm sure you know."

"Papercuts? You don't bleed like that from a few papercuts, tell me what the fuck you've done, Josh."

"I swear, look," Josh said as he peeled back the dressing. The whole of his hand was stained red with blood, but Mike could indeed see just the smallest series of cuts along the inside of his middle finger.

"It just won't stop bleeding, so it quickly builds up, just like my cheek." Josh turned his head to show the patch of black, clotted scabs that ran down the side of his face.

"Josh," Mike said, worry coating his words like syrup. "Seriously, what the fuck is going on?"

He let out a sigh that carried the weight of the battle-worn and once again shrugged nonchalantly. "It's in my blood. I don't know what, or how, but it is."

"You're starting to scare me, man."

"It's like every pain, every injury, no matter how small, it lingers. Imagine the second of any injury, and then make it a constant. Imagine it doesn't go away. It doesn't even diminish."

"What do you mean it doesn't go away?" Mike was trying to wrap his head around what he was hearing.

"Remember I told you I stubbed my toe? Well, I can feel that happening right now. Over and over, just like the sharpness of this cut on my face. Just like I can feel the elbow of that drunk asshole driving itself into my temple. Over and over, Mike."

Mike felt sick to his stomach. Either Josh was completely losing the plot, or this was some bizarre illness that he had never heard of.

Josh ran a finger along the trail of blood at his jaw. "It started with this little nick. I think I'm cursed. You might have been right about the vibes at that yard sale."

"We need to get you back to the hospital, like right now." He was already standing from the sofa, not wanting to wait even a minute longer to get his friend the help he needed.

"If we must," Josh said, defeat heavy in his voice. "You won't mind driving again, of course?"

The car sped along the street, doing ten above the speed limit as Mike tried to focus on getting Josh to the hospital as fast as possible. His attention should have been entirely on the road, but he found himself constantly looking across to Josh who, seeming to have let his guard down now that Mike was preoccupied, was twitching and shuddering in what Mike now understood to be constant waves of pain from various injuries.

He had taken his eyes off the road for just a second, but that was all the time needed for the small boy to step out in front of their car while chasing the red ball he'd lost control of.

Mike slammed on the brakes and swerved to narrowly miss the kid, who was dragged back just in time by an alarmed mother.

The car smashed into the metal barrier that lined the other side of the road, and the entire hood folded in on itself, a wreckage of steel on steel as the impact halted their travel with excruciating immediacy.

Mike's face bounced off the steering wheel, and he was knocked out immediately, slumping forward like a rag doll.

Josh on the other hand felt his ribs crack under the sudden tautness of the seatbelt, and his head was flung forward and back, the whiplash of muscle damage wracking his body.

The scream that left his body would chill the blood of anyone within earshot, and the agonizing pain of his ribs snapping again and again was too much to bear. In mere seconds he felt like we would go completely out of his mind.

Gritting his teeth through the pain, he unclipped the seatbelt and fought against the wave of nausea and agony as he tried the handle on the door.

It clicked open with ease.

Holding the door shut, he looked to his unconscious friend, and then to the wing mirror, the road behind him a reverse image of oncoming traffic.

He knew Mike would never forgive him, but at this moment he was barely holding onto the thin threads of consciousness, his vision becoming cloudier by the second, and there was no way in hell he was going to live out what he had left of this life in constant torment.

The white van in the mirror was quickly coming into range as he gave his friend one final goodbye glance.

One more pain.

As the van closed on their location, Josh took a deep, painful breath and flung the door open, simultaneously throwing himself from the car, into the street and the path of the fast-approaching tires of the van.

One more pain. That was all it would be. He could handle it.

Any Which Way You Slice It

BY S. C. FISHER

I nside the gully of Robbie's pocket, warm nickels slid against dimes. Three whole dollars in total: the most money he had possessed in eight years of life.

"Buy Mom somethin' pretty for her birthday," Brad said as he pushed the bounty into Robbie's hand. Judging from the crumbs and pieces of lint stuck in the grooves of the metal, at least half of the coins had been fished from between the couch cushions. Nevertheless, it was the nicest thing any of Mom's boyfriends had done for him—and Mom had had a lot of boyfriends since they'd buried Dad. Guys just never seemed to stick.

The poster for the yard sale was tacked to a telegraph pole at the end of his street and, since he knew the house, Robbie took off on his bike—the unlikely fortuity of it never dawning on him. It was only as he walked amongst tombstone tables set out on daisy-jeweled grass that Robbie realized he was picking through the rubble of somebody's life. He proceeded more reverently, then, taking the time to marvel at each item his eyes roved; from antique mirrors, over a harem of naked fashion dolls, to an old VHS player that likely no longer worked. Unfortunately, three dollars was still only three dollars, and there wasn't much within his budget that Mom wouldn't be compelled to throw in the trash within a week.

He had been hoping for a bracelet or a necklace. A vase, at a push. Something to show Mom and Brad that he had tried his best. Spotting the cake stand was a stroke of luck at the eleventh hour, right as Robbie was preparing to leave the yard empty-handed and cross. It governed an otherwise desolate table, its pristine porcelain shining in the beams that filtered through overhanging branches. A pattern of dainty, yellow, spring daffodils decorated the stem, which was squat though ornately pretty, regardless. Perhaps it had been part of a larger set—something grand with matching teacups, saucers, and side plates—but the cake stand was all that remained of that, now. On the whole, it wasn't a bad find. Robbie considered it for a full minute before reaching the conclusion that Mom liked cake enough to make this a suitable choice. He paid a dollar for the stand, oblivious to the knowledge that, in the end, it would cost him much more than that. With the treasure stashed in his rucksack, Robbie rode for home, mindful of the looming storm clouds that might make good on their threats at any moment.

In the absence of gift wrap, Robbie formed a cocoon from a bath towel, which he presented to Mom that evening, straight after dinner. She peeled away the cotton with a trill of excitement and a grin that highlighted the wrinkles beginning to set in around her eyes.

"It's lovely! Thank you, Robbie." She pulled him in for a hug then littered the top of his head with kisses, whilst Robbie tried not to breathe in the stench of cigarettes that clung to her cardigan. She had quit when Robbie was a baby; however, Dad's accident had been the catalyst to her taking it up again. These days, the whole house stank of tobacco, and the ceilings had jaundiced where smoke drifted up to caress the plaster.

"Brad helped," Robbie muttered, almost loathed to share the praise. From his position at the head of the table, Brad lifted his beer in salute.

"You must have coordinated!" Mom's attention flitted from boyfriend to son, then back to the gift sitting in the center of the table. "It'll be perfect for the cake Brad picked out. You boys are so thoughtful."

Whilst the stand may have indeed been perfect for the cake, the reverse was certainly not true. Robbie fought the urge to raise a brow as Mom slid a badly dented chocolate cake with crooked frosting out of a box that had surely come from the discount section at the store. In fact, when he squinted, Robbie could see the remnants of glue from the clearance label that had been slapped over the barcode. Still, he didn't comment. Brad was the first guy to treat Mom in a halfway decent manner. There'd been guys who were broke and begged for money, guys who were too generous with their fists or feet, and guys who didn't call after a sleepover. There was only one guy who turned up on the doorstep on Mom's birthday with cake—no matter how pitiful that cake might be. So, fixing a smile in place, Robbie waited as Mom sank a knife through layers of sponge until the chink of metal on china echoed around the room like cannon fire.

"Brad, you should have the first piece."

"Nah, 's'not my birthday." Brad leaned back in his chair to drain the dregs of his can. When he had finished, he crushed it against the table.

"You, then, Robbie—to thank you for the wonderful present," Mom insisted. Robbie shook his head.

"It's your birthday. I don't want the first piece."

He was certain that proper etiquette prevented anyone save for the birthday girl from accepting such an honor. Mom, on the other hand, was no fan of the spotlight; if she could direct the beam elsewhere, she would do so every time.

"Oh, don't tell fibs." She concealed her smirk behind a pretend pout. "It's my birthday wish."

Recognizing when he was apparently beat, Robbie shrugged. Mom slipped the generous slices onto plates and scooted the first across the table to her son. Ordinarily, Robbie would have been fine with diving in with his hands, but it was Mom's special day, and there was something in the air that warned him this night was different; deserving of respect. Robbie picked up a fork and teased a splodge of frosting from his slice.

"How is it?"

Robbie sucked the icing into his mouth, holding it on his tongue to test the quality: chemically sweet and an almost chalky texture. With his mother and Brad watching, awaiting the verdict, he forced himself to swallow.

"Not as bad as I thought."

Brad guffawed, amused rather than offended, whilst Mom swatted a hand at Robbie. They settled side by side at the table, exchanged smiles, and dug into their dessert. Not one of them noticed the spidery crack that snaked across the top of the cake stand.

"So, how's your birthday been?" Brad asked, mouth crammed full. Crumbs showered the front of his shirt, and he brushed them aside with one hand as he kept on chewing.

"Quiet." Mom raised the ghost of a smile. To Robbie, her eyes seemed teary as she added, "Lonely. Nobody spends time with me anymore."

Both Robbie and Brad paused, forks in the air. Mom's cheeks reddened, and she ducked her head to avoid the combined weight of their eyes.

"Sorry, that wasn't appropriate. Guess I'm getting old." She bit off another chunk of cake to silence herself.

"How was your day, kid?" Brad turned to Robbie, instead, ready to shrug off the maudlin blanket Mom had tossed over them without warning.

"Boring. None of the kids on the block like me. They think I'm weird. Sometimes, they call Mom names, too."

A hush fell across the table as cutlery stilled once more. Mom dabbed at her eyes with a napkin whilst Brad fixed Robbie with a long, hard glare that pinned him to his seat. Why had he said that? He never told Mom about the teasing or the way the neighborhood kids ran from him, shrieking, whenever he tried to join in.

"Sorry to hear that, Robbie," Brad said, eventually, though he sounded more angry than sympathetic. Robbie couldn't be sure whether that anger was directed at him or not, and so he chose to keep his mouth shut until he felt compelled to shovel in another morsel of cake. It honestly had started to taste better and better by the second!

"The yard sale was good," Robbie blurted, hoping to redeem himself with some positive news. Brad was more approving of this topic so Robbie steamed ahead with it at full speed. "That's where I found the cake stand. It only cost me a dollar. I spent the other two on popsicles on the way home."

Brad clenched his teeth, smashed another beer can beneath his palm, and popped the top off the next. "You told me there was no change. Said it cost all three dollars."

He had said that, Robbie recalled, as the color drained from his cheeks. What was wrong with him tonight? He forced his eyes away from Brad's purpling face. When his gaze swept the cake stand, he realized that he had failed to notice the three thin cracks weaving across the top. Maybe his gift wasn't as great as he had first thought.

With trembling hands, Mom dug into the pocket of her cardigan to pull out a pack of cigarettes and her lighter. She rarely smoked at the table. Brad hated it—said it ruined the taste of his food. It was Mom's birthday, though—and Mom's house—so Robbie figured she could do whatever she wanted. She lit the butt and brought it to her lips, whilst Robbie reached for more cake and Brad chugged his beer.

"Doesn't matter, I guess," said Brad on the tail end of a belch. "It was only two dollars. You'll pay me back soon enough."

Robbie would have readily agreed; however, he was too busy licking his fingers clean to comment. Mom puffed a cloud of smoke that enveloped her whole head before gusting across the table into Brad's face. His back stiffened, fingers flexing, and he grimaced in distaste. Mom looked apologetic, although she did not snuff her cigarette. In fact, she appeared to Robbie to breathe harder and deeper, like she was fighting to drag every last particle of smoke into her lungs.

"You know, those things will kill ya. 'S'not sanitary."

Briefly plucking the almost-spent cigarette from her lips, Mom nodded.

"I know. That's why I do it."

Misunderstanding, Brad frowned. "You smoke to piss me off?"

Robbie stopped eating, which he had been doing like a man on the brink of starvation. Mom blew out a chuckle with her next bank of smog. She was like a factory chimney, spewing pollution without a care.

"No, not at all. I do it because they'll kill me—maybe make me suffer first—and that's what I deserve."

The silence that descended was ruptured not only by the series of gurgles that emanated from Brad's stomach but also by the clink of splintering porcelain. Robbie looked to the cake stand just in time to watch as another crevasse—this one more livid than the others—burst into existence. With dread settling over him, Robbie stretched his hand out to the cake.

"I don't understand," he said.

Mom foraged in her pack, slotted two new cigarettes between her lips, and lit them both on the same flame. It would have been strange to Robbie—were he not preoccupied with tugging the cake stand towards himself. Plate empty, he lifted his fork and started in on the three quarters of cake remaining. Nobody said a word. Nobody moved to stop him. Mom added a further cigarette and Brad squashed another can so viciously that the table rocked.

"I deserve it." Mom had to speak out of the corner of her mouth, thanks to the wedge of cigarettes, which she seemed loathed to remove even for a second. "Because I killed him, ya see. I killed your father."

That brought Robbie to his senses. He stopped eating, eyes bulging. There were five smoldering ends in Mom's mouth, now, yet Brad paid no mind. He eased back in his chair, releasing his belt buckle to provide much-needed relief to his distending stomach. Satisfied, he sighed, then opened a beer. When he drank, liquid streamed down his chin, cutting a path through the individual whiskers in his beard.

"Dad?" Robbie echoed. His fork clattered to the table, chipping his plate on the way down. "You killed my dad?"

He no longer felt hungry, though the cake was calling his name. It was a persistent voice—deep in the recesses of his mind—that urged him to heed it.

"You were so little. I knew you'd never remember. Dad survived the accident. We visited him in the hospital every day. They told me that he might pull through, given enough time, only he'd be different. 'Dependent'."

With jittering fingers, Mom retrieved two additional cigarettes. When she wanted to speak again, she was forced to remove the bundle with her fist.

"I couldn't face it. I already had you to look after. I couldn't take care of your father, too. When they gave me the choice, I decided it would be better if they let him slip away. Let nature take its course."

A series of coughs wracked Mom's body suddenly, hunching her shoulders and con-caving her stomach. She covered her mouth with the back of her hand, and as she straightened, Robbie saw that the cuff of her cardigan was splattered with crimson flecks.

"I told them to turn off the life support. His mother begged me not to: I did it anyway. I did it. I killed him."

A shudder rippled through Mom and she bared her teeth against it. Her gums were bleeding so fiercely that yellowed enamel pinked. Nonetheless, she returned her cigarettes to her mouth and added three, so that her lips no longer stood a hope of union.

"I swore I'd never tell you, so you wouldn't hate me. Do you hate me, Robbie? Do you hate me because I killed your dad?"

She stared at him, expectant. A trickle of blood oozed from her nose, over her top lip. Mom didn't notice. She breathed in deep, savoring her cigarettes with eyes closed. The cake stand in front of Robbie juddered, and as two more cracks appeared like lashes from a whip, Robbie dove forward to lift the remainder of the cake to safety. Brad—who had not reacted to the revelation—suckled on an empty can like a calf at its mother's teat. When the yield ran dry, he broke another away from the package. Robbie was sure there had been six at the start of the meal.

In the end, it was Brad that saved Robbie from having to answer. Good, old Brad, who was more generous with his couch dollars than the rest of them, who brought delicious cake around for Mom's birthday, and who occasionally tossed the pigskin round in the back yard with Robbie—like Dad might have done, had Mom not signed his death warrant.

"That's nothing," Brad said, nonchalantly. He burped with a wide open maw, then flashed the kind of predatory look that Robbie had seen during *Shark Week*. "I killed a bunch of people. You guys were next."

For a split second, the cake stand simply vibrated in its spot. Then, with an almighty screech akin to metal grating against metal, it exploded into shards that rained upon the diners like a hail of bullets. Robbie felt a piece of porcelain sink into the apple of his cheek; however, his mouth was too stuffed with cake for his cry of pain to amount to much. Although Mom was partially obscured by the smoke circling her face and head, Robbie realized with a jolt that the fragment that had struck her had embedded in her left eyeball. The lid fluttered around the foreign body, whilst the eye itself wept blood and viscous fluid. Mom went on smoking.

"It's kinda my M.O.," continued Brad, after he had necked most of the can grasped in his hand. "'S'why I travel a lot. Pick a town, find a woman, gain her trust, then take care of loose ends. Never come close to bein' caught."

He was pleased by the revelation, despite the porcelain spear wedged at an angle in the middle of his throat, a half inch to the right of his Adam's apple. Blood streamed around it yet Brad downed another beer to the best of his ability. When he swallowed, the shard wobbled, and the wound bled more profusely.

"I was gonna finish you both tonight, once you were asleep. Suffocation. 'S'real quick, real quiet; wouldn't have felt a thing. Then, I take what I need and move on."

Mom made no move to react, beyond stubbing out her collection of ends. No sooner were they gone than the next batch was lit. She coughed around them, this time, hacking and hacking until she managed to spit up a gelatinous, black clot. It splattered onto the table and, regardless of his disgust, Robbie nibbled at the mess of cake in his hands. Brad wasn't quite done, though.

"A few things around here I got my eye on." He trailed off to look at Mom with her ruined socket then let go a guffaw that ended with more belching. He was beginning to slur his words, alcohol and blood loss taking effect in equal measure.

Finally, Robbie set the remainder of the cake down on his placemat, appetite waning.

"Why?" he demanded, as he scrubbed his hands on his pants, leaving smears of brown that looked vaguely obscene. "I thought you liked us?"

Brad patted his belly. It had swollen to three times its typical size, popping the last few buttons of his flannel shirt so that it gaped open to reveal the top of his boxers and his naval.

"Nothin' personal, kid," he said, mopping at the sweat dappling his brow with the back of his hand. "It's business. Guy's gotta make a livin', right?"

Robbie did not answer. There was nothing worth saying anymore. Not to his mother, and certainly not to Brad. He was deliberating his next move—a dash for the door, a scream for help—when more wheezing and choking from Mom served as the distraction Brad had apparently needed. Whilst Robbie's gaze went left, Brad's whole body lurched right, and he made a dive for the kid who was privy to the darkest of his secrets.

Robbie managed to reel back from the table, knocking over his chair in the process, before Brad's fingers could close around his arm. Brad went down on his knees with a grunt. He grasped the edge of the table in an attempt to pull himself back up whilst Robbie pressed his back to the wall, out of reach. Brad had barely made it to his feet when he doubled over, issuing the sort of animalistic wail that Robbie had only heard at the zoo.

No time left to waste, Robbie dashed to his mother's side and shook her shoulder in an effort to rouse her. She was a ragdoll, flopping in all directions with her boneless limbs flailing.

"Mom, we have to go! Come on! Get up!" Robbie implored, refusing to rip his eyes from Brad, who was writhing on the floor as he scratched at his shirt. The rest of the buttons pinged free of the material, scattering across the dining room and allowing Brad access to massage the flesh of his belly with hands curled into claws. In the dim light, Robbie was sure that something rippled and wriggled underneath the man's skin.

Even as he suffered, Brad reached for the leg of his chair.

"Beer ..." he ground through gnashing teeth. "I ... need ... a ... beer ..."

"Mom!" Robbie pleaded. "Please!"

At last, Mom reacted, but not in the way that Robbie had hoped. She reached for her son, only to bat him away when a further coughing fit forced her over the table. She retched and gagged and rasped, then, fell still—collection of cigarettes glowing between blue lips.

Heart sinking, it dawned on Robbie that Mom was not coming.

He should leave, Robbie realized, almost numb. Run for help. Police and paramedics. Anyone who could save Mom, because – no matter what she had done – she was all that Robbie had left, and he could never hate her.

He should move. Regardless, he found that he could not force his legs into action.

He sank back into his chair, ignoring Brad and his inhuman screams as he ripped through the skin and muscle of his own stomach, all the while pleading for a drop of beer.

Robbie knew he really should go for help.

He would, he told himself, as he batted at the tears that leaked from his eyes; eyes that fixed on the mound of abandoned chocolate cake sitting on a table puddled with blood.

He would go for help, soon.

Very soon.

First, though, one more slice of cake.

Room for Two

BY BERT S. LECHNER

Meg knew what the smile on Erin's face meant the moment she stepped through the doorway, her hands behind her back.

Oh great ... she found another yard sale ...

She could only sigh with bemused frustration. When they had bought their tiny condo together, their own little place with just enough room for two, she had dreamed of a clean, slick look: shelving for potted plants and family photos; elegant furniture for the living room, enough for hosting but not too much to make the space of their long living room seem crowded; wide spaces on the walls, reserved for art she hoped she could one day afford. She had put so much effort into achieving that dream, taking on the painting herself, assembling the furniture. The toolset her parents had gifted her had become a near-permanent fixture in the living room as she assembled her dream.

Instead of that cozy dream, every other month she found herself buying new shelving to store Erin's growing horde of knick-knacks and treasures. Yard sales had a magnetic pull for Erin: sometimes it seemed as though she had a supernatural sense for sniffing them out, as if they called to her, appealing to her need for treasures. And, at least once a month —maybe more in the summer— she would find things to bring home: well-worn dolls and antique toys, fractured porcelain kitchenware, and bizarre, ambiguous pieces of art. And far more morbid trophies as well, things Meg made sure stayed in a secluded corner where she didn't have to look at them too often.

It's a conversation starter, Erin would always say, her voice full of pride at the securing of her treasures, her gestures the grandiose performative actions of an overzealous car salesperson.

Though it frustrated the hell out of her, Meg couldn't bring herself to be mad at Erin: that glint in her eyes whenever she brought something back, that bright smile, that way her cheeks pressed up as though inflated by excitement, showed just how much it meant to her to go to these yard sales. Finding things made Erin happy. And to Meg, Erin's happiness meant the world. Reminding herself of this, Meg took a deep breath and began her well-practiced monologue.

"Ok, what did you find this time?" she said, putting on an air of amusement even as she repressed her frustration. Meg put down the claw hammer and dowels for the new bookcase she had spent the last hour assembling to give her partner her full attention for the unveiling of her new prize.

Erin's huge, infectious grin painted her face, warming Meg's heart. She said nothing, but from behind her back produced a rectangular box, maybe half a meter or so in length, built from beautiful dark wood. She held it aloft, displaying it with pride, her grip tight enough around its corners to drain the color from her knuckles.

Meg's heart skipped a beat, surprising her. Her prepared amusement, her canned reaction to Erin's finds bubbled away. In its place burned a searing feeling of fascination for the softness of the light against its surface, for the perfect, unmarred polish in which she could see the blurry outline of her reflection. A hint of baking spice hit her nose, and old books, and the soft, bright scent of pine.

"You know what? I actually really like that," said Meg, getting closer to admire the grain of the wood and the silver gleam of the elegant latch that kept it closed. "Where did you find it?"

"Just down the street!" Erin replied, her grin getting only wider with Meg's affirmations. "You're not going to believe how lucky I was! It was an estate sale, and they were giving away literally everything. I talked with the guy running it, who I think was one of the sons. He was really nice, told me all these wonderful stories about his parents and all the things for sale. Nothing really interesting about the box, though.

"He couldn't remember anything special about it, and at first he wasn't sure about giving it away. Took a bit of convincing, but eventually I talked him into a price! I also know I've been going a little crazy with getting things and it's a bit much, so I figured something small and simple like this would be ok. It is ok, right?"

Meg only half listened, her eyes fixed on the box. In its reflective surface she saw that blurred image of herself, of her desires to reach out and embrace it. Only when she caught that Erin had stopped talking did she snap out of the enchantment, putting on a smile, giving an emphatic nod of approval.

"Of course it's ok! I really do like it." She paused for a moment, distracted by the sense that her reflection on the box's surface moved. "Is there anything in there?"

"Dunno. The latch is stuck shut. Like, really badly stuck." She fiddled with it to demonstrate, proving its stubbornness to move before she brought the box to her ear and shook it.

"Doesn't sound like anything's in there, though. Do you know if we've got any WD-40? I've been dying to see what's inside."

"Maybe? I'll check later," Meg said, despite the feeling in her stomach that she wanted to see *now*. "I've been hammering nails in the wall to hang up pictures the past thirty minutes, and I'm done with tools for the day." She looked around the room for a good place to put it, settling on an empty space between some of Erin's other treasures on the mantle above their unused fireplace.

"I bet it'll look really good over there," Meg said, gesturing with a nod of her head. Erin nodded back, and with a bounce in her step set the box in its place with care.

Literally perfect, Meg thought. The box filled up the space, giving off a pleasing vibe of coziness. The rich, earthen hue of the dark brown wood stood out against the off-white paint behind, drawing her eyes, filling her with a sense of coolness. And a vague feeling of sadness she could not place. *What's in there?* The question burned into her head with a frenzied curiosity that scared her.

"What are you thinking of putting in it when we get it open," Meg asked.

"Dunno. Looks like it could be good to store some envelopes and cards or something, though."

"Well, whatever goes in there, I think it should be something special. I can't say enough how much I like it, Erin. You really found something good."

Erin's proud smile lit up the room. She danced over, planting a deep kiss on Meg's lips that sent butterflies through her stomach. Meg held her close, taking in the tender moment, knowing full well that once it passed the day would return to its normal pace: to late afternoon chores, to preparing dinner, to the slow dissolution of the night as they retreated into their own private spaces to wind down and relieve the stress of the day.

Even in that moment of love, Meg found herself staring at the box, curiosity planted in her head, a need to see what within expressed such mournful feelings. Her reflection stared back at her, its alluring smile visible despite the blurriness, its piercing eyes plunging into her soul.

That night Meg found sleep elusive.

The oppressive warmth of the blankets; the omnipresent whine of electronics and Erin's rhythmic, heavy breaths beside her; the uncomfortable burn in her chest from chronic indigestion: all the usual foes in her nightly battle for rest.

And the subtle, yet overpowering, thread that tugged at her. *I want to see what's in that box. I need to know.*

Meg didn't know how long she lay there, her brain charged, flying at a hundred miles an hour, staring into their living room. The box sat there, on the mantle, looking back at her: a dark rectangle against the light wall, the faint glint of its silver latch in what dim light shone in from the streetlamps below. Beckoning her. Calling her with its secrets, with its profound loneliness.

"I'm not sleeping anyway," she muttered to herself after an eternity of restlessness. With a groan in her joints she pulled herself from the bed, not at all concerned about what noise she made. She knew very little would wake Erin: not even a fire drill could pull her from slumber, from that deepness of sleep that Meg envied. Her feet touched the floor, the warmth of her skin accentuating the chill of the floorboards. With hastiness unfamiliar to her at this time of night, she left their bedroom, and closed the door to the bedroom behind her out of courtesy for Erin. Or was it rather for her need for privacy?

Enough light made it into the apartment for Meg to navigate without colliding into the furniture. Many nights, when she couldn't sleep, she would sit at the table by the window, watching lonely cars traverse the dim city streets far below, glancing past what rooms remained lit in the building across from hers: silent commiseration with the others who found themselves up long before the sun. Tonight, however, she grabbed the box from the mantle and brought it to the couch, turning it over in her hands the way one would inspect a Rubix Cube.

The box possessed a soothing coolness. A welcoming softness, that well-worn feeling that antique wood takes on when it is well-cared for. Meg swept her hands across its surface, delighting in the texture, a feeling of longing for her touch sparking at her fingertips. A strange emotion touched her: loneliness. A sense that the box had been deprived of a company that it craved with rabid desperation.

"Don't worry, you don't have to be alone anymore."

Meg surprised herself with her whispers, that cold wave that comes with terrible realizations sliding down her neck. A sinking feeling dragged through her guts, a feeling that her thoughts, her actions, answered to another beyond herself. Worse still, she felt the box's excitement at her words, felt the power her whisper carried. Her invitation. *What am I doing?*

Her eyes locked onto the silver latch. She couldn't remember opening it.

Awareness of another presence sparked in her mind. A goading presence, brimming with zealous anticipation, with dire need, pressing its happiness at her actions into the back of her skull. A gentle caress fluttered across the back of her neck, an almost imperceptible pressure weight itself upon her shoulders: hands, the color of night, their skin the texture of soft fabric. A whisper crept into her ear.

"Go on. Open it."

Her hands shaking, she pushed up the lid.

Emptiness stared up at her. The inside of the box pulled at her sight, the scant light trickling through the windows doing little to illuminate the dark fabric. It looked far deeper than it should have been. Vivid images washed over her, fragments of light and color, hints of elegant curved branches and marble arches, of soaring towers reaching for amber twilight, of splaying paved roads through beds of moss: an entire world behind a door of dark fabric. And something waiting within, waiting for her company. Wanting to bring her into this world of beauty.

A burning desire filled her, an unquenchable need to test the texture of that fabric under her fingers. Her hand moved to fulfill her wish before she could think to do so, a tinge of fear growing in her stomach before all rational thought got swept away by the texture under her fingertips.

So cool, so soft.

Delectable.

Comfortable.

The perfect, delicate wear of a well-maintained blanket. Meg pressed her whole hand into the box to feel every inch of that fabric against her skin. And found the bottom had some give. It let her push, gave her extra space, as though it too relished her touch. As though to prove that deep within lay passage to a world that longed for her. The fabric tested the softness of her skin, velvet fingers just below the surface pressing against hers, desperate to hold, to clasp her hand.

Within the texture of that fabric, in those soft fingers, she felt the precipitate of some deep loneliness, some urgent longing. A need to be comforted.

Compulsion overpowered her. A compulsion to soothe that loneliness that she felt. A sense arose that something deep, deep within that box demanded to be seen, experienced. That world, that lonesome being. Infinity, perhaps.

But the box was far too small for her to fit.

"I won't let that stop me."

She would fit. She had to fit.

A heavy, ecstatic idea bloomed in her mind, one laced with joy and excitement and portents of pain, but pain worthwhile.

With rabid impulse Meg grabbed the hammer from the table. She tested its weight in her hand, admired the dull glint of its steel beak: a disturbing, flat, logical understanding wriggling through her mind that she would need to use both the blunt and chiseled ends to complete her task.

She tested her aim, the chill of the metal stinging her arm as she searched for the right place to make the break. So that she would fit.

I must fit, she thought. *I must.* The gentle hands on her shoulders slid down her arms: guiding hands, strengthening hands. She felt the welcoming pressure of the thing behind her, the goading force. Felt the warmth of its breath in her ear, carrying words of comfort.

"Let me help you."

She raised the hammer.

A wet *crunch* dragged Erin from her slumber.

Terrible energy buzzed in her chest, her heart pounding, her eyes wide, staring into the darkness before settling on the empty side of the bed where Meg should have been.

She lay still, alert, unsure if her dreams had conjured the noise.

A loud, sickening series of snaps echoed in the silence, the sound of twigs breaking. And Meg's muffled, distorted groan of pain. Erin commanded her limbs to move but found them disobedient, paralyzed. Her heart pounded in her mouth, her eyes burned, staring into the dark, every shadow a menace. Her quick, frightened breaths drowned her in the sweet, iron-tinged smell of fresh meat laced with pine-scented polish.

Erin struggled against herself, pushed, begged her limbs to obey her, hot dampness stinging her cheeks. It took an eternity to break her paralysis. She kicked the blankets off of her, the chill of the air prickling at the hair on her legs. Panic raging through her she shot upright, dizziness assaulting her, threatening to topple her. Out of fear, out of concern for Meg, she pushed herself from the bed despite the dizziness, the wooden floors frigid under her feet swaying for a few treacherous moments before she grounded herself.

But fear alone did not pull her out of the bedroom, into the little hallway that filed out into the living room. An unsettling curiosity, a sneaking urge spurred her onward, an undeniable need: even in her dreams, the desire to see what lay in that box she had found devoured her.

And riding that wave of conflicting emotions she found herself across the room from it.

The box sat on the mantle; the lid open.

In the dark Erin thought she saw movement at the lip of the box: the shadows of fingers, retreating out of sight.

"Meg?" Erin's voice quivered, unsupported by her short, hollow breaths. Her eyes darted around the room, her finger hovering over the light switch, afraid of what she might see if she flipped it.

A silent affirming groan answered her. Answered her from the box.

Erin's spine froze, her mind ablaze, her thoughts tugging her in all directions. She looked for a sign of Meg in the living room, looked to catch sight of her on the couch, her go-to place when she couldn't sleep. Anything to counter the belief that she had, in fact, heard her partner's voice from within the box.

More groans filled the air, more cracking, snapping sounds. Her throat closed, Erin flipped the switch, flooding the room with light. The slick sheen of fresh blood on the floor caught her eye first. Blood, speckled with crimson-dyed chunks of bone and strips of errant flesh. A trail of gore from the couch to the mantle, to the box.

Besieged from within by panic, fear, and urgent, sickening compulsion, Erin tiptoed across the gore-slicked floorboards, the sticky dampness clinging to her feet, the chunks of bone catching on her skin. She reached the mantle, reached the box.

And looked within.

No language possesses words for the cacophony of confusion and raw terror that churned through Erin's body. With a scream fighting against her constricted tongue, she looked down upon Meg's severed head, compressed into the box, her mouth contorted into a twitching chasm of horror, a scream caught on the tip of a tongue that had no space to move. Meg's one visible eye stared back at Erin with agony, with terror, with a maddening sense of delirious joy. Her broken fingers, askew at odd angles, pressed between her forehead and the blood-slicked, dark wood, twitched and writhed, scratching at her skin, trying with what strength remained to pull her deeper into the box.

Beyond screams of terror or anguish, beyond sane thought, beyond her ability to comprehend, Erin took the box into her hands, levying a tender touch on the mangled face of her partner. In one last conscious thought, before her eyes settled on the bloodied hammer at her feet, before she felt the soft, velvet touch of unfamiliar hands on her shoulders, she wondered if the box had room for two.

Fishcore

BY CONNOR BOYLE

"What do you think?" Cam flashed a pale white calf, dipping his ankle daintily like a ballerina mid plie'.

Lara's expression was something beyond disgust. It was existential revulsion. Disbelief that such ugliness could exist in this world, followed by an attendant horror that such ugliness *did* indeed exist, and had made its way into her home.

"They're called fish flops."

Resting atop each of Cam's feet was a greenish-brown rubber sandal fashioned to resemble a river bass. The fish lay on its side, a single eye looking upward. Where the gill flap would be on an actual river bass was a slip into which Cam had slid the top half of each foot. His stubby toes protruded from the bass' gaping mouth like rows of Vienna sausage.

"I got them at a yard sale," he continued. "Only cost me a dollar."

"You bought those things used?" asked Lara. "You mean someone wore them before you?"

"I'll clean them off," Cam said guardedly.

"You're already wearing them," Lara replied deadpan.

"They're comfortable. Besides, I needed new shoes."

Lara chuckled. "You're not telling me you plan to wear those things out in public?"

"Why not?" said Cam. "They're funny. Besides, I've been wearing them all day."

"They're ugly and clownish," replied Lara.

"But I like them," repeated Cam.

A thought suddenly occurred to Lara. The job interview. The only one her brother had landed in weeks. It was this morning for a part-time gig at the public library. The money was far from great, but it would get Cam out of the house and create some much needed buffer room in their relationship.

"You didn't wear them to—"

Cam cackled. "I did!" he said. "You should've seen the looks on their faces!"

"Oh Cam," said Lara. "That is so not good."

"Why?" said Cam. "I'm inventing a new punk scene. It's called fishcore." Cam performed a hopping jig, bouncing from one fish flopped foot to the other. "I wonder if I can get some matching gloves."

Cam was only supposed to stay with Lara for a few weeks. Enough time for him to get a new job, bank some money, and find his own place after being kicked out of the house over on Somer Ave he'd shared with his roommates. Cam was sketchy when it came to the details of their eviction. Something to do with a kitchen fire that Cam "absolutely had no part in." The only thing Cam spoke in definite terms about was that his previous landlord was an "absolute asshole" and had "no right" to kick him out.

Lara didn't dispute that his previous landlord was an asshole but wondered if maybe there was more to the whole kitchen fire business. She hadn't bothered to press Cam on the matter. What was the point?

Lara's mind returned to that same idea now: *What was the point?* Growing up with a brother like Cam, she knew it was best to pick her battles. Besides, she loved him, as hard as that could be at times. As much as he managed to get in his own way, she loved him, which meant that she could never kick him out on his ass over something as petty as a pair of fish flops.

"I guess they're okay for house shoes," said Lara.

Cam grinned.

Later that night, after Lara cooked them both dinner (vegan fish sticks and sauteed kale), they watched reruns of *The Office* together in the living room. Cam always chided Lara for her love of *The Office*, calling the show "the white bread of comedic television."

"Remember when we used to watch *Looney Tunes* as kids?" Cam remarked sleepily. "Now that was funny."

Sleep came unbidden for Cam, and he soon slumped over face down on a couch cushion. Lara turned him on his side, propped a pillow under his head, and tossed a blanket over his inert form. She then retired to her own bedroom.

That night she dreamed of swimming in a great blue lake surrounded by snow capped mountain peaks. As she paddled to the center of the lake, she noticed a dark shape trailing beneath her. Lara was treading water on her back, enjoying a view of the pristine alpine sky, when suddenly her perspective shifted, and she was looking down on herself from above. Beneath her floating body was an enormous fish head rushing up from the depths, its gaping mouth wide enough to swallow Lara whole. The fish's head broke the water, and Lara let out a piercing scream, jerking her awake in a pile of sweat stained sheets.

When she emerged from her bedroom two hours later, Cam was already awake. The TV was on again, turned to the local morning news channel. Cam had his feet propped up on the coffee table and was inspecting his toes with the file on a pair of nail clippers.

"Please don't cut your toenails in the living room," said Lara, pouring herself a cup of cold brew.

"I'm not," said Cam. "Come look at this."

In between each of Cam's toes was a thin film of semi-translucent skin. Cam inspected each of the fleshy interstices closely, pulling the toes apart and poking the skin with the file. The skin stretched like the surface of a balloon.

"What is that?" asked Lara.

"I'm not sure," said Cam. "I just woke up and it was there. My first guess was athlete's foot, but now I don't think so."

He smelled the fingers with which he'd been inspecting his toes.

"Doesn't have that athlete's foot stink to it."

Lara gagged.

"You've never had anything like that before?"

"No," said Cam, turning to face his sister.

"Your face!" said Lara. "You're so pale, and—"

She ran a hand along his cheek, taking away a palmful of dry flesh.

"You're scaly, Cam. What the fuck is going on with you?"

"I don't know," said Cam. "I feel fine. Nothing hurts. It's just itchy."

"It's probably those sandals," said Lara. "Probably did have some toe fungus on them. Something heavier than athlete's foot. Did you touch your feet and then touch your face?"

Cam paused. "Maybe. Most likely."

"That's probably it," said Lara. "Jock itch can transfer the same way. You put your foot in your undies and your toe brushes against the inside of the fabric, next thing you know you've got crotch rot."

"What should I do?" asked Cam.

"Put some calamine lotion on it, and don't itch it."

An hour later, Lara was dressed and off to the office. When she got back home later that night, Cam was gone. In the space he usually occupied on the living room couch was a large wet spot. Lara threw a towel over the spot and cursed her brother.

"Please don't be piss," she thought. "I don't know if I can handle piss."

Lara was watching reruns of *The Office* again when Cam returned. Soaked to the bone and shivering, he traipsed through the living room leaving muddy footprints behind him.

"Where have you been?" asked Lara.

"Swimming," said Cam.

"Swimming where?"

"The lake," said Cam.

"Jesus, Cam. It must've been freezing."

"It was," said Cam. "I need to get in the shower."

As Cam turned down the bathroom hallway, Lara made out a gleaming gold piercing extruding from his cheek.

"What the hell is in your face? Did you get another piercing?"

"A hook," Cam replied flatly.

"A hook?"

"There was a fisherman. He used nightcrawlers. I couldn't help myself."

Before Lara could respond, Cam had locked himself in the bathroom. Lara wanted to chase after her brother and make him explain what the hell was going on, why he decided to go for a dip on a day the temperature was in the low fifties, how that puddle on the couch got there, why he was eating fish hooks, and if he planned to clean up his muddy footprints.

She stopped herself. When it came to her brother, she had a sixth sense about things. It was probably just a sister's intuition, or maybe it was a real psychic power like Charles

Xavier had in the X-Men comics; whatever it was, it told her that something was wrong, that something dangerous was going on with Cam, and that hollering at her brother would do him no good.

The shower was still running three hours later when Lara turned in for the night, and it was still running six hours later when she woke up the next morning. Lara forced the bathroom door open, snapping the cheap balsa door frame as she shouldered through. The air was thick with steam. Lara briefly panicked at what her water bill would be this month, then pushed the thought aside.

As she slowly pulled back the shower curtain, her mind recoiled in horror at the sight before her on the tiled floor.

Cam lay naked on his side, his skin faded to a milky white hue and covered with hundreds of diamond shaped striations. The insides of his legs had fused together with a thin layer of skin, similar to the tissue between Cam's toes they'd observed together the morning before, forming what looked like a single long fin that stretched from his hips down to his webbed toes. Identical flaps of skin connected the undersides of Cam's arms to the sides of his chest. Just below where the arms connected, on each side of his chest, were lengths of blood orange flesh peeking out between lips of white skin. It was as if someone had slashed Cam open and revealed the muscle beneath.

Worst of all was Cam's face. His soft blue eyes had been replaced by enormous globes of glassy eyeball tissue punctuated with huge black irises. His thin red lips were now rounded, purple, slimy things that puffed for air.

"You were right," he gasped. "It was the fish flops."

"How?"

"That night I fell asleep on the couch, I never took them off. The next morning they were gone. I think they ..."

Cam stretched down, pointed a flippered hand toward his feet.

"Fused," he made out weakly.

Cam croaked and flailed until his gills were under the stream of water once again. He seemed to catch his breath.

"What do you want?" said Lara in a panic. "Should I take you to the hospital? What do you need?"

"The lake," replied Cam. "Take me to the lake."

Lara soaked a bundle of towels in the shower and then wrapped them around Cam's chest, pressing them tight against his gill flaps. The water allowed him to breathe, although only in shallow breaths. Enough to get him out of the shower and in Lara's car.

Lara raced to the lake. By the time she got there, Cam's skin had taken on a pale gray complexion, and his face had started doing that awful puffing thing again. Lara helped him from the passenger seat and shuffled him across the gravel parking lot to the water's edge.

"Goodbye, Lara," he groaned unceremoniously, then collapsed backwards into the black brackish water. Cam's body floated there for a while, a hazy gray shape hovering beneath the water's surface, until the body seemed to come to life again. A whip of its tail fin, a jerk of its upper half, then it was swimming away, toward the center of the lake.

Lara would visit Cam each morning, bringing him old loaves of bread to munch on, and a cup of fat nightcrawlers on Saturdays and Sundays.

One Monday, several months after Cam's transformation, Lara awoke early, ripped from sleep by the awful sensation that something was wrong. It was the same feeling she had when Cam had come home that night with a hook in his face. She rushed to the lake and sprinted to the usual spot from where she'd feed her brother.

Standing on the shoreline was a middle-aged man in a flannel shirt and nylon fishing vest. His rod was bent nearly in half, and his reel was screaming like a banshee as the line let out.

Lara knew it was Cam on the other end of the line.

The man loosened the drag and started cranking. The reel's scream diminished to a high-pitched hiss, and he started to pull Cam in toward the shoreline.

"No!" screamed Lara, racing to the man's side and swatting at the reel. "You can't do that! You'll kill him!"

"That's the point, little lady," said the man. "I think I'm about to set a state record with this baby. Wooohee!"

Lara looked from the man to the water. Cam's head broke the surface fifty yards out. Although his human features had almost disappeared entirely by then, she could make out the same look of pain and fear she'd seen in her brother's face when they were kids and he'd fallen out of a tree or crashed his bike. Her heart sank.

Lara scrambled along the shoreline until she found a long, flat rock. She struggled to free it from the mud, until finally it released itself with a loud sucking sound. Lara stumbled and swayed, until she was behind the fisherman with the rock raised above her head.

"Wooheee! She's coming! She's coming!" the man hollered.

She brought the rock down with a loud, hollow thunk, and the man collapsed at her feet. The lake was silent again but for the soft trickle of blood flowing from the man's cratered skull.

Lara was in a daze. She wondered if she might try to remove the fishing hook from her brother's mouth; maybe the fisherman had some pliers in his tackle box. But she thought better of it. She needed to get away from the body before anyone saw her.

"How long can I keep up with this?" she asked herself on the drive home.

There would be more fishermen. Would she have to kill them all? She didn't know if she was capable of such a thing. Sure, if she saw someone trying to hurt her brother, she would intervene without a second thought. But would she be able to live with the knowledge that she had murdered innocent human beings? She didn't think she could. And what if the police caught her? Would they believe her story? That her brother had turned into a fish person and that he was now living in the lake?

At home, Lara stripped off her blood-stained clothing and threw it in the garbage. She scavenged around in the hallway closet for a heavy cardigan she liked to wear when she was feeling depressed or exhausted. The sweater was nowhere to be found, and she wondered if Cam had done something with it when he was still living there.

Lara got down on all fours and started scooping handfuls of gloves, hats, and old jackets out from the back of the closet. At the back of the space, concealed beneath a pile of scarves, was a gift-wrapped box with a notecard taped to its front. Lara pulled the box into her lap, opened the card and read:

Dear Lara,

Thanks for letting me crash at your place. It means the world to me, and honestly it's been a lot of fun spending more time with you. I picked these up at the yard sale and thought you might like them. Don't worry, I cleaned them in the washing machine.

Love you, Cam

Lara's eyes welled up with tears. She tore off the wrapping paper and opened the box. Inside were a pair of canary yellow cotton slippers resembling Tweety Bird, Lara's favorite *Looney Tunes* character. Lara slid them on her feet. They were soft and comfortable, just what she needed. She wore them to bed that night.

The next morning she woke up feeling refreshed. The events of the previous day seemed far off, almost as if they'd never happened. Her anxiety was replaced with an intense desire to be outside, to feel the wind blowing along the contours of her body.

Lara's taloned feet clicked across the tile floor as she collected a scarf from the closet, wrapped it around her neck, and went out the front door. She headed toward the lake, whistling a tune. She'd say hello to her brother, maybe watch him from high up on a tree branch, collect some grubs and feed him a snack. And if anyone tried to hurt her brother, well, she knew what to do with bad old pussycats.

Epilogue

By Nadine Stewart

Everything felt hollow now, mere echoes of memories bouncing between empty rooms. There was nothing left of them here, nothing but a few trash bags, a couple of boxes of leftovers destined for the thrift shops, and Dad's old steamer trunk. They'd only briefly rummaged through it before the sale looking for their parents' will and sat it aside when they discovered it contained dozens of their dad's old journals. As far back as Rae could remember he took one of those journals with him everywhere, scribbling down notes here and there.

Rae sat cross-legged on the floor of her parents' living room. The house was eerily quiet now that her siblings had all headed back to their lives. It was the kind of silence that came after a shrill, high-pitched ringing in your ears. The kind of silence that only lasts for a few moments, devoid of all sound as if someone pressed pause on the world. Lost in thought, Rae watched as the shadows from the trees outside bowed and swayed across the carpet. Then, she heard something so faint she would have missed it if it hadn't been for the absence of sound at that moment. A swishing static in her ears like the grey noise of a fuzzy old television screen. She snapped her head around straining to hear where it was coming from. Her eyes fell on the trunk. Lifting its heavy lid the static turned to muffled whispers. *That's weird*, she thought to herself. Tucked up against the inside edge of the trunk she pulled out a large, yellowing notebook. It looked to be a ledger of some kind.

The whispers increased in volume and pace as she pulled it from the trunk, becoming urgent, unintelligible chatter.

Rae reverently opened the ledger and thumbed through the pages of itemized lists. The first column listed various objects or belongings; the second column was titled "Reported Incidences"; the third, "Origin Known or Unknown"; the fourth, "Current Location"; the last column was titled "Date Acquired." There were dozens of pages filled out with detailed notes. When she stopped flipping through the pages, the book settled to a set of notes near the beginning. As Rae began to read, an invisible ether seeped out from the book and took hold of her senses. In a trance, suddenly, Rae was no longer reading the words on the page. She was sitting on their old sofa, the date on the wall calendar was three weeks ago. The day her parents died.

Jean and Howard had been the average all-American couple in their youth. High-school sweethearts who married young when Jean got pregnant with their eldest son. Howard, an amateur paranormal enthusiast, had been more than happy to play the role of supportive husband and stay-at-home dad while Jean pursued her dream of becoming an archeologist. In grade school, Jean had been fascinated by Egyptology, learning about Pharaohs, tombs, and buried cities. This coupled with her and Howard's hobby of collecting rare, unique items and the rush of investigating their provenance eventually led them down a path neither could have imagined.

Jean's career took her around the world, to sites and digs she had only read about in journals and books. To archeological locations that gave insight into past civilizations and ancient ways of life. Their young family grew between each assignment. She studied human bones found near Stonehenge that suggested it could have been the site of ritual sacrifices. She had climbed the steps of Chichén Itzá imagining the ancient city at its bustling peak. She had stood in the shadows of the Pyramids and Great Sphinx of Giza guarding the tomb of Pharaoh Khafre. She explored the hidden city of Petra and studied the Acropolis of Athens. She had even worked at historical sites closer to home like Cliff Palace in Colorado, home to the Anasazi 900 years ago, and various Native American

Mound sites in Mississippi, Illinois, and Ohio. And all along the way, Jean collected mementos from each city to remind her of where she'd been. Long forgotten tchotchkes hidden at the back of a dusty antique shop or buried amongst other treasures in market stalls.

Jean's work caught the attention of universities and museums wanting to employ her or invite her to be a guest lecturer. Many of which she turned down to balance her career and family life. But one offer soon came to both her and her husband that they could not refuse.

While Howard remained at home raising their children, in their quiet suburban neighborhood, his fascination with the paranormal and his investigation of "haunted" objects grew as the popularity of ghost-hunting shows rose. He stayed up to date with all the latest technology and social media platforms, which was quite impressive for an aging baby boomer. When all of their kids were grown and gone, the empty house allowed him to waste away the days on his hobby turned obsession. He spent many an afternoon being sucked down YouTube rabbit holes about haunted places and objects, scouring message boards, and tracking down reports of strange incidents around the country. He shied away from the limelight and wouldn't soon become the next Zak Bagans or Jack Osbourne with his own show or YouTube channel. He simply was curious about a phenomenon that had been researched and occurring for as long as anyone can remember but is still not fully understood or believed despite countless reports of its existence. Perhaps it was his way to find meaning in a random chaotic world or to try to answer his questions about the purpose of life and what was to come after. Do we fade into nothingness devoid of all light or was there more? Do we leave behind a piece of ourselves, or do we simply move into a parallel dimension of existence and our actions there leave trace echoes of us in this timeline?

Whatever the answers were Howard was curious and kept journals about the unusual things he read about it. He loved tracking lore and myths and marveled at how something so simple as an internet challenge could years later be told and retold as urban legends and that they'd go on to also be featured in movies and videogames and even compel teenagers to commit acts of violence in real life to appease these made-up fables. Separating fact from fiction became a game for Howard. He even started delving into dark web territory when he would hit a brick wall in his deep dives. Swapping information and digging around in the underworld of the internet. And that is how he suspected they were found.

Jean spent the better part of the day making notes about anything they had acquired over the years that they could have possibly missed. She hoped a colleague would find it before her children. As Jean laid the ledger back into its trunk with her husband's journals, she felt her limbs becoming leaden as if a heavy weighted blanket was wrapping around her extremities. Her legs felt stiff and tired, the sensation of pins and needles slowly creeping its way up her body. She tried to move but was anchored to where she sat. With weariness setting in, it became increasingly harder to breathe. Her lungs felt like deflated balloons no longer able to hold the air within. As she waited for the inevitable, Jean couldn't help but think about the day their lives changed forever.

Rae, still locked in a trance, gasped for breath as she felt, saw, and thought about every-thing her mother had in her final moments of life.

At first, the offer felt like any other Jean had had over the years. A mysterious benefactor of a museum wanted to hire her to oversee and curate a new collection. She was fully prepared to turn it down when they said they wanted her husband to join her in their meeting. Not many people outside of their immediate family knew much about Howard's extracurricular activities, nor could they link them to her and her line of work. He kept his digital footprint contained to a few different screen names, and there wasn't much you could find of his personal life online. So, for a potential new employer to be interested in her stay-at-home husband, curiosity got the best of her.

The meeting with the museum director was surreal, to say the least. Jean and Howard were being recruited to join a team of individuals to track down artifacts that had rumored histories of bad things happening in their presence. They would be given assignments to research the validity of certain claims and would be tasked with acquiring said objects by any means necessary. Suffice it to say, this would be a collection that would not be seeing the light of day. Jean had always been on the fence about her husband's hobby and until that very moment, she didn't know if she believed in ghosts, possessions, or entities, (evil or otherwise), being able to imbue their energy into objects or spaces. But the job intrigued her. Being empty nesters, this could be a thrilling way to spend their golden years together whether she believed in such things or not. It would combine her knowledge of antiquities and use her and her husband's skills in tracking an item's origin story. However, what she thought was going to be an exciting adventure turned out to be a more terrifying ordeal as they encountered things that couldn't be explained.

In all of their years working for their employer they were very careful not to mix work with pleasure. They rarely brought work home except for their notes and the ledger. All artifacts were contained and hand-delivered to the museum vault. Yes, they acquired souvenirs from some of the places they visited, but they never expected anything else to follow them home. Until it did. Was it contained in the wooden box from Germany they bought at an outdoor Christmas market? Was it attached to the beautiful antique hairbrush Howard bought her for their anniversary while in Australia? *How could they have been so careless?* she thought as her eyes became too heavy to keep open. Perhaps it attached itself to Howard on their last job. They'd never know now, and as Jean took her last breath,she worried about what would happen when they were both gone. Who could contain the curse that had taken over their home so quietly like a thief in the night? A curse so powerful she was afraid it had completely transferred into everything in their home it had touched. A curse that had ultimately led to their untimely deaths. Who ... would ... know ... it ... even ... existed...

"Hey Rae, I forgot my coat in the garage, and I just wanted to check before I head out again if you were done and needed help loading anything else into your car," Donavan called out as he unexpectedly burst through the front door. He saw Rae kneeling on the floor in front of the old steamer trunk but she didn't move. "Rae?" he called out again as he approached her and laid his hand on her shoulder.

With a large intake of breath, Rae's body arched and heaved as she turned towards her brother, the ledger falling to the side. Donavan backed away terrified at the sight of his sister, only the whites of her eyes were visible as they rolled back. She snarled and hissed, teeth bared, crawling towards him like some kind of animal, just before she pounced.

About the Authors

Nadine Stewart is an author, poet, and media creator. Her short fiction has been published in several anthologies including Terrorcore's *Doors of Darkness*, Voices From the Mausoleum's *That Old House the Bathroom Anthology*, *Autumn Tales II* from Anatolian Press, and the charity anthology *Gridiron Gates of Hell*, just to name a few. Nadine has always been an avid reader with a wild imagination. Born into a creative family of artists, from a young age she was always "performing" for family and friends and creating poetry only ever seen by those closest to her. She was born and raised in beautiful British Columbia, Canada, and she now resides in Washington State. You can follow her on Instagram @nadine.stewart.author @house_of_the_macabre @stewartsocialcreations

Ivan K. Conway wrote his first book at four years old using crayons and construction paper. He's rarely stopped writing since. Yet, it was only after graduating from college that he finally chose to share his tales with the world. His short stories include *The Cursed Items Anthology*'s "Til Death", *The Thanksgiving Horror Anthology*'s "Barnyard Blood", and the *No More Resolutions Anthology*'s "Zombees". Ivan's first novella, *Goblins & Gunslingers: Fresh Blood*, is due for release this summer. Ivan currently resides in his hometown of Helena, Montana.

A.W. Mason lives in Florida with his cats Wallace and Belle, retired extreme parkour artists (who look so dapper in their little helmets and knee pads). He enjoys all the nachos, getting lost in the woods, and naps. Mason has published several books including *A Haunt of Travels*, *The Cleanup Crew*, *The Scampering* (co-authored with Alana K Drex), and *Judy Martin's Final Curtain Call*. His short stories have appeared in various anthologies. Find him at the social media below:

IG/Threads/TikTok: a.w.mason.author

Twitter: awmasonauthor

G.M. Pugliese enjoys life with his wife and son in Northern Georgia. While completing his undergraduate degree at the University of South Florida he spent time as a staff writer for the daily Oracle student paper. After spending a decade in college administration he pivoted to his passion into the world of golf course maintenance. As a writer, Mr. Pugliese has always enjoyed science fiction, historical biographies, and classical mythology as a source of inspiration.

AudraKate Gonzalez started writing horror stories when she ran out of *Goosebumps* books to read as a child. Her love for horror grew, and now she has a BA in

Creative Writing and is working on her MFA. Her written works include her YA Horror series, *This is Noir*, her Middle-Grade Mystery series, *Welcome to Noir*, and numerous poems and stories in various anthologies. She likes to use frequent themes of paranormal, monsters, villains, good versus evil, family values, and coming-of-age. AudraKate's books will appeal to fans of *Goosebumps, Fear Street, Christopher Pike, and Point Horror*. AudraKate is a current member of the Horror Writers Association, Sigma Tau Delta, and enjoys her time working as Editor-in-Chief at Twenty Hills Publishing. She lives in Ohio with her handsome husband, and her adorable furry bad boys, Zero and Scrappy Doo. When AudraKate isn't writing, you can find her reading, watching scary movies or sleeping. You can follow her on Instagram and TikTok @lets.get.lit.erature or check out her website www.authoraudrakategonzalez.com

Kirsten Craig has held a lifelong fascination with the weird, unseen corners of the universe. She wrote this story in between downing cups of coffee and reading way too many books at one time. She is currently pursuing her Bachelors in Library and Information Sciences. Kirsten lives in Chattanooga, Tennessee, with her kiddos, three cats and ten backyard chickens. You can follow her on any social media platform with the handle @TheSpineOfMotherhood

Alana K. Drex, an eternal horror reader (among many other genres), has always been compelled to write it! So far she has written the Gothic horror novella, *Sleeping Celeste*, and the B-rated/campy novelette, *Shsskish*. She also co-wrote the absurdly squirrely short story, *The Scampering: An Extreme Horror Story* with A. W. Mason to show people it isn't wise to mess with nature—all proceeds go to the Animal Welfare Institute. Currently,

Drex is furiously writing away in Missouri where she lives with her family and Boston Terrier, Phantom.

Carolyn O'Brien lives in Pennsylvania in the USA. She started writing horror, dark fantasy, and speculative fiction when she stopped working due to a physical disability. At the age of 50, she published her first story to a podcast and has published several short stories since. Your dream does not have an expiration date.

Dan Rafter has worked as a writer and editor for more than 30 years, writing for publications such as the Washington Post, Chicago Tribune, Mental Floss Magazine, Chicago Reader, Phoenix Magazine, Grist and many others. He's finally starting to build a fiction writing career and is thrilled to have his story "The Billiken" appear in this publication. He lives in Chicago with his wife, two kids, and dog.

Brad Wilkins was raised in small town Alberta where he encountered science fiction and fantasy early. He reads voraciously and loves science fiction, fantasy and crime drama. He also loves monster movies. He has written a yet to be published novel. He is a father of four, grandfather of seven, and great grandfather of three. He supported his family for thirty four years as a law enforcement officer and firearms safety instructor.

Lance Loot Whether creating at-home comics or opus-like stories, a lifelong love of all things eldritch and macabre brought Lance to writing. Taking inspiration from daily life and distorting it like a funhouse mirror for your reading enjoyment is what he does best. Lance lives in a centenarian haunted house in Illinois with his wife and three cats.

Robb Basham had always wanted to be a spinner of sinister stories, as far back as he could remember. Even as a youth, he rooted for the malevolent antagonists in movies such as *Star Wars* and *Predator*. This anthology will be his first chance to unleash one of his horrors upon the unsuspecting masses. Along with film, Robb is an avid reader of horror novels by established masters as well as his fellow aspiring voices. His musical tastes vary across an eclectic spectrum of genres. From punk to traditional country to even grindcore, all of these sonic templates fueled Mr. Basham's creative exploits (including "The Blank Cartridge," available in this anthology).

David-Jack Fletcher is a gay Australian horror author and editor, specialising in work that emphasises the everydayness of LGBTQI+ individuals. His debut horror-comedy released early 2022 titled *The Haunting of Harry Peck* and was an international Amazon #1 bestseller in several categories. It has recently been sold for a second edition with

Lethe Press for a 2024 re-release. In June 2023, his debut novel, *Raven's Creek* became a #1 bestseller in several international Amazon categories and subsequently won the 2023 Bookstagram Award for LGBTQ+ Novel of the Year. He has also appeared in several anthologies across the US, the UK, and Canada, with a short story featuring in the highly anticipated anthology *The Earth Bleeds at Night*, featuring acclaimed international indie authors Caitlin Marceau, Richard Thomas, C.M. Forest, Ally Wilkes, and Christi Nogle. He has just released *The Count*, with upcoming titles including, *Hell is other People* (November 2024), *Stowaway* (2025), *Wires in the Gut* (2025), and *Indentured* (2025). David-Jack is also the co-founder of Slashic Horror Press, an emerging queer indie press focused on promoting under-represented voices—and stories—in horror and dark fiction.

Joey Powell is the Owner and Operator of Mad Axe Media, a publisher of dark and spooky genre fiction. In addition to championing the works of others through his publishing company and his podcast Creatives Getting Coffee, he is a writer and an actor. His upcoming published work includes *Squirming All the Way Up*, an anti-fascist horror novella from Madness Heart Press.

Jason A. Jones is an industrial painter and writer. He has works in several anthologies and is looking forward to the release of his debut novella, *Starving Alice* sometime this year. He lives in Central Indiana with his wife, two cats, and one dog.

David Washburn lives in the Greater Cincinnati area (in Northern Kentucky for any locals who choose to argue about geography) where he lives with his two teen sons and the lady of the house. When David isn't fighting imposter syndrome as a writer he is probably working out, watching horror movies, baseball, or wrestling. David is also the author of other independently self-published works and has short stories published in several anthologies.

Caleb J. Pecue is the owner and editor for Terrorcore Publishing, which specializes in bringing back the vintage feel of the 80s. His short story, "The Turning of a Card", was published in the second volume of *Horrorscope*, edited by Harriet Everend. Another of his short stories, "One More Time for Old Time's Sake", was published in *Gridiron Gates of Hell* by Loki DeWitt for charity. By day, he works at a university in Illinois, advising students; by night, he works to find short stories to publish and writes his own that he hopes to publish.

Dr. Stuart Knott is a PhD graduate and a writer of horror fiction. A lifelong fan of videogames, comic books, and horror, action, and science-fiction films, he is primarily influenced by the writing of Stephen King and H.P. Lovecraft and the films of David

Cronenberg and John Carpenter. Dr. Stuart Knott has published several short stories, novellas, and novels ranging from traditional slashers to surreal terrors. Unafraid to push the limits and always seeking to try something different with each story, Dr. Stuart Knott aims to infuse the mundane nature of everyday life with dark comedy and macabre events.

Eric Todd's only goal in life is to hug a bear in the wild. He quietly eeks out a meager existence working sometimes, sleeping little, and doing whatever he can to ensure his sarcasm level is over 9000. Despite that reference, he's not into anime, but he has read some manga. Karma kicks his ass on the regular. Ironically, his dog is also named Karma. He is much stronger than his dog though and could easily take her in a fight. Fuck around and find out. Snitches get stitches. Forgiveness is divine, but never pay full price for late pizza.

David E. Kruegger writes horror fiction, mostly about the Upper Midwest. He lives in Minneapolis with his wife and their collection of RPGs and cookbooks. You can see his house when you land at the airport, if you know where to look.

A.D Jones lives in the North of England where he spends his time favoring books over people and can be found writing or devouring said books to review online. He loves

Coca-Cola, *Twin Peaks*, all things horror, and cult movies. He dislikes the movie *The Karate Kid* with a passion that burns brighter than the sun. His debut novel *Umbrate* was released in October 2023 to positive feedback, and his next book *Sacrificial Waters* was released April 2024. You can find him on Instagram @the_evergrowing_library

S. C. Fisher is the author of horror series *Base Fear*, as well as short story contributions that have featured in anthologies such as *That Old House: The Bathroom*, *Sinister Stories by the Ten*, and *Horrorscope Volume 4*. She lives in Britain with her husband, their children, and more animals than she can count on one hand.

Bert S. Lechner is an autistic indie author from the Bay Area, California. After years of pursuing odd jobs, from pizza making to troubleshooting excessively fancy phones, he decided to pursue his dreams of becoming a published author and now writes cosmic horror full-time. He has two cats, who are extremely needy but make up for it with their marketing prowess. When he's not writing Bert can be found cooking, baking, watching horror films, and playing video games, often simultaneously.

Connor Boyle's work has appeared in the aquatic horror anthology *Rampage on the Reef* and the mall horror anthology *Escalators to Hell*. His aesthetics are informed by the

1998 Taco Bell-*Godzilla* cross-promotion campaign and the *Resident Evil* video games. His favorite authors include Harlan Ellison, Joe Lansdale, Owl Goingback, and Brian Keene. When he is not writing fiction or working at his day job, he enjoys bicycling, collecting rare genre paperbacks, and watching B-horror movies with his friends. He lives in Santa Fe, NM. You can find him on IG: *@thylacinebooks.*

Nico Bell is a horror author and editor who offers developmental/line edits and proof-reading. She loves working with writers of all levels of experience and is passionate about helping authors achieve their writing goals! Her social media handle is @nicobellfiction, and she can be found pretty much on all sites including TikTok, Instagram, and Substack. To learn more about her, check out her website at nicobellfiction.com or email her at nicobellfiction@gmail.com to learn more about her services!

Acknowledgements

I would like to thank everyone who played a part in bringing Curbside Curses to life. To all the friends and family who supported my vision from the beginning. The ones who kept coming back to me and saying "hey this is a great idea, you really need to do something with it." To the ones who held my hand and walked me through the self-publishing process and answered all my questions every step of the way. You all know who you are, I'm so grateful for you and your support and encouragement. To all the authors who trusted me with their stories and gave this project a chance, you are a truly talented bunch. To the horror writing community in general for being so collaborative and kind. To my wonderful editor Nico Bell who is a truly talented author herself and whose skills really helped polish this book. And last but not least, to the readers who have given this book a chance and have been enthusiastic about the project from the beginning, you guys rock! Please remember to leave us a review on Amazon and Goodreads! #curbsidecurses

9 798990 680807